The Big Score

Tales of the Wild

Peter Thomson

Published by Peter Thomson, 2023.

This is a work of fiction. Similarities to real people, places, or events are entirely coincidental.

THE BIG SCORE

First edition. August 20, 2023.

ISBN: 979-8223994602

Written by Peter Thomson.

Also by Peter Thomson

Tales of the Wild

Distracted

The Servant's Story

The Big Score

To all those who helped make it a better story.

The Lands Around the Green Sea

Interested readers will note that the events of The Big Score follow on from those recounted in The Servant's Story and largely precede those in A Walk in the Wild and The Forked Path. Nevertheless this Tale can be read by itself.

1. A Bad Start

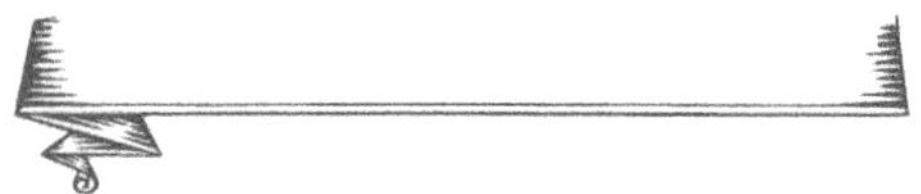

At least it was not snowing, thought Jayas. Not that it made much difference. The wind was chill enough, and if the cold did not kill him, something would come along, find him hanging here, and then make a meal of him. He had no wish to die watching predators squabble over his entrails. He looked across at Seyvyar, dangling from the next tree. He too was naked, pale skin blotched and marbled with cold, his lean body stretching as the branch to which his hands were tied swayed in the wind.

"Any ideas?" Jayas asked.

A wordless grunt. No help there. Jayas could understand; Seyvyar was shut out from the ether, unable to cast even the pettiest of spells, and missing most of a hand besides. Enough to make anyone despondent, really. He was pretty down himself. They make the big score, wealth enough to make a tax-gatherer happy, or at least moderately content, and then that bitch of a housemaid hits him with a poker. Him, a hardened warrior, fresh from killing two magicians and a skilled swordsman, felled with a poker. He could still feel the lump. Next time he would keep his helmet on until everyone was dead or in chains.

His mind was wandering. He had better do something – anything – before the cold deprived him of will. If he had the use of his hands he could be warm in moments. He arched his back and looked up. His wrists were lashed together above the branch. Stout side-branches kept him from sliding along the bough to freedom, and he could not reach the ropes from below. He studied the foliage above him, took several deep breaths, then arched his body, bringing his legs up to snatch at a hold with his feet. At the first two tries his feet slipped on the bark, then he had a heel over. Another heave, a pull with his arms, an awkward moment and then he fell back, barely keeping his leg on the branch. Another try, a swing of the leg for momentum and he was half over the branch. Jayas clenched his teeth as sensitive parts scraped across rough twigs and the spiky seed-balls of strangler vine. Another heave and wriggle and he was lying on the branch, scratched and bleeding, uncomfortable and precariously balanced.

"Wild-cats and bears can climb, you know." Well, Seyvyar was talking. That was something.

"I know. Now shut up and let me chew." Jayas hooked his ankles around the branch, leaned out to one side, dipped his head and brought his wrists to his mouth. The lashings were tight and he could only bring his front teeth to bear. A rat would make quick work of this, or any rodent really. He was stuck with these inadequate human fangs. No help but to gnaw away, keep balanced despite the spikes against his naked flesh, keep spitting fibres out. Ankles sore, chest raw, gums bleeding, teeth aching, chew on. Finally a strand parted and the ties loosened a fraction. More chewing. Now get a canine in and pull the rope apart. More chewing. A loop came free. Prickles of rope stuck in his lips. Another loop loose, then another, and the cursed rope fell away. Jayas' wrists were deeply scored, his hands swollen. Sharp pains coursed through his flexing fingers, adding to a myriad others.

Jayas lay there a moment, panting, then leaned over to drop to the ground. His knees gave way and he staggered, then brought himself upright. By ancient and universal custom no-one was left in the Wild without a weapon. Their own knives were stuck in a fallen log a few paces away. Jayas limped over, and a few moments of sawing had Seyvyar moaning on the ground, rubbing his abused flesh. Jayas let him be for a little time, then nudged him with a foot.

"Up you get. We need to find shelter before nightfall."

Seyvyar dragged himself to his feet and looked around. At this time of year the branches overhead were bare, letting the fading light through to the forest floor. The hummocked ground stretched away, littered with mossy rocks and fallen timber furred with lichen. Orange bracket fungi were spots of colour against the muted browns and greys of bark. Ferns lined a small stream down-slope. The wind was as chill as ever.

"Which way?" Seyvyar asked.

"That way. Due south, as near as we can manage," Jayas told him. Seyvyar looked at the ground and his feet, and sighed. Jayas supposed he was recalling a long walk barefoot, not all that long ago, also the result of ill-luck and enemies. It was all to do again, only this time without clothes, in winter, with but a single companion. He must feel his life cursed, or the Powers angry with him. Seyvyar took a brave step forward and sank to his ankle in a muddy hole.

THEY SPENT THE NIGHT huddled together under a fallen tree. Seyvyar gathered piles of dead leaves and heaped them in the earthen hollow, while Jayas chipped away at the stem of a bush until it parted. It served to barricade their refuge. Something sniffed around in the dark, pawed briefly at the thorny stems and then wandered away. There was plenty of water, but they had eaten no more than a few withered berries, a handful of nuts and a mushroom that Jayas thought safe. It was a poor night, cold, tired and hungry, a pair of improvident squirrels, the leaves scrunching against their battered skin as they shifted restlessly.

"I heard of a craft-spell that grew fur all over the body," muttered Jayas. "I thought it was only good for laughs, or maybe a certain kind of party. Wish I'd learnt it now." Seyvyar grunted.

Morning brought only a dismal grey light, a deeper hunger, and more walking. Jayas took the time to cut a stick for Seyvyar and a longer one for himself. He whittled the end to a point, then scooped up a few pebbles from the bottom of a small creek. Seyvyar cursed as the water chilled his ankles, but then he had also cursed thorns, a hillside covered with sharp scree, the rock-hopper that had chittered angrily at him, the weather and much else. His conversation was basically a steady drizzle of cursing. It passed the time.

At last Jayas squeezed his companion's arm and motioned him to silence. A few cautious steps forward, the slow raise of an arm, a whiplash throw and a small body fell from a branch. Jayas was on it in an instant, severing the head with a flash of the knife. The tang of blood brought saliva to his mouth. A few quick jerks of the blade had the carcass skinned, gutted and split in half. He handed a bloody portion to Seyvyar and bit into the raw flesh. It was gone in moments, leaving them to walk on, sucking the bones. The meagre meat and a few other morsels – a handful of leaves plucked from a swamp, two dried mushrooms, a dozen nuts gleaned from a shrivelled bush – gave them the energy to keep going through the day.

"How much further?" asked Seyvyar. "To a town? Or a village? Or even a farm? Out of this Wild?"

Jayas considered. "Not too far, I think. Another day at most."

"Isn't there something you can do? Some craft that will ease hunger, or speed our feet?"

"There is," Jayas told him. "I can keep myself warm for an hour at a time, be warned of danger and more besides. I prefer hunger and cold to being dead, which is why I am reserving my use of craft for real need."

"Well, I'm dying of exposure here. I don't know whether my feet or my bits will fall off first. Which would be worse?"

"Your feet. Because then you will not be able to run from the things behind us."

Seyvyar whipped around, stumbled, cursed; his head jerked as he scanned the forest behind.

"What things? Where?"

"I don't know, but the birds have been making alarm calls for some time, back along our path. It's getting closer." Jayas led Seyvyar up a slope and along to where brambles overhung a steep bank. A leaning tree had made a gap in the thorns and provided some shelter overhead. It was as defensible a position as they were likely to find, and would have to do. He pushed Seyvyar to the back and waited, makeshift spear angled forward. The birds continued to call from the trees below. A movement caught his eye, a stealthy dappled slide from cover to cover. He brought the spear lower and waited. A second big cat joined the first, they lowered their heads to sniff the ground, then looked up straight at Jayas, amber eyes meeting his. Lips curled back from long fangs.

Jayas shifted the spear to the crook of his arm and played his fingers together, drawing on craft to toughen his skin. The cats tensed, leaned forward. He brought the spear back to ready, smiled.

"We are just passing through. Why don't we talk this out?"

The cats blinked, looked at each other, backed away a little. There was a moment of shimmer, an eye-defying twist in the air and two women stood there. They were in tunics of coarse weave, belted with rope. At one waist was a dagger of bone or ivory, at the other a blowpipe and pouch. Bare feet gripped the mould of the forest floor. Both wore their hair short, one dark brown, her companion lighter. They were unalike in feature – sharp cheekbones and pointed chin on the left, long nose above a full mouth on the right. Neither was smiling.

Jayas did smile, accompanying it with a look that swept from toes to face, expressing blatant admiration at every part of the journey. They both preened slightly, then frowned. *Ah, cats*, Jayas thought. He cocked his head to one side and waited.

"You are on our land, and weak," Cheekbones stated.

"True," conceded Jayas. "But with nothing worth taking, naked as we are." Here he gestured at his lower body. The cat-women sneered. "Also, my friend is a magician of some power, and I am not without resource myself."

"A magician and his friend, just out for a nude stroll in the Wild," sneered Cheekbones. "Or maybe just a pair of inadequate exhibitionists who got lost."

"An interesting hunt, perhaps," allowed Long Nose.

Jayas shook his head sadly. "Alas, no. We intend to rest here for some time." Cheekbones pouted.

Long Nose patted the pouch at her side. "Skin is a poor armour, and you have a lot of it."

"So it is," smiled Jayas. "But I'm quick. Try me."

Long Nose scooped up a pebble and threw it hard at Jayas' face. His hand came up and it smacked into his palm. "Good throw." He tossed the pebble about, cleared his throat, adjusted the spear and suddenly threw the pebble back, aiming low. Long Nose caught it easily with a graceful dip. Jayas acknowledged with a tilt of the head. The pebble went from hand to hand, then back at him with a lightning flick. Jayas twisted to let it thump into the earth behind. Long Nose went to say something to her companion, caught at her throat in shock, turned an angry glare on Jayas and Seyvyar, her mouth opening and closing soundlessly.

"Is something wrong?" asked Jayas.

"What have you done?" growled Cheekbones.

Jayas shrugged. "I? The Wild is full of oddities, and spirits are playful."

Cheekbones cast her eyes about. "I sense no spirit. No, *you* have done this. Release my friend at once!"

"Is it that she has lost speech? I believe there is a herb that remedies this. It grows in open country, often where cows have grazed. Is there any such place nearby?"

Long Nose raked the earth with a clawed foot in frustration, snatched a dart from her pouch and threw it at Jayas. Seyvyar squawked in alarm. The dart hit Jayas' naked chest and bounced off. He brushed a hand across his scaled skin and carefully did not smile. Long Nose melted into cat shape, lashed her tail, re-formed into a woman with smouldering eyes.

"You took my voice," she growled.

"I am not a hare for your sport, not while I can draw on craft," responded Jayas. Long Nose lifted a lip and took a half step.

"Ladies, ladies," soothed Seyvyar. They both bristled. Seyvyar edged into half view and held up a placating hand. "Surely interesting people like us can find something better to do than *fight*." He followed this with a leer and a thrust of the hips. The women looked at each other, one made a step forward, lips drawn in a scowl, then halted as the other muttered something. A pause, and they both turned and left, not deigning to look back.

"Did you just try to crack on to that pair?" demanded Jayas. "You're lucky they are not cooking your balls in front of your eyes right now."

"Give me some credit," explained Seyvyar. "The worst they could do is go lounge under a tree and watch us die of starvation, because we'd be dead or worse in an instant if we came out to fight in the open. So we had to make them either attack us here, where we have some advantage, or go away. I turned them off, and they went away." After a pause he added "Of course, they could have taken me up on the invite. That would have been really interesting."

"Fat chance," Jayas told him. Seyvyar gave back an unrepentant grin, leading Jayas to a reluctant laugh.

"Might as well spend the night here. I'll see if there are any frogs in that stream while you gather leaves."

THEY SAW THE FIRST signs that the Wild was giving way to settled lands next morning. A beaten path crossed a stream on a bridge of three logs, the tops adzed flat; a small clearing where trees had been felled, the stumps orange with clustered fungi; a bramble pruned back to allow passage. If the land permitted these, pasture and farm could not be far away. Jayas and Seyvyar staggered on with fresh energy, despite gnawing hunger and chilled flesh.

The first farm was a disappointment, an isolated house guarded by moats, thorn hedges, closed walls and a chorus of deep barks. The cattle were shaggy, sharp-horned, wary, lifting their heads from the wintry grass to track the pair with suspicious eyes. Rather than brave the defences they went on, crunching across frosted grass until a second came in sight. This was scarcely less formidable, but at least had no audible dogs and a gate giving on to a path. The stone creature on the gate pillar screamed as they entered, evoking an answering cry from the iron harpy atop the house. Seyvyar and Jayas winced as the gravel dug into their soles but hobbled on gamely. The house stood on a mound above a ditch, the door reached by a narrow bridge. As they stood at the foot, uncertain, a voice called from above.

"Who's there?"

Jayas put as much pitiful anxiety into his voice as he could. "Two who have lost all in the Wild, cold and hungry, seeking only what your charity might provide. I can work," he added, "for food and a rag to cover our naked shame against the winter's bite. My companion is maimed."

When there was no response they shuffled back, resigned to a desolate trudge onwards. Jayas had half turned away when the door creaked open. A tall woman, broad-shouldered and stoutly built, looked them up and down, from bleeding feet past cold-shrivelled parts to scratched torsos and pinched faces. The corner of her mouth curved up.

"A sorry pair indeed. Well, the powers smile on the charitable, and the district will get a bad name if you wander around like that." Her gaze flicked to the knife Seyvyar cradled awkwardly in his left hand and the blade loose in Jayas' grasp.

"No weapons in the house, and your words on no harm to any within."

"Freely given, our word on no harm, by the Powers and our honour," Jayas replied for them both. He laid the knife carefully on the bridge rail and stepped forward, hands open. Seyvyar followed, to be led down a flagged passage into the blessed warmth of a large kitchen. A thin man looked up from chopping vegetables, snickered and went back to his task. A sizeable lump of brown fur snored from a basket in a corner. Jayas' gaze went from it to the woman, he tabulated a number of clues and abandoned even the tiniest thoughts of mischief. One trifled with the shape-strong at one's peril.

A bowl of porridge lent Jayas the strength to barrow manure from the stables to the garden, there to spread it over the chill earth. A worn kilt and a thin shirt did little to keep him warm, but he felt safe enough to draw on craft for that. When dusk fell he put away his tools, washed the dirt from his feet and came inside to bread and a large helping of stew. Seyvyar's hand kept him from doing too much, but she allowed him a shirt and kilt too, remarking that she was not so abandoned as to keep naked men around the house. They slept on the floor next to the hearthstone and thought it luxury.

In this way they worked their way from farm to farm. Jayas grew gills to clear a blocked intake in a well, earning two pairs of shoes and an old coat. At another he drew on craft to lure a troop of hurler possums from the roof of a barn, adding more clothes to their mismatched collection. At this last place he woke in the night to find Seyvyar weeping quietly. At his soft-voiced query Seyvyar looked up, letting the tears drip to the floor.

"I have my ether-sense. I can feel the surround, and know the world as it truly is. That vile potion has left me. I am a magician again." Jayas reached across to grip his shoulder in sympathy. He would feel the same if deprived of craft, as that dab of potion had cut Seyvyar off from the ether-sense essential to his practice of the art. The thought kept him lying awake for some time, listening to Seyvyar's joyful sobs fade into an easy sleep.

JAYAS TURNED OVER THE quandary in his mind as the slow journey continued. What would he do if he lost his command of craft? For that matter, what had it brought him so far? Since he had left the order – no, he corrected himself, let's be honest, at least in our thoughts; since he had been *expelled* from the order that had first taught him to draw the ether through his fingers, he had wandered far, seen much, learned some. What had he gained? Some knowledge, some tricks, some scars. Few friends, none lasting; sudden flushes of wealth, soon dissipated. He had invested a lot of hope in this last job; not much at first, but more and more as it unfolded. It was going to be the big score, the one that set him up for life. Now, after it had crashed in ruin, he wondered what he would have done had it succeeded. What exactly would he have been 'set up' for? Would he have bought a house, made prudent investments, lived the hedonistic bachelor life or found someone and made a family? Bought a bar, as old soldiers were wont to do? These last years had hardly fitted him for such paths. He reflected that he had hardly ever met any older venturers, and never a retired one. After a time he gave up such thoughts. He would figure out what to do with his life after he made the big score.

Jayas did communicate his musings to Seyvyar as they trudged down a muddy lane. The frozen ruts and sudden soft patches made for treacherous footing, made more so by a sleeting rain gusting across the dismal landscape. Seyvyar, head down, hand and half-hand tucked inside his ragged coat, merely grunted. An hour later he spoke up. They were sitting by the hearth in the taproom of a village alehouse, nursing two mugs of mulled wine. Jayas had noted the sword and crossbow mounted on pegs behind the bar, the cropped iron-grey hair and upright carriage of the barkeep, the regimented tables and benches, and remarked that it fitted one of his visions of a future.

Seyvyar swept a disdainful eye over the scatter of other patrons. "Well, if a life serving drinks to yokels would make you happy, so be it. Not for me. I want fame and fortune and the heights of the art."

Jayas refrained from pointing out that they were themselves by far the worst-dressed people in the place, and certainly the poorest to boot. The wine had cost the last of the few coppers his odd jobs had earned. Another gust rattled the windows. He swallowed the last of the wine and pulled himself to his feet. Perhaps the barkeep had some work he could do, enough to earn another mug, or even a meal.

The barkeep was forthrightly negative. "There's nought to be done that I can't do myself, in this season. There's not much around the village either." She raised her voice, asking the room if anyone had some work for these men. One spoke up to say nay, another shook her head, the rest stayed silent. The barkeep suggested they look in the next village, or perhaps in Irrense. At this Seyvyar lost his temper.

"And how the bloody hell do we get to Irrense, or even the next village, on two swallows of cheap piss? I'm a magician! Even this shit-hole must have some use for magic."

Jayas stepped over to the door and outside, waited a minute, then opened the door to allow Seyvyar to be ejected violently. Seyvyar picked himself up, wiping mud from his face

"Bastards! The only reason I didn't kill them all is, is..."

"Because you couldn't? Possibly also because you had no mind to be hunted across the Four Kingdoms? I believe one of the privileges of the Association is the right to punish convicted magicians. I am told they do it with magic, adapting the spell to the crime."

"And you would come to watch," said Seyvyar sourly.

"Of course. What sort of person would not go out of their way to say a last farewell to an old friend? Come on. There will be a barn somewhere."

2. Skulls Talking

On the north side of the port town of Ilkina, a short walk beyond the last push-stone that allows the operation of sedan chairs and lift-poles, sits a house. It has a broad view over the sea from its perch on a small cliff but is otherwise unremarkable. The house is of local stone, roughly dressed, the black roof tiles pitched against the sudden downpours of summer. The path to the front door winds among rocks and shrubs, as is usual in this province. The door itself speaks words of welcome in five known languages and two as yet unidentified, an idiosyncratic but ordinary piece of magic. Likewise the copper stoats on the roof that apprise the residents of visitors are nothing special, and to be expected in a dwelling a little out of the way.

The sole resident is a dealer in old and rare books. Every morning when the weather is fine he walks down into the town, takes his accustomed chair in a harbour-side restaurant, has a glass of white wine and a bowl of fish soup and walks back. He is widely known but has few acquaintances and no close friends. He has mentioned that much of his time is taken up with a philosophical work on the interaction of the material and the extra-material. As part of this he is compiling a complete and accurate compendium of the known Powers, domains and other spiritual entities of the lands around the Green Sea. Any who give it thought accept that this explains his correspondence and the visitors from out of town.

From time to time someone makes casual inquiry as to how the work is coming along, and are answered with a discourse on such topics as the metamorphosis of spirits or the non-ergodic nature of domainal evolution. The erudition is undeniable, but the delivery leaves listeners no better informed at the end than the beginning. Inquiries had dwindled away until nearly everyone confined themselves to remarks on the weather.

On this particular morning the resident took his accustomed walk into town, had his wine and soup, exchanged a few words on the weather (cold but clear, with a light wind from the east), and walked back. He let himself in and proceeded to his study, a large room at the back of the house, whose glass doors looked out on the restless waters. A movement caught his eye as he opened the door, and he glanced across to see a woman waiting on the terrace. She was simply standing there, hands at her sides, looking out over the sea. A flutter of the light dress she wore had been the movement that attracted his attention. The resident hurried across to open a door and usher her inside. The woman picked up a cloth bag and stepped past him, acknowledging his bow of welcome with a slight dip of the head.

"Lady Fleuri, this is an honour. What may I offer you?"

"You may provide me with information, Jochem. That is all I require." She crossed to his desk and let two skulls fall from the bag. They were both clean of flesh, mottled brown rather than the white of old bone, complete with jaws. They sat askew on the desk, sending their vacant stares into the corners of the room.

Jochem showed no surprise. He pulled on gloves and gave her a querying look."They are free from possession or taint?"

The lady nodded.

"Then first I shall move them from my copy of Pradiger's *Theosophical Investigations*. It is both rare and fragile." He lifted the skulls and set them on a cloth, then took a pair of calipers, a small hammer and an ear trumpet. Lady Fleuri watched as he measured, tapped and listened. At last he straightened up.

"Both male, in their early twenties. This one had advanced in the art magic to a considerable degree, but was still some way from the higher levels. The other was of a similar level in craft, and had been schooled in one of the darker orders. Both died of violence, the magician quite unexpectedly."

"I need their names, the names of those who killed them and the names of any they recently killed," said Lady Fleuri flatly.

Jochem's mouth tightened, but he made no overt protest. "I may not be able to obtain much. Their own names, certainly, their places of birth and their learning. They may not have known the names you seek, and faces are often indistinct. Memory is uncertain even in the living, the more so in times of stress."

"They knew the killers, if not the killed," stated Lady Fleuri. "Do all that you can, as soon as you can."

"That will need me to use more, ah, intrusive methods. I may have your answers in two days, more likely three."

"Three days, at sunset," was the reply. Lady Fleuri walked to the door and vanished around a corner of the house. Jochem sighed. He knew that if he went and looked she would have vanished. He did it anyway. Back in the house he looked at the skulls.

"Well, boys, we're going to become very well acquainted." He picked up one. "You were a magician, so you liked something a little exotic. For you, pike with Dravish spices, a silver pot, and a garnish of tongue-stabber. For your friend, something from a colder climate. Root vegetables and lamb bones, I think, with some eggplant for the darkish side. Garlic for both, of course. I only have the one large pot, so you will have to take turns. You first, magic-boy." Jochem left the room for the kitchen, humming absently as he went.

The next evening found Jochem in his cellar. A stockpot steamed gently from a stand next to a raised earthen bed, the dome of the skull rising briefly above the liquid before sinking again with a hiss and a gurgle. The rich smell of a spicy fish stew filled the air but did nothing to lessen the chill. Jochem fussed about with candles until the shadows cast by three triangles set into the floor were to his satisfaction. At last he crossed to the bed, pulled off the thick robe and stepped out of his slippers. A shudder went through his thin frame and goosebumps sprang up on pale flesh.

"This is not the most comfortable of ways to ask questions, you know," he grumbled to the bobbing skull as he lowered himself gingerly on to the dark soil. Jochem's body sank into the loam, which shifted until it cupped his head and spread over his torso like an inadequate blanket. "This is too much like my student lodgings to amuse. You're warm in your bath, and I'm freezing my old body into an early grave. It should be the other way round. Mind you," he went on in a fair-minded tone, "I suppose there are less comfortable ways, and I think you experienced some. Well, let's see what you remember." He dipped a bowl into the broth and sipped slowly, mindful not to burn his tongue, then closed his eyes. It was half an hour before he stirred. He grumbled his way into the robe and slippers, picked up the now luke-warm stockpot and shuffled upstairs, muttering names under his breath.

Lady Fleuri returned as promised on the third day, appearing on the terrace as the setting sun was still glimmering on the water. Jochem looked up from his desk at her rap and hastened to let her in. As before, she wore only a simple linen dress and light sandals, despite the brisk weather. She opened without preamble.

"Do you have the names?"

"I have names, and more besides. First, let us discuss payment for three days of my time, some expensive materials and considerable spiritual wear and tear."

Lady Fleuri did not frown. Rather, a puzzled expression crossed her face. "Payment? Are you not a valued client of our house?"

"Indeed I am, and one well-compensated previously."

"We gave you *money*? Was not our patronage enough?" asked Lady Fleuri.

Jochem was firm. "Frankly, no. The Patrician is generous with both favour *and* silver."

Lady Fleuri stood a moment, then said curtly "Tomorrow at sunset." She turned and left. Jochem closed the door and returned to the *Theosophical Investigations.*

Lady Fleuri was true to her word. At sunset she walked in and dropped a bag on the desk. Jochem was not so crass as to examine the contents, and proceeded straight to his findings.

"The magician was one Rudrin, from Kadlus in the southern provinces. He gained his scroll three years past, and had spent much time in the Wild. He is no stranger to death, and most recently helped kill a magician. He did not know the man's name – there was some dream-like farrago of flying and monstrous ants. He himself died suddenly, in a moment of unguarded elation, struck from behind. He died bewildered, but his fellow here solved the mystery."

At this Jochem gestured at the two skulls on the desk. One – the hapless Rudrin – wore a wreath of crocus flowers, while two sprigs of rosemary stuck jauntily from the ear-holes of its fellow. Jochem resumed.

"This was the more interesting. Name of Kelve, well-versed in craft, a member of a dark order and a thoroughly devious sort. He had some years of experience in theft, violence, deceit and betrayal. It did not serve him in this instance. He was in a fight to the death shortly before his own demise, involving people with kilts and a fellow in black armour, but met his death at the hands of one of his fellows – another versed in craft and also of a dark order. As ever, those people do more to each other than they do to their supposed enemies. Kelve's grievance at being the betrayed rather than the betrayer lingers yet."

Lady Fleuri dismissed this with an impatient wave of the hand. "The name of the killer, and of his fellows, did you get those?"

"I had to delve further back than is usual, and fit together fragments from both into one whole. But the answer is yes. The killer of Kelve was one Jayas, and both Kelve and Rudrin spent their last months with Jayas, a magician named Seira, a buffoonish fellow they both thought of as 'lamb-chop' and – the only one they trusted - a soldierly sort named Sarm. The fracas in which they died resulted from a falling out among this group."

Lady Fleuri absorbed this, absently tapping an arched foot on the floor. "Jayas, Seira, a buffoon, a soldier. I have reason to doubt all four survived, but which? Was there any memory of further deaths?"

"Alas, no. What I glean is not so much memory as the echoes of events. It took much effort to get as much as I have, and I cannot answer that what I have told you is the un-distorted truth."

"What of places? With these names alone I could search the Four Kingdoms and be no nearer finding them."

"Birth places usually leave a strong resonance, but Kelve was silent on this and much else. His was a hidden life. For the other, well, the Wild overlays much, but I caught a smell that reminded me of Kaber, and a fondness for the wines of the Duneep. I would look along the road from Kaber to Azbai."

"That does not offer as much guidance as perhaps you think it does," said Lady Fleuri acidly. Jochem spread his hands apologetically, then offered two further suggestions. With the aid of a craft-spell a layer of earth was persuaded to shape itself over the bones into the features they had in life. Lady Fleuri approved, and was adept at drawing. When the likenesses were to her satisfaction, Jochem told her that the craft could interrogate any objects closely associated with the four, although details faded over time. This might yield more information on the four she sought.

"If I find something of theirs, likely I have found them," said Lady Fleuri.

"And what then?"

"Death," she replied "Death or worse". She scooped up the portraits and left as unceremoniously as ever.

Alone again, Jochem took time to study the two faces. In life Rudrin would have been a cheerful, open sort, Jochem supposed. The earth had shaped a round face, broad at the cheekbones, a low nose and a wide mouth, now set in shock and surprise. To be expected, Jochem thought; few people anticipate a stab in the back.

Kelve now, well, Kelve was a very different sort. A wide forehead, pointed jaw, narrow eyes. A face made for suspicion, or perhaps suspicion had made the face. Jochem wondered idly if physiognomists had determined cause and effect in this matter. He picked up a skull in each hand and weighed them.

"Shall I put you together or keep you apart? Apart, I think, for you may have company later. Kelve here can go next to that fellow who washed up two months back, while you, Rudrin, can be with the magician who exploded. She will have some advice for you."

He departed the room, fingers tapping a tune on Kelve's dome.

LADY FLEURI SAT AT the window of her apartment in Seimo. The milder climate of the Islands suited her, she found; that it was nearly as distant from the tax authorities as one could be in the Four Kingdoms was also a distinct advantage. Her late husband had been adamant that no single penny of his should go to pay taxes, and it was a tradition she saw no reason to alter. The window was open to a spring air redolent of the herb-covered hillsides above the town. The Lady was reading a page of small print easily, although it was near dusk and the light was poor.

Inquiries were made at towns, villages and other suitable sites along the Northern Road, starting from Kaber on the 11th of the Month of the Polecat. No conclusive results were obtained until I reached Zyich on the upper Duneep. It is a town often used as a base for ventures in the West Wild. I made inquiries here in a variety of guises, and was able to obtain positive news of Rudrin, Kelve and their associates. In summary:

> *Rudrin was a member of a band that engaged in ventures into the Wilds, a band that had suffered recent losses and had very mixed fortunes. The leading member was the magician Seyvyar Trist, recalled as a vain and boastful person but well-versed in the art.*

Apart from Seyvyar, the band most recently comprised:

> *The magician Rudrin, young, likeable and earnest;*
>
> *Kelve, sworn to a northern affiliate of the Companions of the Road. Reserved, steady, made people a little nervous;*
>
> *His friend 'Cutlet' (a nickname), a sergeant in the Brothers in Glory. The words brash, loud, handsy and nuisance came up repeatedly;*
>
> *Saram, a former soldier with the River Guard. Very strong but a peaceable fellow, easy-going, the best-liked of the band.*
>
> *Jayas Zrei, a lieutenant of the Holders. He spoke of this as a minor order based in the High Dinau in the eastern hills, and was recalled as joining the band some days before they left on their last foray into the West Wild. No-one had anything much to say of Jayas, good or bad.*

I enclose sketches of all six, drawn from the minds of those who agreed to cooperate. The band left for the West Wild on or around the 3rd day of the Month of the Mouse last year. There has been no news of them in Zyich since.

It is possible that inquiries in Hierrez, Leax and Perry will yield further information. It is also possible that the band left the Wild to the south, in which case I may be able to find traces in Irrense Province. If you wish any of these avenues explored, please remit a further one hundred Azic crowns to cover fees and initial expenses together with instructions. I attach an itemised list of expenses.

Tol Henze, Inquirer

LADY FLEURI PUT THE document aside and glanced at the pictures. Kelve and Rudrin went to one side. Jochem had examined various objects and been able to tell her that the owner of the axe was dead. That must be Saram, pictured as a large man with a friendly smile and an axe. His portrait joined the discard pile and she turned to the expenses. These she scrutinised line by line, hissing through her teeth and marking several claims. That done, she again picked up the pictures and leafed through them. She studied Cutlet's cheerful vacuous countenance and murmured '*I* would kill him, given the opportunity'. All or some of these three were possibly alive. She intended to change that.

For now, though, it was dark enough that she could go to dinner. She climbed the stair to the widow's walk above, studied the sky a moment and then shimmered into owl-shape. A leap, a spread of wide barred wings and she was wheeling above the town. There would be one less spring lamb frolicking in the hills tomorrow.

3. Second Move in the Game

Tol Henze, inquirer, felt her purse, shrugged and turned into the street diner anyway. She *needed* a hot drink and something to eat, for it had been a long and fruitless day. Her hooded cape, damp from rain, went on a hook and she settled herself in a back corner to brood over a mug of hot beer and a stuffed roll. She was, Tol decided, sick of Kaber City. Sick of being poor, and damp, and her talents unappreciated. Her first years as an investigator had been exciting, full of new things to learn and a new side of life to navigate. Then it became routine, and ever more evident that she would never make more than a meagre living. It was that job a month back that had unsettled her, she reckoned.

She went over that job in her mind. A former client, Shefin Skan, had asked her to find out what she could about several people, looking along the highway from Kaber City to Zyich. She had accepted eagerly, the first commission to take her any distance out of the city in three years. It had been a real adventure, even if the per diem was at the low end and the expense allowance less than generous.

Tol's mind returned to a recurring puzzle. Skan dealt in paint, with a sideline as a rental agent. An odd combination. Her previous commissions from him had involved finding tenants who had skipped out in arrears. What had he to do with a motley group of footloose adventurers? Still, she had gathered the asked-for information and sent in her report. Since then? Nothing. A couple of small jobs, just enough to pay the rent. She had checked on Skan a week back, to find he had left the city, moved his whole business, paint and all, to Leax. The cheese wholesaler on the next floor said he had a lover there. Another oddity. Leax was a small port clinging to the coast of the West Wild. He would not collect rents there, or sell much paint, she supposed.

Tol finished her roll and stood up. This was getting her nowhere, and she had to walk home. A spell for flight was in her book, and often used at the end of the day, or earlier when people would not answer the door. A knock at the window was somehow more compelling, especially when they lived on the fifth floor. Today, three tracing spells had not left her enough ether-access to fly. She pulled the cape about her and set off through the drizzle. She had one foot on the stair to her room when the concierge called out from his cubby. What did the dratted man want now? A letter? It was probably a bill. She took the envelope ungraciously and went up. It was not until the flimsy door closed that she examined it.

Good thick paper, her name and address in a firm hand, the lettering careful, as if the writer was not used to the script. She turned it over; sealed with black wax, no impress. Out of habit Tol checked for poisons or hostile spells. From time to time someone resented an inquiry enough to take measures to discourage the enquirer. Nothing obvious, so she opened it. Three slips of paper.

Tol looked at the bank draft first. One hundred and sixty-two crowns. A welcome amount. Next was a single sheet giving a box number at the Seimo branch of Green Sea Mercantile. The third was another sheet, with two terse lines in that same foreign hand.

Look from Zyich to Ilkina and find all those named in your last report. Advance and expenses enclosed. Receipts required. Report from Irrense to enclosed address.

It was signed with a looping 'F'.

Tol read it again. This must relate to her commission for Skan, although 'F' was unknown to her. She was to follow up. Leave Kaber City for at least a month, more probably two. She looked around the rented room. A thin hard bed, a wardrobe that leaned a little to one side, so that the door stuck. A carpet so thin the lines of the floorboards showed through. A small table that wobbled. A chair that also wobbled. A washroom down the hall just as bleak. The only virtue she could give it was it was clean, although the landlord's dust-weasel shambled rather than scurried, with small tooth-tightening squeaks. What was there to miss?. A loud step outside and a wobble of the table gave her a small push, but it was really no choice at all. Stay here and find lost dogs and delinquent tenants or delve into a major mystery with travel thrown in? It might be an irresponsible jump, but she was taking it. The next day she pushed a note under the landlord's door – 'I have left', and she was down the stairs and out into the streets of Kaber Old Town. The coaching inn for the south road was only half an hour's walk from the bank.

TOL SAT ATOP THE CARRIAGE, reflecting on life journeys and the current fashion for vegetable magics. The latter had shown itself a fruitful (she snickered at her own pun) avenue of research, although few successes had been replicable. The absorbent squash was mostly reliable, and messy rather than disastrous when it went wrong. A pity that one could only carry so many pumpkins. The parsnips were erratic enough to make even senior mages wary and the kale unpredictably vicious. She herself had three carrots, picked up cheap because no-one, including the maker, had any idea what they did. Well, that was making new Items, best likened to trying to teach a three year old to cook a souffle: sometimes a fluffy triumph, more often a flat failure. In magic's case, often a failure that ate the cookware or grew tentacles and chased the cat.

In the present instance, a definite success. Someone had turned to vegetables in the continual quest for etheric transport that worked on the open road. Two cabbages, each wider than she was tall, were harnessed in tandem to the carriage. They had been fitted with yokes and steel-studded wooden rims, and dragged the carriage at an unvarying pace, guided by long reins. At each stop arms dropped to lift them off the ground, still turning, to churn away until the carriage was again set in motion. How long they would last she did not know, but it saved a deal of fodder in the meantime. It was possible some mage-wrights had a cabbage-breeding farm out there, and she mused awhile on a vision of cabbage-racing as a sport. Since this was the first and only pair of carriage-cabbages she had encountered, it was more likely that repeat trials had done something else – perhaps refused to grow larger than sprouts, or run off into the Wild to go hunt wolves. No matter; the pair out front were no thoroughbreds, but they managed a decent pace.

Tol had made three previous trips along the road that linked Kaber to Azbai city, the not-quite-capital of the Four Kingdoms, never reaching as far as Azbai itself. The first had been north, from her birthplace of Duneep-Seffra (so-called to distinguish it from Seffra-on-sea, Seffra-out-east, Little Seffra, and Seffra-in-the-Huff), away from her overbearing mother and her obnoxious siblings. That had been the slowest, a tedious creep up the Duneep valley in an oxcart, a three day wait in Zyich for a caravan to assemble, another five days through the Wild that divided Kaber from the Four Kingdoms, then this last familiar piece of tilled land and into great Kaber city itself, with all its new sights and smells and sounds.

She vividly remembered that anxious walk into the city, her meagre luggage a weight on her back, asking directions in halting Kabinese until at last she knocked on the door of the academy. The second and third trips had been recent, the precursors to this current journey. The second had been a slow walk from village to village, then as quickly across the Wild as possible, then more villages. At each making patient inquiries, showing around portraits, spinning whatever tale seemed likeliest to produce results. A cheese-monger in Failli had provided one name. A man she was fairly certain was an ex-bandit had spoken at length and with some bitterness about two others. A woman had pointed to one of her portraits, smiled and said she was sure he had given a false name 'But, you know, it didn't really matter. If you find him give him a kiss from me.'

It was not until she reached Zyich that she hit pay-dirt. Shop-keepers, street-loungers, the habitués of the town's famous inn all readily put names to the faces, along with stories of boastful success and abject failure, claims for monies owed (and in one case credit due) and varied assertions on character. Associates were mentioned, including several deceased. A salesman in dried shrimp, seaweed snacks and like marine tit-bits, recently from Kaber, thought he had seen several of the band in the coastal town of Hierrez some six months back. Tol committed it all to memory and spent her evenings with a pen.

The third had been the quick return to Kaber. Now here she was again, this time behind a fine pair of winter whites. The carriage met the first steep climb, but the pace did not slacken even as the driver hauled on a rein to turn the lead cabbage into the bend. This steady pace would cut at least a day off the trip, maybe two. She put this to her fellow roof-passenger, a sturdy woman with the beaky nose, brick complexion and tawny hair typical of the Islands. As she wore stout leather, had a helmet dangling from her luggage and a long-handled axe close to hand, it was no great deduction that she was some sort of fighter. A professional guard, perhaps? She had no insignia and her gear was plain and well-worn, if in good order.

"Tol Henze, lately of Kaber," Tol offered after the first exchange of calculations on journey times.

"Serriet Habse, sword-crafter. Well, I'm best with an axe, but I make do with the sword and bow. Currently looking for work. I'm hoping to find some Wild-runners looking to make up a party in Zyich."

"I was there recently and it seemed pretty quiet on that front. Sorry to disappoint. A band I heard about has gone missing, believed mostly dead, and no-one was looking to follow them."

Serriet sighed. "If it's as you say, I'll keep going. There may be something down south, or over in the Islands."

They chatted for a time as the scenery rolled past, finding commonality in age, precarious professional prospects and distaste for their respective families.

"Mine are all in orders, mostly the Companions, except for the snooty few who opted for the Pure Land. I have no gift for that side of craft, and no desire to be ordered about," was Serriet's summation of her relatives. Tol responded with her autocratic mother and her several siblings, all obsessed with their prestige among the landed gentry of the district, and all disdainful of the art or indeed any other higher learning.

"So I applied for a scholarship with the Association, and they granted me a place in Kaber. I gained my scroll four – no five - years back."

Serriet swore as the carriage lurched through a pot-holed stretch, one out-flung hand gripping the strapped-down luggage piled behind them. The cabbages splashed through a shallow ford, the carriage tilting as wheels sank into the soft gravel, then set out briskly up the next slope. Tol felt the surrounding ether begin to shift from the sedate and even cadences of settled lands into the skirling rhythms of the Wild. Another hour at this pace and she would be wholly immersed in these livelier, more demanding, deadlier tempos.

They asked so much more of her, challenged her nerve and wits. She met it as a fencer might enter a tournament packed with worthy opponents, as a chance to better her command of her art. She turned to see Serriet had the same sparkle in her eye and a small fierce grin.

"You feel it too?" Not really a question. She went on, curious, "How does it work for sword-craft? I was taught that our ether-sense was peculiar to the art."

Serriet stretched out a muscular arm and sketched a series of quick movements in the air. "A little weapon-skill is the beginning of the art, no? You take it and let that access flow through to the mind. In those with high craft, such as my cousins in the Companions, the access flows through the fingers. With us, we tune our whole bodies to the flow. I do not see the surround, nor can I draw it through my hands, but when I swing my axe or let an arrow fly I am in tune with it in every nerve and sinew. You talk to the ether; high craft plays tunes with it; we *dance* with it."

The coachman glanced back over his shoulder. "Might need some of that dancing a bit later. A few things out here see these green horses as food, and other things make mistakes. Had a big drop-bear try for the leader last trip. Got its claws in and went around and under. Didn't come up – these beauties weigh as much as a draught horse."

Serriet turned around to reach between bundles and pulled out a bow, the unstrung ends making elegant curves away from the central grip. Another reach fetched an open quiver, the arrows arranged head-down much as a carpenter might rack their chisels, from narrow armour-punching bodkin to cutting broad-head.

"Usual terms?" she queried the coachman, who grunted reply. "You have to say yes or no," pursued Serriet, which elicited a muttered yes.

"You can witness," Serriet told Tol. "On second thought, if you throw a spell you're covered too." She dropped her body over the rail and down to call to the inside passengers.

"The coach agrees to the usual terms for passenger help if we are attacked. That's half the fare and free medical or funeral. Can I have a witness?"

A voice answered. "Baive sees my heart. I so witness." Serriet pulled back from her alarming lean, satisfied.

"Medical or funeral?" Tol asked uneasily.

THE COACH ROLLED PAST the usual first stop while the sun was still well up, to Tol's satisfaction, and reached the second an hour before dark. This was a small piece of level ground, sheltered on the side away from the road by a rock wall. A line of squat stone pillars marked it off from the road, and the passengers were assured that they were safe from the Wild unless they strayed beyond these bounds. The coachman and his assistant unloaded tents, set a hearthstone to heating a stew and directed people to privies that were no more than a plank over a hole in the ground. Tol had no need of a tent, as the Circle of Shelter would keep her dry and warm. She invited Serriet to share and took her bowl over to collect stew and flatbread.

The circle around the hearthstone included three brothers from Chiran going home after a visit to relatives in Kaber, a dealer in furs with a bale of winter pelts, a priest of Baive, the divinity of tilled fields, and an older man in faded blue and silver robes who introduced himself as Guiding Light.

"That is the meaning of my life-name in my native Brahnak," he explained. "I took that name when I was called to devote my remaining years to telling outland folk of the teachings of Sebres Brahn, that they might walk the Path in full knowledge."

When the priest of Baive asked the Brahnak to tell him more, Tol listened as Guiding Light outlined his foreign faith. The Path, he said, was the route to perfect understanding beyond the brief life of the mortal body and the longer life of the soul; beyond even the vision of the greater powers. For such as Baive - here with a bow to the priest – were known lords of field or forest or other domain, yet beyond them was the world itself entire, and beyond that the necklace of worlds, seventeen strung like pearls on a string, each with its divinities. Great as these might be, there must be a greater beyond, source of all. For where does justice come from, or truth, that the highest powers must bow to? Whence the mysteries of the ether, that sometimes knows our subtlest thoughts and at other times refuses the simplest request? What gives law to the Wild, that lets no house be built here? These questions we can ask, went on the Brahnak, but answers we have none. And by this absence we know our understanding is imperfect, yet our conviction in justice and truth tells us that a better understanding is to be had. As we may look at a mountain and know, though we cannot see it, that there is a land beyond, so we may know a more perfect world.

The man looked around. "We may reach that place of understanding, that abode of the Highest, source of all. The Path is the way, where every right act, whether of hand or speech or thought, will take you upward, ever closer to the Highest."

This speech was met with mild interest. "Baive is the limit of my vision," was all the priest said, and the conversation moved on to the spring planting and the current fashion for curled slippers.

Tol did return to the topic when lying in her blankets, the light green glow of the Circle overhead. Serriet was lying next to her, rolled snug in her own blankets. "What did you think of the Brahnak's creed?"

Serriet considered, lying there with her hands behind her head. "I dance with the ether, but I don't know what it is. I don't know that anyone does. I met a priest of Sthenae once. They attend on the powers of knowing, or so they claim. I asked him if the powers told him what it was all about, and he said no. Then he tried to knife me, so I took his head off." There did not seem to be anything to add to this, so Tol went to sleep.

The coach rolled on the next day, easily outrunning a horde of caterpillars that humped down from the hills in pursuit of fresh cabbage. Tol thought this a good thing – some of the caterpillars were as big as cats, and would they have stopped at cabbage? She was looking forward to a hot bath at Zyich when the coachman called a warning. Bounding from rock to rock down the slope ahead was a mob of goats. Not goats such as might be found in a farmyard, or even the wary creatures that ran free in the hills, but goats of the Wild. Horns as sharp as spears pointed forward, hooves boasted sharp spurs, cunning sent one part of the mob across the road so that attack would come from both sides. Tol sorted through her spells and made ready to cast when they came in range. There was almost no need. Serriet had strung her bow in one movement, snatched out an arrow and was standing on the swaying roof, a foot braced under the side-rail. A draw, a pause to aim and the bow sang. A goat dropped, the shaft sunk deep. The bow sang again and another fell. The charge faltered, veered away. Serriet shifted aim to the other side, missed a shot, sent another which pierced a neck through. With the first hit she called "That's half fare, coachman."

A bold or foolhardy goat darted in close to the lead cabbage, neck twisting as it angled for a bite. Tol leaned out and emitted the Silent Scream, freezing it. Momentum and the rolling cabbage did the rest, the yoke rising briefly as it crunched over the animal. The others were scattering away, and Serriet did not waste arrows. "That's two half-fares, coachman."

ZYICH WAS AS TOL REMEMBERED, a cluster of houses at the head of a long valley fading away south, the road a pale thread thinning into the distance. They rolled in a little before dusk, skirting the crumbling town wall and the battered old fort to haul into the caravan yard on the east side. Tol clambered down and stood, stretching legs cramped from sitting so long. There was a short bicker above and then Serriet dropped down beside her, landing easily, to hand over a wooden token. "The coach office will discount your next fare or – if you push – give you a cash refund in exchange for this."

Tol thought of a night in one of the inns around the caravan yard, a night of noise, the smell of stale beer, a hard bed and a cold washroom; a night, in short, that her expense allowance was calculated for. She shouldered her pack. "The coach office and cash it is, and then the Xanfred. It has five beers on tap and a bath-house."

She left the next morning, walking out on the country road that led eventually to the highway from great Azbai to Irrense. The West Wild loomed to her right, a dark mass of trees that rose away into the hills. To the far north Mount Ledeka brooded over the landscape, a presence ever vigilant that no seed be planted, no path laid in its long watch. Village after village followed, hard beds and soft, good beer and bad, poor dining and some unexpected delights. In all of them, no news of her quarry. At last she reached the Irrense road at Eum Ang, where her pennies saved paid for a luxurious bath and laundered clothes. No news here either, although she did not really expect any. Eum Ang was too busy to notice strangers.

Ahead the Ozrai Hills reached out from the West Wild nearly all the way to the coast, a long finger of Wild. Tol walked half a day, then flew over to the other side to resume her village to village queries. Nothing this side of the road to the dwarf mine at Nau (and how the dwarves had gained permission of the Wild for their road and mine was known only to themselves). She skirted Irrense town to take up the trudging task in the hamlets that dotted the country down to the coast. Here at last her inquiries bore fruit. The two vagabonds that had turned up naked at Mistress Rebrin's door had spawned a wealth of remark and too many bucolic jokes. An arrogant tramp had been thrown out of one ale-house here, the pair chased out of a barn there, suspected of chicken-theft in that place. The barn and another place allowed Tol to collect signature traces for both targets, although these were of little use when the trail led back to Irrense, lost amid the comings and goings of the town.

At least Tol had something to report. The Association offered rooms to visitors at a modest charge, so she lodged there, sent her report and expenses claim off and waited. Irrense had a few sites of interest and the Association a decent library. Tol spent a morning first at the famous Sighing Bridge, which groaned in sympathy with the lovelorn, and then at a cake-shop that had served as cover for three notorious pirates – all excellent pastry-cooks. Their story was famous; the magistrates had declared that one might live on condition they give up piracy to teach their skills. The three had been unable to agree on which, and left it to chance. Each had baked a last cake, two concealing a deadly poison and one harmless. The apple torte had given life and was now the signature dish of the province. Tol thought it very good indeed.

She was in the library after lunch, leafing through a volume on the Dravish system for classifying spells, when a conversation behind caught her ear.

"One hundred and forty-three thousand crowns! Really, the price of a decent retreat is becoming absurd. Might as well stay in town."

The second speaker differed. "It does not seem unreasonable to me. The place is a castle, and very prettily furnished too, I understand. My father knew the old Patrician, and said he had collected some fine pieces. Convenient to town too, as so many of these places aren't. I dare say Merrife will be able to find guests, especially if she can persuade her cook to move there."

The first grunted, clearly unwilling to accept this argument. "What happened to the son anyway? I thought he had sworn never to set foot in the Four Kingdoms."

"I gather he met with an accident. It's his widow has put the place on the market. Don't know the details, but I was told that fellow with half a hand, the one who was here for a month, was mixed up in it."

"I remember the fellow. Gave himself airs, for all he was doing still-work to pay for the restoration. Sevyon, Sevye, some silly southern name. You don't mean he was a murderer?"

"It *is* the Wild, so murder is not the word. He may have just won a fight – the son was not above a bit of robbery, for all that he followed his father into the Silver Glove, then had something to do with that new order – the Reaching Hand or some such."

The reply was a humph and a rustle of paper.

Tol put a casual query to the desk clerk that evening. "Do you know a Seyvyar Trist? I have a message for him."

The clerk spread his hands in apology. "He was here until late last month. He left no forwarding address. Turne, do you know where he went?"

The other clerk scratched his head. "Not really. He was looking at maps of the Green Sea and I recall he asked about the cost of passage from Ilkina to western parts. What he finally settled on I don't know, or maybe he went off by land. He was not the chatty type."

Tol thanked the pair and went off. The next day she visited the basement, confirmed Servyar's presence and enhanced his signature trace. Her strongest detection spell circled aimlessly, unable to give even the faintest hint of direction. It seemed he was far away, deep in a Wild, overseas or shielded by some Item. She guessed the third of these most likely. It seemed the trail would stretch some distance yet, and perhaps inquiries with the Silver Glove or the Reaching Hand would yield some more information. Her first report was gone, but this merited further investigation. She decided to follow up here first and then in Ilkina. More walking, and probably one or two days spent poring over passenger manifests, if that clerk's gossip was accurate. Such was the life of an inquirer, but at least she would at least smell sea air again.

4. Irrense and Beyond

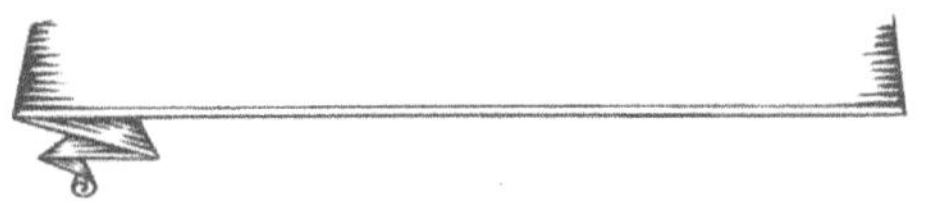

They spent the night burrowed into a pile of sacks at the back of a shed. It was smelly but dry, and mostly out of the wind. Seyvyar could cast a spell to create a warm and sheltering dome, but the green glow might bring the shed owner down on them. This way, if they were discovered they could pretend to be rats, Jayas thought. It would not be hard. Tomorrow it would be back to the road and on to Irrense. Seyvyar resentfully observed that a journey of four or five days had taken them over two weeks, most of it cold, hungry and comfortless. Jayas shrugged and replied that hero-tales rarely dwelt on the awkwardness of relieving oneself in a freezing wind, or how hard it is to get fur out of your teeth.

Seyvyar picked up bits of gossip on the last stretch into Irrense, news which did not improve his temper. That Powers-curse-her poker-wielding servant was, it seemed, respectably established in Irrense, no housemaid but a lawyer and trustee of an order in craft. His gloom persisted until Jayas' quick hands and a passing purse provided a hot meal and a drink. As they scarfed it down they tossed ideas about. Revenge was briefly considered but rejected. No, what they needed was new pastures, places where bad luck could not follow them. By the time this was settled the staff and other patrons were giving them pointed looks. Well, they had to admit their appearance and perhaps their hygiene rated poorly. They adjourned to a bench in a small square, one situated out of the wind and in the weak sunshine.

"What now? If fortune lies across the sea, we need money for passage to reach it," Jayas said, ever practical. "I can heal, and harm, and do some other things. If I can find the right people, a couple of jobs would let me buy some decent gear. With that, I can make money easy enough. Surely the Association can find you something?"

Seyvyar reluctantly admitted that he had fallen behind on his dues. The Association would be no help unless he first paid up. Jayas admitted to an emergency stash, unfortunately cached two weeks' travel away. This reminded Seyvyar that he still had a small sum with his banker in Kaber. Perhaps a bank here could arrange a transfer? They asked a passerby for directions, walked two streets over and were firmly refused admittance by an impassive doorman. Seyvyar's protestations and demonstrated command of magic yielded him nothing but directions to a charity for mendicants.

As they were retreating a plaque caught Jayas' eye. "There is our stake. We'll tell our stories to the Archivists."

"They will pay handsomely for stories?" asked Seyvyar sceptically.

"They will pay something. If not money, then clothes, a bath and a meal. Enough to get us into a bank." As he approached the door the bronze lamps on either side stretched down to sniff at his skin and peer at his face. One nodded to the other and tapped the door lightly. It opened on to a small room, bare but for a bench and a statue of a small dog on a pedestal. Jayas entered without hesitation, Seyvyar following more gingerly. The dog scratched an ear then spoke without preamble.

"What knowledge do you bring to the Order of the Learned Archive?"

Jayas spoke. "The Names of two demons, eight deaths in the Wild, doings of a Patrician, a trail of silver from Kaber to Irrense. All first-hand, recent and hitherto untold."

The dog scratched the other ear reflectively, gnawed on a toe, then spoke again. "What do you ask of the Archive in return?"

Again Jayas spoke for them. "At the least, befitting clothes, a bath, a night's rest and a meal, or silver enough to buy these. For each demon Name, one hundred Azic crowns."

The dog laid down, head on paws, and they waited. After a little it sat up. "Your first request is accepted. The Names we will discuss. A bath first. Follow the green light."

They were decanted on to the street the next morning, clean, decently clad, breakfasted and well rested. "Where now?" asked Seyvyar hoarsely. Their listeners had been attentive, thorough and relentless in their questions. After some initial prevarication Seyvyar had followed Jayas' advice to be frank about their dealings in the Wild. "For the Archivists hold their secrets well, but do not pay for half tales."

He still had misgivings. "What we did in that castle was totally justified; I mean they were going to do us, and all we did was get in first. But others might not see it that way. What if word gets out and we find the Brothers in Glory challenging us at every fork in the road?"

Jayas was sanguine. "The Brothers know as well as anyone that death goes with ventures into the Wild like taxes go with kings. The same goes for the friends and family of the others. As for the Patrician and his retainers, all are dead. The lawyer-lass let us go. So who's got an issue? Anyway, it's not the first time you have lost companions – same for me – and no-one's come back about it before. So let's check with a bank, look for some gear and see how much the Association wants."

Seyvyar let it go, acknowledging that Jayas was right, and for him getting his fingers back was the first priority.

SEYVYAR LEANED ON THE rail and watched the coast recede, enjoying the wind, the sea-smell, the prospect of new lands and the flex of his new hand. Even though the Association had given him a discount, it had still taken a month to cover the cost. A month of boring spell-work in a basement, every meal coarse bread and vegetable stew, nights sleeping on a pallet in a dormitory. Jayas had left one morning, only saying he would be away for three weeks. Whatever he had done – and Seyvyar assumed it was something shady – he had come back decently equipped and with his passage money. Jayas had then vanished again, only dropping by every few days. So now they were on the *Safe Delivery*, bound – slowly - for fame and fortune on the far side of the Green Sea. Just where these were to be found Seyvyar had no immediate idea, but he was sure something would turn up. He had his hand, his spells, a brace of virgin steel knives and a stout dagger. They had been enough before, and this time nothing would go wrong. Soon he would have money, and be able to afford something better than these wretched off-the-shelf clothes. Something in a soft weave, tailored of course, the style more in the cut than the decoration, although with a hint of richness here and there.

Jayas interrupted his dreams by joining him at the rail with a strip of smoked eel. He bit off a piece and chewed reflectively, then another, ate the last, spat a thin bone over the side and just leaned there. The sails above thrummed, pulleys squealed with each shift of wind, ropes slapped against wood. The two stood in silence for some time, Seyvyar returning to his reverie, Jayas scanning the varied rigs of the fishing craft dotting the waters. Both paid idle attention to the features of Holtin Island as they slid past to the north.

"We'll need to find two or three companions before we can try for anything big," observed Seyvyar finally. "People we can trust, this time," he added.

Jayas nodded. "People who trust us would be good. I have grown tired of watching to all sides. I think that one's a buss," he said, pointing at a red-sailed craft off the starboard bow. Seyvyar was uninterested, preferring to pursue his first remark.

"We will need another magician, and at least one arms-man. Another such as yourself, good with craft and steel, would not come amiss."

Jayas pointed out a nobby, two fifies and a dogger. Seyvyar ignored him. Jayas suggested off-hand that two of their fellow passengers – women wearing the red and yellow arm-band of the Guardian Avengers – might be suitable recruits. Seyvyar gave an exaggerated shudder.

"You know they are sworn not just to protect women, but to deliver retribution to any who harm women?"

"So? As far as I know you have never harmed a woman who was not trying to harm you," replied Jayas.

"Well, yes," Seyvyar conceded. "But they'd go haring off on their own, and they'd want to donate half the takings to homes for orphans."

Jayas agreed that this would be an unacceptable diversion of profit and dropped the idea. He went back to cataloguing the vessels within view, mostly as a way of keeping Seyvyar from talking about clothes. When Seyvyar spoke again it was at least on a different subject.

"What do the Archivists want with demon Names? They must know dozens, maybe hundreds. Do they have enemies? There's a spell that makes objects speak and they could wreak havoc by using it to summon a mass of demons."

Jayas considered. "It's a pleasing notion, but demons are like devil-rats - they cannot abide each other. Put two free in one place and you have an entertaining fight. I think the Archivists just like knowing things, although I suppose they can sell the knowledge.

Knowing the Name of a demon can be a handy thing if you are in its domain, although it does not give as much control as people think."

"I thought they could appear anywhere they are called," Seyvyar said.

"Some are confined to one place, some are free," Jayas told him. "I have known both."

"Your familiarity with the habits of demons does breed suspicion, you know. Best you keep quiet on the subject," Seyvyar told him.

Jayas shrugged. "You brought it up. In any event, demons never manifest on the sea. Since this is the *Safe Delivery* and not the *Fast Delivery*, I have several weeks free of worry about them. I intend to spend them polishing my Merllan. If I seem distracted at times, it will be because I am – I will be drawing on craft to help me learn."

Seyvyar asked if Jayas could cast the spell on others. When told that, like most such craft-spells, they could only affect the user, he spent some time grumbling about the inadequacies of craft when compared with his own noble art, but had to acknowledge that he knew of no comparable spell available to magicians. Jayas told him he had spent the last weeks exchanging language lessons for instruction in craft with a Merllan merchant, looking very smug as he did so. Seyvyar rolled his eyes and asked what help he could provide. Jayas handed handed him a booklet of basic phrases in Merllan.

'*My lowly status does not permit me to pay such an exalted amount*,' read Seyvyar. He flipped a page. '*My mother is offended. Will you apologise with steel or spell?*' '*I cannot accept a challenge at this time. Please call tomorrow/in three days/at my mother's*'. Am I going to have to fight for my life as soon as I step ashore?"

Jayas passed on what he had learned about the Merllan. They thought it demeaning to bargain over ordinary things, which were always sold at the posted price; haggling would be met with scorn and derision. For goods of high status, such as works of art, novel

Items or fine clothing (here Seyvyar paid close attention), one was expected to pay according to one's status. Hence sellers would greet all loudly as lordly benefactors, open-handed and generous to a fault, while buyers would pretend to modesty. The price finally agreed balanced one's means against one's reputation.

"Of course, as foreigners and transients, we have little reputation to lose, and can cheerfully claim to be lowly paupers," Jayas noted. He went on to explain that both formal duels and assassination were major pastimes among the Merllan nobility. The great merchant houses were ruled by matriarchs whose retinues were eager to advance in the eyes of their patrons. Fights were commonplace, although the Syndic's guards punished any that damaged property or disrupted commerce. Large sums were wagered on the outcomes and house rankings were followed eagerly by people of all degrees. Seyvyar took this in while thumbing through the booklet.

'*I will have the stuffed squid with seaweed*'; '*Is this bath-house for the left-handed?*'; *What day are the eel-races?*" He turned to a page listing the appropriate forms to use in greeting, going from Senior Syndic at the top through House-Mother and merchant all the way to servant and slave. The last gave him pause.

"Slavery is permitted in Merllan lands? I thought they were civilised folk. It has been gone from the Four Kingdoms these last three centuries."

"The Merllan will trade wherever there is profit," Jayas explained. "I asked my tutor, as I heard slavery was not forbidden and had no mind to end up on the wrong side of the auction platform. She said almost everyone around the Green Sea has agreements with the Syndics that they will not be enslaved. The Four Kingdoms do, so we are safe. The exception is the Brahnzhever, where the religious have taken to exiling people they don't like. The exiles don't fall under any agreement, and often end up being sold. The Saka likewise sell some criminals abroad, and the Merllan enslave captured pirates. They hate pirates."

"I never really thought of piracy as a career choice, and now have another reason not to," Seyvyar said.

Jayas grinned. "Oh, I wouldn't worry. No-one enslaves magicians. They are too much trouble to keep around. No, they just kill them straight away. 'Get the magician first' is good advice."

Seyvyar preened. "We *are* the most dangerous enemy."

SO THE VOYAGE PROCEEDED. Jayas quickly became fluent in Merllan and Seyvyar mastered the basics. The *Safe Delivery* plodded south under plain sail until the island of Bogue hove in sight. They laid over two days in the small port, unloading sacks of grain, bales of cloth, grain and joints of meat kept fresh by alchemy, then loading spices, resins and dried herbs. The next day was enlivened by two pods of whales, dark backs rolling over with huge breaths as they travelled to their northern feeding grounds. One leapt high out of the water, to fall back in a cloud of spray, a most wonderful sight to Jayas and Sevyar.

Some days later they reached the first of the Fire Islands, a ring of dark jungle below a cone-shaped mountain. As the *Safe Delivery* altered course to pass by, a sailor told Seyvyar that it was Tweli – "a fine place to visit, masters, if you keep to the hills. The strangler clams have arms as long as this here ship." Jayas and Seyvyar stayed away from the rail.

Tweli fell astern but was still in sight when the next island came into view, to be edged around in favour of a third, larger island. This, they were told, was Magh, and they would dock at the town of Merkil on its eastern shore. The *Safe Delivery* made its stately way towards the harbour, sails came down, lines were thrown and they were hauled alongside. As their purses would not support a visit ashore, Jayas and Seyvyar took up their customary position on the rail and watched as hatches were opened, booms rigged and cargo hoisted from the hold and swung over to the wharf. The Fire Islanders were a short folk, teak-skinned and flat-nosed. Both sexes wore the hair piled up and cut flat at the top, to Seyvyar's eyes an odd fashion that gave them the look of all wearing the same hat. The common garment was a sarong, tied at the waist in men and the shoulder in women.

Seyvyar told Jayas that the Islands boasted a famous college of magic, attracting students from around the Green Sea, and certainly there was a fair number of non-Islanders in the crowd – tall black Dravish draped in linen, tawny Brahnaks, red-haired Krohls sensibly wearing wide hats to keep the sun from pale skin. The waterfront was a babel of shouts, cries, the squeal of blocks and the thump of crates and bales on the planks. A similar medley of smells assailed the nose, from the tar and old water of the wharf timbers to wafts from the cook-shops along the waterfront. It was a lively scene and, to judge from the busy commerce, a wealthy one. As they each speculated privately on the possibilities of transferring some of that wealth from the Islanders to themselves a young man staggered up the gangway. Staggered because he was laden with two rucksacks, three bags and a satchel. He dropped the bags on the deck and came over to them.

"Hello there. I was told by him," - here a jerk of the chin at the sailor at the foot of the gangway - " that you could show me where we berth. I'm on this tub as far as Mer Ammery."

The three looked each other over. Jayas and Seyvyar saw a slim young man, olive-skinned, dark-haired and sharp-featured. A bright red and blue sarong left his upper body bare, showing a trimly-muscled torso. The greeting had been delivered in Merllan. For his part, the newcomer saw two men, both a little older than himself, one with dark skin, tight black hair and a wide face outlined by a fringe of short beard, the build of a wrestler and an air of relaxed watchfulness. The other was taller, thinner, lighter in colour, his carefully-tended hands and hair at odds with his rough clothing. It had taken him a moment to puzzle out the meaning, so clearly his Merllan was not fluent. They each tested the surround at the same moment and recognised each other as magicians, notionally brothers in the art. He gave a magician's greeting.

"Seyvyar Trist, Chiran, five years ago."

"Delfe se tiene Frehuar, Mer Ammery two years ago and just this month here," was the reply.

Seyvyar hesitated as he tried to put together a sentence in Merllan, then gave up with an apologetic glance at Jayas and changed to Dzai, the language all magicians had in common. Jayas shrugged and went back to watching the passing scene. It was not that he didn't trust Seyvyar, he thought, it was just that a secret told is lost forever; so best that his command of Dzai stay unremarked. It was not a very interesting conversation anyway – the two were comparing academic experiences, mixed with anecdotes of life in Mer Ammery, Chiran and the Fire Islands. Jayas did pay attention when Delfe expressed surprise at Seyvyar's off-hand mention of a powerful spell, one only an experienced magician could use. How had Seyvyar risen so high in the art so quickly? Seyvyar told him of the invigorating effects of the Wild, where one learned fast or died young. Delfe was intrigued, even interested. Here, Jayas thought, was a possible addition to their little group. Delfe should be sounded out in more depth. In the meantime, Seyvyar could show him the room they slung their hammocks in.

The *Safe Delivery* spent two days in Merkil, then plodded back out to sea. A large Fire Island trader was coming in as it cleared the harbour, its bluff bows and high sides shouldering aside the waves. Delfe drew attention to a cradle hanging between the masts.

"That's the nest for the sea-dragon. It will have flown ahead to give the harbour notice and will then go and add to its hoard."

"Sea-dragon?" queried Seyvyar.

Delfe explained that the local dragons, a relatively small breed that lived off fish and marine mammals, partnered with the Islanders. They went on voyages, acting as scout, messenger and guard in return for valuables to adorn their caves. Delfe added that negotiating shares was always long and tedious and the make-up of the dragon's portion usually a matter of intense argument. Sometimes Islanders deposited things with a dragon for safe-keeping but 'depositing is easy, withdrawal rather hard'.

Delfe went on to point out places of interest as the *Safe Delivery* worked its way north about the island to the open sea. A line of stone pillars half way up a mountainside were there to quiet the volcano; an elaborate horned tower on a shelf of rock was a temple to Nakoro, patron divinity of the purple squash that was a staple of the Islander diet. Seyvyar grimaced. He had tried the squash and did not like it. He could only hope it would not be on the menu all the way to Mer Ammery. At last the ship laboured around the northern cape and settled on to a course south-west by south with the wind on the quarter. This was the *Safe Delivery*'s best point of sailing, and she picked up the pace, lumbering along like a cart-horse with a light load and a stable in sight. The island dwindled astern until only the peak of the mountain was visible, then that became a nick on the horizon, and then they were in a circle of empty sea. Seyvyar went below and watched as the cook ladled squash into his bowl.

SEYVYAR AND DELFE SOON fell into long discussions on their use of magic, comparing what they had been taught, swapping spells and plotting lines of advancement in the art. The *Safe Delivery* boasted a professional sea-mage, a weather-beaten Fire Island woman who deigned to join their conversations from time to time.

Jayas was amused by their intensity. He was not so naive as not to see that Seyvyar was largely motivated by greed, but that left considerable room for devotion to the art. All the magicians he had known had been like that. He thought of his own high craft as a skill, like any other. Indeed, many people had some degree of craft, just as most people had some degree of skill. If his high craft had a wider scope and reached further in effect, it was still of the same kind. One brought the image to mind, twisted the fingers just so to tie the ether to oneself and things happened. Magicians were different; they sensed the ether directly, or so they claimed, and were drawn into its complex currents and shifts, matching their Words to the surrounding flows. Seyvyar had remarked that one never cast the same spell twice, and Jayas supposed that this accounted for the fascination the art exerted.

These musings led to other reflections. If Seyvyar was greedy, what did he, Jayas, want from life? His last two tries at riches had both led to disaster, both very nearly been fatal. Before that there had been ups and downs - more downs than ups, to be honest. If his experiences had given him a greater command of craft than others of his years, they had not made him rich, or earned him a position. Seyvyar would always have his art, those in orders their vocations. The Companions of the Road saw travellers safely home, the Guardian Avengers looked out for women, the Waifs minded orphans; had he graduated into the Grey Cloaks he could now be happily breaking legs and menacing merchants. Well, his life had gone another way and he could not regret it. He had some good stories; perhaps he would turn writer.

MER AMMERY IS KNOWN for many things – the Great Market, the splendid harbour, its Houses and their duels, the wild abandon of carnival, several prestigious schools of magic, the fish dishes at Sulei's

Restaurant and the Mazere. The Mazere is a street that curves around behind and above the wharves. It is wide, paved in stones of many colours, shaded by old trees placed down the centre. The seaward side offers benches and kiosks overlooking the water, the landward side has restaurants, cafes, shops selling luxuries and exotica and the Oberis, Mer Ammery's most exclusive hotel – five stories of pink stone and black timber, the facade artfully carved with scenes of conviviality and the whole topped with three glass domes. The Mazere is *the* place for assignations, challenges, displays, seeing and being seen.

Two days after the *Safe Delivery* made port Jayas, Seyvyar and Delfe were strolling along the Mazere. Delfe pointed out the sights, while Jayas and Seyvyar dreamed of the day when the shopkeepers of the Mazere would welcome them as customers of wealth and taste. That day was not today but they could dream, and Seyvyar took particular note of two tailoring establishments. A stir in the crowd ahead attracted their attention, and they pushed through to see a moustached fellow confronting a woman in House colours of white and purple.

"Juleize has offended, and I am here as the arm of House Pens, ready to clean away the slight with your blood."

"It is Pens that is offensive, and my blade is here to prove it on your skin," came the reply.

"A challenge!" cried the crowd, and formed a loose circle about the two. Two of the Syndics' guards arrived, to take station at either side, and several people started calling odds on a yield, first blood, maiming or death and the standing of Houses Pens and Juleize. Jayas cast an experienced eye over the pair.

"I'd put my money on the moustache," he told Seyvyar.

Seyvyar had been listening to the odds. "That's the general opinion, so not worth it – even if we had any spare money."

The general opinion was right. Three ringing passes, moustache batted the woman's blade aside with a bare hand and cut through her bicep. Her arm dropped and the sword fell from her hand. She raised her head to look her opponent in the eye, swaying as blood drained onto the stones. Moustache gave her a deliberate cut on the cheek, another on the forehead and walked away. She fell to her knees, blood-blinded, desperately trying to staunch the flow from her arm.

"Juleize must be in low straits, to have no healer, nor duellist with craft," remarked Delfe. "The House-Mother will look in vain for support." The woman had fallen prone.

Seyvyar and Jayas exchanged looks. Here was opportunity, from what Delfe had told them of Merllan Houses and their duellists. Seyvyar stepped forward, murmured Words and reached down to the woman. The blood-flow stopped as flesh knitted under the Beneficent Touch. Jayas helped her to her feet and bound a cloth about her brow, ignoring feeble protests. A guard called out. "If you aid, then this mess is yours. You have to clean the street." Seyvyar inclined his head and cast that spell known as Clean Spirit, evoking a small whirlwind that shortly had the paving spotless.

"Which way to Juleize?" he asked Delfe.

THE HOUSE-MOTHER OF Juleize glared at the final set of figures in the ledger. "Three thousand, four hundred and twenty gulls." She repeated the sum. "We feed the House, we pay our dues and then what? We have a ship due this month, another the month after, but the likely profits will keep us fed, no more. Hmm. The *Jewel of Juleize* finishes refit in two weeks. Dekkes, can we raise enough to cover a few short voyages – Brahnker or Brafa?"

Her chief adviser played with the tassel dangling from his headband of office while he considered. "At our current standing? Any lender would want another five or six per cent, with sureties."

The House-Mother looked at the shelf empty of ornaments, the lighter patch on the wall where a tapestry had hung, glanced down unhappily at the frayed sleeve of her robe. Dekkes spread his hands in silent commiseration.

"Where is Zarisse?" asked the Mother, changing the subject. Dekkes adjusted the headband on his bald pate, touched on a set of hanging rods, listened to a bowl.

"She left the house an hour ago, Domina, saying Pens would not go unanswered."

"Did I not tell her to accept no more challenges without my word? She is our last sword."

"She may have felt it touched her honour," offered Dekkes.

"The powers grant she return unharmed," muttered the House-Mother, and went back to her accounts and plans. She was no happier, nor her plans more feasible an hour later, when a rod chimed. Dekkes listened and reported.

"Ill news, Domina. Zarisse has returned, badly wounded. She met Pens on the Mazure and was defeated. Three strangers – one of Frehuar and two outlanders – brought her back. They ask audience."

"With their hands out, no doubt. Frehuar? Where do they come into this? Well, let us see."

"Outlanders? They could be assassins, Domina, careless of the Syndics."

"Then we shall receive them in the Eel Room, I shall wear my Taint Chime and you will monitor their auras."

JAYAS' FIRST THOUGHT on seeing the Juleize House-Mother was 'she's too young'. A high formal headdress, enveloping robes, and a stiff posture as she sat cross-legged above where he kneeled did not hide that she was scarce older than he, thirty at most. And a good-looking less than thirty, he added mentally. Skin pale as the snow that never came to these islands, hair black as a crow's wing, a small straight nose, slender hands held perfectly still. Her adviser, the bald old man to her left, that would be one to watch.

"What brings you to Juleize?" asked the Mother, her tone distant, disinterested, her voice pitched low. Jayas had taken note of the signs of financial stress: minor maintenance left undone, an absence of younger faces, an air of nervous calm. She expects us to demand a reward, he thought. Well, he had paid careful attention to Delfe and then to the crowd gossip.

"Care for a fighter wounded, now delivered to your healer," he replied. She gave an acknowledging lift of a finger. "The opportunity to serve, Domina," he went on. *That* surprised her; for a moment her cheek quivered.

The House-Mother took real note of the trio, for the first time. Delfe she summed up in a glance: a young man of a provincial House, well brought-up, probably a magician – they all had that slightly abstracted air, as if listening to music no-one else could hear. Perhaps they were. The third one, he too was a magician if she had her guess. Not a rich one, and recently arrived, by his clothes. The long pale hair, held back by a plain leather tie, light skin and thin features all pointed to an origin somewhere north-east of the Green Sea. The speaker, now, he was a puzzle. His Merllan was perfectly fluent, barely accented. Dark hair and skin, a closed face, plain clothes offered few clues. His stance, hands and a certain relaxed awareness told her experienced eye he was advanced in craft. How far advanced? Again, hard to tell.

"How so? You would serve Juleize?" in the same distant tone.

"I and my friends are recently come to Mer Ammery. All three of us are open to opportunities for mutual gain. House Juleize needs to improve its standing; Seyvyar here and I need employment," stated Jayas.

The House-Mother was interested, but cautious. "If you have the skills, many Houses would pay well."

Jayas grinned. "We are unknown here. Too many people ignore the old advice to never bet on a dark horse. We are better – much better – than we appear, and the Juleize colours will do nothing to alter that impression, at first. Your House is on the brink of relegation; several well-placed wins could alter that. I expect the odds to shorten after the first four or five duels, but before then?"

The House-Mother leaned aside to confer with her adviser. When she straightened it was with a calculating gleam in her eyes.

"We shall speak more on this."

5: Loose Hounds

Lady Fleuri slid a long fingernail under the flap of the letter and gave a quick jerk. The seal parted and she unfolded the thick paper. The writing was the same small, neat hand.

Inquiries along the road from Zyich to Irrense yielded no new information (see attached itinerary). Further investigations made between Irrense and the coast were more fruitful. Two men appeared at a farm on the edge of the Western Wild, both unclad, one missing most of his right hand. They worked their way to Irrense, earning clothes and food with odd jobs and craft (the maimed one boasted of being a magician, but was apparently unable to speak to the ether). At Irrense the magician – one Seyvyar Trist – paid for the restoration of his hand by working for the Association. The other – Jayas Zrei – left Irrense and returned some weeks later in a more prosperous state.

Seyvyar Trist and Jayas Zrei left Irrense together for Ilkina, where they took passage on the Four Kingdoms vessel Safe Delivery *for Mer Ammery via the Fire Islands. The* Safe Delivery *left Ilkina on the 11th of the Month of the Fox and was expected to arrive at Mer Ammery late in the Month of the Badger or early in the following month. I have information to hand that these two were the only survivors of the original band.*

The table below sets out the places and dates at which the pair were seen until their departure abroad.

As before, an itemised list of expenses is attached. Please remit as soon as possible. I await your further instructions,

Tol Henze, Inquirer, at Ilkina.

LADY FLEURI TAPPED the polished table with sharp nails. The murderous scum must have been at Irrense not many days after she left. By so little had she missed them. What to do? She would not give up her vengeance, but was of no mind to follow the pair abroad. Post a bounty? She intended to return to her homeland shortly, and hunters would be reluctant to chase their quarry as far south as the Merllan Islands only to then trek back north to Hadawa for the reward. It would take a princely sum to tempt them, and this pair – she curled her lip – were not worth so much. This Tol Henze seemed capable and – here she looked at the expense list – was certainly affordable. She would commission her. A magician against a magician. For the other? Tol could find someone, at the same cost. She picked up her pen and began to write.

TOL PAID OVER THE COINS, took her three letters from the clerk and walked slowly from the receiving office. A cafe opposite offered a table in the spring sunshine, where she ordered a glass of berry liqueur and opened the first. It was from her mother with the social news from Duneep-Seffra. Over several pages she learned of the nice young men who had moved into the neighbourhood and her youngest brother's appointment as third steward to the Duneep Valley Root Vegetable Collective. She laid that aside, took a swallow of liqueur and opened the second, a gossipy missive from a friend in Kaber. She skimmed that, tucked it into her jacket and went on to the third, a post from the Islands.

You are hereby empowered to pursue Seyvyar Trist and Jayas Zrei and visit upon them a punishment appropriate to their crimes, viz murder, trespass, theft and derogation of the Patriciate. The funds necessary to this end will be released to you on receipt of your written concurrence. Should you feel the need to engage a suitable partner, an additional amount will be made available on their presentation and co-signing. The Ilkina branch of the Green Sea Mercantile Association has been instructed in this matter.

To forestall any unpleasantness in Mer Ammery, a warrant attesting your status as agents of a House-Mother will also be available to you and any associate. On presentation of proof of success in this endeavour, a further sum of two thousand Azic crowns will be paid each to you and any single associate. Application for this may be made at any branch of Green Sea Mercantile; the code-phrase "The Patrician's Due" will cause them to seek instructions.

I enclose a draft reimbursing you for your expenses to date, together with the agreed per diem.

AS BEFORE, THE PAPER was signed only with a looping 'F'. Tol recalled the conversation she had overheard in Irrense. They had mentioned a Patrician, who had died at the hands of Seyvyar. Could her correspondent be the grieving widow, out for revenge? She sat back and considered. This investigation was starting to resemble the children's stories where one started with a goldfish and ended with a whale. First a trip to Zyich, and now a voyage to the far side of the Green Sea. That was well beyond a goldfish, or a turtle. It was up around the seal level, she thought. Yet here was foreign travel, adventure and the possibility of a significant reward. Of course there would be risks if she actually tried to collect – say, by killing Seyvyar and Jayas. She doubted that anything less would be regarded as an appropriate punishment. Could she kill? She had never done so, and her spell-book ran more to eavesdropping than lethal force. Perhaps she could hire someone in Mer Ammery. By repute the place was rife with assassins. Or it might not come to killing after all. She would travel and see what happened.

"Hey, Tol!" Tol was shaken from her reverie, and looked around to see Serriet grinning and waving from the steps of the receiving office. She waved back and Serriet came over to flop into the other chair.

"What are you doing here?" Tol asked.

"Getting my letters," was the reply. "Oh, you mean in Ilkina? You were right – there was nothing much going in Zyich. I picked up a couple of small escort jobs into the hills out east, then went on to Azbai. Too pricey, so I came over to Eum Ang and did shuttle runs through the Ozrai Hills. Last one had a run-in with razor-tails. One guy lost a leg, so I replaced him down to here, thinking I might see what's on offer in the Islands. Got in two days ago. You?"

"I was hired to find a pair of rascals – a magician and a crafter. Traced them here. They left for Mer Ammery over a month ago. The sponsor wants me to chase them and," she added candidly "kill them (or at least see them dead) if I can."

Serriet whistled. "Tol the bounty-hunter. Does it pay well?"

"Expenses, four a day and two thousand each on proof."

"Sign me up."

Tol put down her drink and looked straight at Serriet. "Are you serious? I'm allowed to bring a partner in on the same terms and, well, you seem pretty competent."

Serriet was positive. "Pays better than what I'm doing, takes me to new places." She paused. "Unless I have a better offer, of course." She rifled through the small number of letters before her. "Bill, bill, threat, relative. Nope. I'm good with Mer Ammery, or even beyond."

"Then let us go down to Green Sea Mercantile and then to the waterfront to see what ships are clearing for Mer Ammery."

TOL STAGGERED TO THE lee rail and took firm hold of a stay. She now knew what the rope was called, and was standing beside the rail, not flopped over it retching. If her legs had not quite adapted to the pitch and roll of the deck, at least her stomach had. She hooked an arm around the stay and turned her face to the brisk spring wind, letting it clean away the memory of the last three days. The tub-like *Wind's Burden* was wallowing along under all plain sail, well out into the Green Sea on its way to Mer Ammery via Salweil, Tonish, Semerai and Uoka. Not the quickest route, nor the fastest ship, but the first available. The bank had been instructed to get them on their way as soon as possible, at the least expense. The *Wind's Burden* fitted both. Hammocks, three meals a day and the smell of tanned hides and Beskish Blue cheese to keep the nose alert. Ten to fifteen more days to Salweil, according to the master – if the wind held and sea behaved. He added those words to almost every statement. Life at sea was clearly uncertain.

Now she was recovered, Tol could take an interest in the voyage. The sea was a circle of blue, dotted with white where the wind kicked the tops off the waves. The sails above were a light brown, curved shapes shifting slightly among a web of ropes and wood, the whole assemblage creaking and squeaking like a flurry of excited bats. This must be usual, for the sailors ignored the noise. The quartermaster at the wheel shifted the spokes only a little, glancing down at the pointer from time to time. A stray eddy brought a waft from the galley forward, reminding her of her empty belly. Perhaps she could stand a little – a very little – food. Something light.

Tol was consulting the state of her innards, to eat or not to eat, when Serriet came on deck in martial harness. A helmet sat on her head, mail covered her limbs and torso, her left hand supported a shield and her right held her axe. She skipped up on to a hatch cover and began to run through a series of exercises. Her feet shifted, the shield angled, raised and lowered, the axe looped through the air in whistling arcs. At first the movements were slow and regular, then faster and faster yet. A last set where the axe was a blur of motion while Serriet twirled, dodged, crouched and leapt, and then stillness. She held the last pose for a full minute, then laughed, jumped down and came over to Tol, loosing the strap and hauling the helmet from the hair braided atop her head.

"Impressive," commented Tol. "Truly dancing with the ether."

"Be better if I had someone to spar with," Serriet said. "But I'll have to make do until we hit land. How often do you have to practice?"

Tol thought about it. Magicians did not practice as such, any more than one practised breathing. Awareness of the etheric surround was a constant. She realised with an internal shock of disappointment that quite distracted from her stomach that sickness had dulled that awareness. She opened herself to the surround, to find it vast, shifting, impossible to grasp in its entirety. How to match Words to this immensity? Tol recalled a conversation in Kaber with a sea-mage, and tried a small spell. The overwhelming surround buried her first syllables. She tried again, this time letting the surround have its way; a wiggle of the fingers and success: a vigorous clapping filled the air. A passing sailor was startled into dropping a bucket and the quartermaster looked up, puzzled. Tol uttered a stop tone, then felt out the Words to an old familiar. A mage-light shimmered into being, wavery at first, then steadying as she let the sea shape the spell. Interesting. She would try more, but only low, quiet spells. Here, she was in the domain of Selm of the Waters, and it would not do to attract *their* attention.

Serriet practised with axe, spear, dagger and a short heavy sword. Tol cautiously felt her way through this new surround and the *Wind's Burden* plodded on. The voyage did allow Tol to share what she knew of their quarry. Serriet looked at the portrait of Seyvyar and twisted her mouth. "That's the face of someone who likes himself much more than he likes anyone else, and lets you know it." She was less judgemental on Jayas. "I'd probably end up punching Seyvyar in the face if I met him. This one? Maybe, or maybe I would kiss him, or have a beer with him. Could go any way."

After twelve days Tol felt the shifts in the surround that signalled the approach of land, and Serriet pointed out shore-birds and sea-bats flying and diving. Another day and low mountains humped the southern horizon. The helm turned to bring the wind more aft, the motion of the ship changed, the first few small-craft rocked past and bit by slow bit the land crept up. Tol had heard mention of Salweil as the site of a respectable academy of magic, but knew nothing else about it. When consulted, Serriet professed a like ignorance. There were no other passengers, so Tol asked one of the mates what to expect.

"Salweil? We'll lay over two, maybe three days. The main town's safe enough, though don't get on the wrong side of the undermen. They talk a kind of Hada, but many of the shop-keeping folk will understand Azic or Merllan."

"Undermen?" queried Tol.

The mate spat over the side. "Big green bastards. They pay some to keep the others in line."

The *Wind's Burden* came in with the morning tide, was towed to a berth and began unloading. To Tol's annoyance, the blue cheese was not destined for Salweil. Tol and Serriet crossed the gangway and set off down the wharf, weaving through a bustle of cranes, carts and lift-poles, shouting longshore workers and clerks wielding clip-boards. The wharf joined another, that led to a paved quayside, they took a street at random and were in the town. At Serriet's suggestion they found an outdoor cafe, ordered drinks with a combination of sign language and the server's few words of accented Azic and sat down to observe the passing parade.

As a port town, Salweil had its share of people from all around the Green Sea. The locals tended to a dusky black complexion, with broad faces and heavy eyebrows, but Tol saw tall glossy-black Dravish, olive-skinned Merllan, red-haired Krohls and all the mixes in between. If the most common garb was a loose tunic over a long skirt, clothing was nearly as various. An adjacent stall offered fruits and vegetables, some familiar to Tol, some not. What was that root with long curling tendrils? Or that square red thing that squeaked when prodded? Perhaps Salweil was advanced in vegetable magics?

Serriet touched Tol's arm and directed her attention to three figures coming down the centre of the street. They were nearly as tall as the Dravish, and far wider, massive shoulders and arms hulking in heavy mail, blunt features, under-slung jaws and orange eyes under shelf-like brow ridges. Loops and whirls of black ink spread across grey-green skin. All three carried thick staves topped with hooks, blades and spikes. The crowd made way for them, they stamped on down towards the harbour and life went on as before.

"Wouldn't like to face one of them over a shield," said Serriet. Tol finished her drink and set about finding directions to the Magician's Association. She wanted to add some more forceful spells to her book.

The *Wind's Burden* left Salweil two days later, having taken on a cargo of gums, resins and barrels of shellfish preserved in brine, along with two merchants returning to Tonish. Tol found she had kept her sea-legs, and fell to studying her new spells. Tonish was a larger, more prosperous, even more varied port than Salweil. To Tol's relief, the blue cheese was offloaded, and replaced with a less fragrant cargo. The stay was only two days, because 'they charge a bleeding fee if you break wind on the wharf'. Hatches were battened down, gear tidied way and they were on their way down the coast to Cape Braise.

TOL WAS LEANING ON the rail thinking that life at sea was more restful but less interesting than travel by land when a sailor called down from an upper yard. There was an immediate stir on deck, and the *Wind's Burden* turned to port, edging away from the land. Her question of what was toward was answered with a curt 'pirates'. She looked over the rail to see three small triangles, the sails of boats making for some point where they would come together with the ship.

"What will they do?" she asked.

"Board over both sides and rob us blind," was the glum answer. Tol looked around. The captain had called for more sail, which was added with methodical efficiency; there was no move she could see to issue weapons or ready any other defence, and an air of resignation. She looked again to where the triangles were now close enough to see hulls leaning over as they raced for their prize. The *Wind's Burden's* crew numbered no more than fifteen, two of them mere youths and one an old man. Serriet had heard the answer and vanished below. Now she came on deck armed and armoured, axe at her belt, bow and spear in hand.

"Tol, I'll take the closest when it gets within bow-shot. You do the second and we'll see about the third. They're not robbing *us*."

The captain reacted with alarm. "You'll just annoy them and get us all killed!" Serriet ignored him and strung her bow. Tol desperately riffled through her spell-book. The Invisible Defence would keep her safe, but how to keep them off? Winged Dagger? She had no virgin steel. Choke? It would take out one, perhaps two. Her eye fell on oars lying inside the ship's boat. Closer range than she would like, but it might do.

The captain continued to expostulate, then called on the crew to restrain Serriet. The response was divided, with some younger members calling that she was right. Serriet forestalled the outcome by stepping to the rail, drawing to the ear and loosing at the nearest boat. The shaft sped across the water into the body of the helmsman, whose lurching fall dragged the tiller over. A gunwale dipped, there were cries of alarm and a hasty scramble to regain control. Several more arrows followed, a second man died, a third was pierced through the shoulder and the craft fell off the wind, sagging away into their wake.

Tol felt the surround, shaped the Words and hurled Choke at a figure on the approaching boat. The only result was a startlingly loud clap. Drat. She mustered another spell and picked up the oar with her mind, lofting it high. The boat rounded under their stern, spilled the wind from its sail and a row of grinning faces readied themselves to spring. She brought the oar down in a great arc, bashing away. One fell, there was a moment of consternation and then one quick-witted fellow seized it, wresting the wood from her mental grasp. Tol let it drop and seized another.

"Don't whack, stab!" yelled Serriet. Tol held the oar vertical and plunged it down as a fisher might gaff a tunny. Boards splintered, the hull opened and the boat was awash in moments. The grins vanished along with the craft.

The third boat had come alongside. A man sprang up with shield raised, only to meet Serriet's axe. The lower horn sheered through the shield-rim, the upper cut through the collarbone and he fell back in a spray of blood. Serriet's axe looped, cut sideways and the head of a second parted from his shoulders; a third was pushed back by a clumsy thrust from a sailor with Serriet's spear. Serriet whooped with delight of battle, Tol scooted across uttering Words that formed a black cloud above her head, a cloud that rumbled and flashed. It was too much for the pirates. They fell back into their craft and pushed off, chased by jeers and calls. As the *Wind's Burden* drew away they could look back to see heads bobbing in the water as swimmers made for the boats still afloat.

"If the rules are the same at sea as on land, you owe us half the fare," Serriet told the captain. The rules were the same, but the captain put them ashore at Uoka anyway.

6: High Stakes

Donde se leise Pens swaggered along the Mazure, one hand on hilt, the other twirling his moustache. An eighth ribbon adorned his hat, a fine new coat in the Pens livery of red trimmed with gold – the gift of a grateful House-Mother - adorned his person and all was well with the world. He kept his eyes moving; a duellist has to stay alert, and there were admiring glances to collect. What was this? Some yokel in the colours of Juleize, daring to to display himself here on the Mazure. Donde changed course to intercept the interloper, causing an eddy of expectation among the crowd. The yokel tried to evade, but Donde moved faster. A cutting insult, brusquely delivered, a hesitant reply curtly dismissed and the circle formed. Two naive country-folk pooled their money and wondered if they should bet on the outsider, wavering until an offer of ludicrous odds overcame their caution. A pity to take their money, really. The Juleize upstart took a mace in a clumsy two-handed grip and awaited his fate.

Donde struck a pose, tossing his sword from hand to hand while considering which part of the fool should feel his blade first. Right arm, he decided, advanced and lunged, murderous quick. The idiot of Juleize twisted aside in panic, flinging the mace out to meet the sword, just keeping the steel from his skin. Donde made a lightning redouble, aiming for the throat. The Juleize fellow escaped by falling over. One hand hit the paving, the other arm flailed the mace about. Quite by accident it met Donde's advanced foot with bone-crushing force. Donde reeled back, shifted balance to his uninjured foot and brought his weapon to guard, blocking out the agony. Juleize scrambled up and pointed to the blood running from the shoe.

"First blood is mine", he said carefully in accented Merllan. The guard agreed, the lucky country-folk scrambled to collect before their debtors could get away and Donde gritted his teeth and hailed a lift-chair. He was not walking home.

WHEN NOT KILLING EACH other, the duellists of Mer Ammery can be quite sociable. Some enmities do not permit anything other than deadly intercourse but, for those less serious, Felisher's Bar is the place. By long convention, no challenges are entertained within, a rule made convenient by the useful exchange of gossip and rarely but brutally enforced by Felisher's deadly aim with a hand-bow.

"This Juleize fellow has been damned lucky five times now. I reckon he carries an Item of protection," was the opinion of a duellist in the colours of House Taliere. There was a grumble of general agreement. Substantial sums had been wagered and lost.

"What of this full challenge?" demanded another. "One Item will not save him in a contest of craft as well as steel, and House Pens has put down a large stake. They will send their best."

"Juleize may well decline," offered a woman wearing blue and green. "They have only the outlander and Zarisse, and we know how Zarisse fared last time. Donde will be out to kill."

"It won't be Donde. Pens will put forward their very best," said a veteran. A compact man with curious hazel eyes sipped wine in a corner. He smiled slightly as names were bandied about, then slid a silver five-gull piece across the bar. "Put that on Juleize."

A FULL CHALLENGE IS a formal affair, not a street brawl. It takes place in an arena close to the Great Market, supervised by Syndic guards, two Justices and two members of the Association. Healers are always on hand, but often not needed.

A Syndic Guard cried silence, then planted the colours of House Pens in a tub of sand.

"House Pens cries full challenge against House Juleize. How does House Juleize answer?"

"House Juleize takes up this gage, and answers Pens with craft and steel." The flag of Juleize thumped into the other tub.

"Then let Pens and Juleize contest."

The champions of each House stepped forward. From the east, Cremione of House Pens, a veteran with twenty-eight ribbons. Her devotion to House Pens was evident in her colours; not only did she wear a red surcoat, but her breeches were red, a red crest adorned her helmet and her shield was bright red. Cremione came as one dipped in blood. Her fingers played as she drew on craft, and her skin pebbled as scales formed. The onlookers shared comments – a toughened skin together with mail would be nearly invulnerable. Her skills with sword and shield were widely admired, and then there was the skeletal spectral hound that paced beside her, reputedly won from a necromancer in the Wild. Its broad mastiff skull matched her hip in height, green fire outlined its jaws and a red scarf at its throat marked its allegiance. House Pens was not taking any chances.

From the west came forward the champion of Juleize, one Jayas of the north, in a white and purple surcoat. He too wore mail and an open-faced helmet, carried a shield and a long-handled mace. The blued steel of its flanged head was dull and wicked. Three darts were holstered on his chest, feeble weapons against steel and scale. He too twisted his fingers, drawing craft to himself, but to no apparent effect.

Cremione and her hound advanced, separating to menace Juleize from two directions. Jayas circled, bringing him closer to the hound. Its shoulders hunched, claws dug into the turf; Cremione uttered a sound, part-howl, part-hiss, and the beast sprang as she sprinted forward. Jayas sprang too, to meet the beast with open palm. As the glowing jaws arced for his throat his hand slapped the bare ribs. The hound disassembled, skull, rib and spine clattering apart, and he ran past, spun and brought up his shield. Cremione's thrust was slid aside, even as his mace thudded off her shield. She backed away, brought forth another unnatural command. The scattered bones did not stir. Her eyes told Jayas that now he had made this personal.

The pair again resumed their circle dance, shuffling in half-steps, shields high. The sword had reach, to slash a face or cut a hamstring; the mace had power, to dent a helmet or break an arm. A few exploratory passes, where the sword was turned aside, the mace met with shield, told each that here was an equal in skill. A quick flurry of feint, misdirection and like ploys showed an equal match in cunning. Cremione fell back, held Jayas away with a quick thrust at the face, leapt backwards, let the sword fall to dangle by a wrist-thong and flickered her fingers. Her mouth opened in a silent scream that could rupture eyeballs. Jayas inclined his shoulder, and the wood of the arena wall erupted in splinters as the force was directed sideways. He bounded forward and swept the mace at her midsection. The shield came down, the sword up, he spat in her face and leapt back. She did not react, but came on, the sword flicking out. It was deflected, deflected again, turned aside on the shield.

Jayas broke contact, she followed to keep him from craft, her sword met the mace, bound to it and was forced aside. Jayas kicked at her knee, tried to plant an elbow in her face. She freed the sword with a wrench and fell back. Jayas played his fingers, closed again. Her blade bit into his shield rim, Jayas punched his hand against his chest, a glass tube broke and a thin yellow mist wafted over them both. Cremione hurled herself away, Jayas circled, and her eye fell on a small plaque, one exactly resembling the highest honour House Pens could bestow. It was worn by a nondescript fellow in the stands, a young Merllan man in modest dress. Her shield dropped as she started towards it at a run, then met her belly as Jayas landed on her back. Cremione was driven to the grass, felt a sharp point enter her neck and then blackness.

Jayas took in a great lungful of air, savouring the craft that kept it clean and fresh. That was very nearly his last ploy, and he did not know how it would have gone if it had failed. He looked down at Cremione, shook his head, replaced his boot knife and walked over to the colours. The guards made no move as he yanked the staff of House Pens from the tub and flung it to the ground.

"Pens' challenge fails!" boomed the crier, and there was hubbub in the stands.

ZARISSE REGARDED JAYAS with a mixture of awe and puzzlement. He did not think he would be welcome at Felisher's, so was celebrating his victory with a beer in the rooftop garden of House Juleize. Seyvyar was somewhere downstairs counting their winnings. Jayas smiled benignly at his fellow duellist.

"The weapon-play I could follow, and I thought she had a slight edge on you in that," Zarisse pursued. "Craft is beyond me, but I was told she was at least your match there."

Jayas smiled. "She was my equal, but thought I was lesser. She would not have brought her hound up against one skilled in the art, but did not think that I might have mastered the Dispelling Touch. It never pays to underestimate your opponents, even" - here he grimaced – "housemaids."

Zarisse was still puzzled. "What of the rest of the contest?"

"Steel for steel she was my match, craft for craft also. She tried the Piercing Moan, I tried Spit. It failed to put her to sleep, but at least it rendered her mute. She had Iron-Skin and the hound. I had potions. Attractant turned her Moan aside, Stickfast bound her blade to mine, Scent of Greed was a fatal distraction."

"Scent of Greed?"

"It is an inhalent that fixes the attention on the thing most desired. People think gold is always desired, yet it is not always the *most* desired. I listened to what was known of Cremione, and believed high honour was her passion. So it proved." He raised a finger. "Never let your obsessions distract you from the job." After a moment he added "I learned that too the hard way," then went on "Also, if you use a trick twice or thrice, it becomes a pattern in your enemies' minds. They expect it, and are thrown by something new. The gamblers of Mer Ammery have learned not to offer odds to country bumpkins, but still listened to the gossip at Felisher's."

They were both contemplating life's lessons when Seyvyar came up the steps to the rooftop. His smug face told Jayas that their bets had paid off. He gave brief thought to whether it was time to take their winnings and move on, and decided not. There was more to be made. Seyvyar plonked himself down, grabbed a beer and told them the final take on their different bets. Zarisse's glee was confined to chortles before she retreated into blissful contemplation of the gear she could now afford.

Jayas let Seyvyar drink half his beer before observing that he was up next for a duel. When Seyvyar's sputters had subsided Jayas pointed out that challenges to himself could only be for personal prestige, as he, Jayas, would be the betting favourite. A House looking to take Juleize down a peg would look to move the contest on to a different ground. What was left but the art?

"That's, that's... *uncivilised*," protested Seyvyar. "The art is not for duelling."

"You have killed with it, more than once," Jayas reminded him. "And magicians have tried to kill me, more than once," he added.

"Everybody tries to kill you soon after they meet you. It's your winning personality," Seyvyar told him. Jayas just smiled and suggested he brush up on combat spells. Seyvyar made a rude gesture, but did pull out his spell-book.

In the event, House Juleize was content to bank its winnings. Pens had been humbled, Juleize's standing restored and three duellists of repute had taken the House colours. Best if Jayas was out of sight for a time and, as it happened, a provincial house had taken advantage of Juleize's moment of weakness. Goods had been diverted from a warehouse, a ship had been placed under distraint, Juleize sailors roughed up. Could Jayas remind them that Juleize was not to be trifled with? Councillor Dekkes would brief him on the correct forms.

THE MERLLAN ARCHIPELAGO is a jumble of islands large and small, embroidered with bays and inlets, sounds and channels and straits. The islands rise to wooded hills slashed with fertile valleys where terraced fields step down to shore-side villages. Winding paths link village to village but, for any distance, the sea is the way to travel. House Juleize made a vessel available to Jayas, and Seyvyar and Delfe elected to come along rather than remain in Mer Ammery. Early one morning they slung their bags over their shoulders and made the short walk down to where the Juleize boat was tied up. It was a short, stubby two-masted affair, crewed by a collection of taciturn oldsters. They stepped abroad, were tersely directed to stay out of the way, ropes were untied, sails hoisted and they were off. The first leg crossed the harbour, a great enclosed stretch of water studded with small islands. They eased their way along, threading through the craft great and small plying their way

– deep-hulled three-masters in-bound from the ports of the Green Sea, coasters, fishing rigs in all their varieties, skiffs and wherries and long, narrow proas bringing fresh vegetables to market. They rounded a point then breezed through a channel that led east to the open sea. Jayas felt the first heave of the deck and let the weight of Mer Ammery's intrigues fall from his shoulders.

Throughout the day the coast slid past, cape after cape. Jayas and his companions lounged by the rail, idly taking in the passing scene. Here inshore the waters were rich with marine life, from flying fish flapping furiously as they fled pursuing dolphins to squabbling birds diving into the waters to bob back to the surface with a catch instantly contested. Once a Merllan warship cruised past, its sleek hull and press of sail overhauling them from astern to vanish ahead. Delfe remarked that he had briefly considered joining the navy as a sea-mage, but abandoned the notion when he remembered how little he liked being shouted at. They anchored in a sheltered bay for the night, and dined off fresh-caught fish fried with onions.

Their destination was the town of Haliek. This clustered around an indent on a channel between an island Wild and a settled land, and was a trans-shipment point for coastal traffic. Their vessel came in at noon, the Juleize flag flying bravely from the mast-head, to dock adjacent to a Juleize warehouse. Jayas noted a broken window, hasty repairs to a door and graffiti scrawled across the front. The Juleize factor was a tall, iron-haired woman with the three steel rings of a far-voyager. She led them through a cavernous space empty but for a few bales in one corner to a cluttered office. An unmade camp-bed took up part of the floor, and the desk held a hearth-stone and several dishes along with some papers.

"Messers, my apologies for the disorder. I have been sleeping here for the last week, as one of our usual guards left and two others are recovering from wounds. I hoped to catch the rascals in the act." A halberd leaned against the wall and there was a steely glint in her eye. Jayas could appreciate the sentiment. He went straight to the point.

"I carry a warrant from the Office of Arbitration allowing us to name and call those we hold responsible. That would be the House-Minor Diense?" The factor gave a terse nod. "Where might we find them?" She gave succinct directions. "Then we will call on them immediately," Jayas said.

Their arrival had not gone unnoticed. It was a short walk to the Diense house, through streets where everyone turned to look as they passed, and some few followed behind. As Jayas, Seyvyar and Delfe approached the house two burly figures lounging against a wall straightened up and stepped out to bar the way. Town ordinances forbade the open display of steel, but they held oak staves and wore armour. Jayas halted only when toe to toe with the first and held the scroll to her face.

"I'm here to serve this order on Diense. I can deliver it to the door or to you. Your choice."

"Diense? Never heard of them. I'm just standing here, shorty."

Jayas' left hand grasped her stave, he kicked a knee, twisted the stave, popped the scroll-holding hand at her face. She found herself lying on her back with the butt of the stave pressed to her throat. Her companion started forward, then met Seyvyar's steady gaze and small shake of the head.

"And now you're not just standing there, so I'll deliver the message," said Jayas with a smile. He stepped over her and up to the door, rapped five times, produced a tube of glue and pasted the scroll to the door. He was turning away when the door opened on a stern-faced man in livery.

"What do you at Diense?" he demanded.

"Read your door," Jayas said, and walked over to where Seyvyar stood. The man stood there uncertain until a voice called from within the house, then tried to remove the warrant without success before retreating. A few minutes later he returned, accompanying a veiled woman. She read the notice and then looked across to where Jayas stood. A brief mutter and the liveried man spoke.

"Who do you name, and for what do you call?" he asked, his voice carrying to the small crowd of bystanders.

"House Juleize names Diense, and calls theft, assault and unlawful distraint of the vessel *Land Breeze,"* called back Jayas. There was another hasty conference, then another loud response.

"House Diense throws back these calls. The *Land Breeze* is under no distraint, and has left Haliek."

"Juleize's charges stand," returned Jayas. "I call a second time." With that he gestured to Seyvyar and Delfe and walked away. Tomorrow he would call for a third and final time. If Diense refused arbitration they would suffer the consequences.

The three were halfway back to the warehouse when a sailor came running to report that the *Land Breeze* had been seen clearing the harbour less than an hour previously. It took no more than a moment to decide. Delfe would stay to guard the warehouse, while Jayas and Seyvyar ran for the harbour. Their ship stood ready to cast off, the captain took the tiller, sailors manned the sweeps and they left the wharf.

"Never fear, master. We'll overhaul them up-channel before sunset. They're deep-laden and under-manned," the captain told Jayas. Jayas nodded, wondering why Diense had sent the ship off at all. Did they have a rendezvous arranged where the cargo would be trans-shipped? Did they plan to sink it out in the channel, so denying Juleize both ship and cargo? Or was it simple desperation? As he ran through the possibilities the crew hoisted sail, hauling in the sheets until the deck was heeling. They cleared the mouth of the inlet and the captain at once sent someone aloft. It was not long before there was a hail from the mast-head.

"I see her, two points off the starboard bow, making nor-west, maybe two leagues off."

The captain pulled at his beard. "Where's she making for? She'll have Siolnes Island under her lee, and us to windward soon, so no escaping us."

Jayas tried to recall the charts he had glanced at in Mer Ammery, but could gain no clear idea of the situation. A query to the captain told him that Siolnes was Wild land, allowing no village or town, so the *Land Breeze* could not be making for there. What if they ran it aground, he asked. The captain gave him an impatient look.

"Then the grabbies will get them, and she's lost to us."

It soon became clear that the *Land Breeze* was heading for Siolnes. The crew were uneasy, muttering among themselves and continually gauging the distance to the shore. Jayas had to admit it looked forbidding. Thick forest came down to the water's edge, a wall of green that closed off an interior hidden under dark vegetation. The mast-head hailed again.

"She's rounded to. They're taking to the boat and letting her drift." Jayas stepped up on the rail and balanced there, holding a stay with his right hand while his left shaded his eyes. There was the hull of the *Land Breeze,* a paler patch against the black bulk of the land. A slow scan finally picked out a small boat, oars rising and falling as it pulled away, keeping close inshore. He stayed there while they closed in until their quarry lay no more than a long bow-shot away. Jayas studied it intently. It was much the same as the craft he was on, squat hull, two masts, flush-decked, to his landsman's eye very little different from any other of the hundreds of coasters plying the archipelago. The sails hung loose, the tiller made small motions as waves pushed the rudder. There was no sign of any human presence, and indeed the small boat was well away by now. He kept watching, puzzled. The wind was light but onshore, so the *Land Breeze* should have grounded in the shallows. Instead it was moving slowly along the land, staying about the same distance offshore. There could be a current here, of course. He put the question to the captain, who shrugged. Even the sea had its own rules this close to a Wild. He would go no closer.

"What if Seyvyar and I carried a line over. Could you tow it off?" Jayas asked. The captain pursed his lips, finally grudgingly agreed. He was so emphatic that any untoward occurrence would see them abandoned them to their fate that Jayas decided to take his gear. The boat was drawn alongside, and Jayas and Seyvyar stepped down into it, scrambling as it rocked until they found their seats. Their gear followed, then one end of a coil of light rope, to be made fast to a stern cleat. If all went well this would pull a stouter line across and the *Land Breeze* taken under tow.

Jayas rowed, clumsily for a few strokes, then more smoothly as he found the rhythm. Seyvyar directed from the stern. Water gurgled around the bow, the line stretched out astern and they moved steadily closer to the abandoned ship. A stray waft brought a smell of rotting vegetation and old mud, together with a sharper scent. Jayas looked over his shoulder, making the boat veer, but saw nothing but leaves and brown water. Seyvyar corrected him, he made a few more strokes and they bumped alongside. Seyvyar grabbed a trailing rope, Jayas stood unsteadily, then reached up and heaved himself over the rail. The deck was bare. He reached down, hoisted their gear aboard and then took the line from Seyvyar. When he gave a pull it came in easily. He pulled again, there was no resistance, another pull and a frayed end appeared. There was a yell from Seyvyar.

7. The Importance of a Good Hat

Jayas dropped the useless rope and jumped over to the side. Seyvyar was standing on a thwart reaching up, while large red crabs poured into the boat. Jayas had to admit the scrabble of claws and array of waving pincers had a certain menace. He reached down a strong arm and hauled Seyvyar over the rail. A slash of the knife and the boat with its cargo of hostile crustaceans drifted away. Seyvyar mopped his brow and looked at the shore moving slowly past, where a tangle of arched roots lifted pallid trunks above the mud.

"We seem to be up the creek again, and without a paddle, again," he told Jayas.

Jayas nodded, also watching the shore. "Paddle or no, the ship is moving," he said. "I cannot think that the people at the end of the trip will be pleased to see us."

Seyvyar darted below, to return with a small iron plate from the galley, of the sort used to cook rice-cakes. He strapped it on top of his head, added a hat, made sure all was secure and gave Jayas a thumbs up. "I'm ready for them."

"If you say so," said Jayas dubiously, and set about getting into armour. If he went overboard he could breathe under water and walk ashore, which was a better choice than taking an arrow through the ribs. He himself had killed three – no, four – people that way, and knew how easy it was. By the time he was done their own ship was standing well off and falling behind. Well, he had known there would be little help from that quarter. He gave a wave just in case they were watching through a scrying ring, then went back to his scrutiny of forest and shore. It slid past while he checked out the mud-hoppers, hover-flies and other wildlife. The canopy above rustled from time to time, but nothing large showed itself. The sun was hot, the armour heavy, the padding underneath sweat-soaked, the smell from the muddy banks awful. Jayas endured. Seyvyar had paged through his spell-book, then muttered Words to no visible effect. Now he watched with Jayas, mopping his face with a handkerchief.

The ship began a slow turn and they became more watchful. The shore came closer, a narrow channel opened before the prow and they drifted under the trees. Jayas put on his helmet and tightened the strap. The channel made a turn, closing off their view of the sea. The heat and damp were, if anything, even more oppressive here, intensified by the confinement. Jayas levered back the string on his crossbow, dropped a quarrel into the slot and leaned it up against the bulwark, out of sight. He flexed his fingers and waited. Seyvyar had picked up a boat-hook and was holding it like a spear.

The boat moved out into a pool and came to a stop in the centre. Stone stairs emerged from the water on the far side, the lowest covered in green moss. They led up to a platform nestled between two enormous trees, the roots and buttresses of which clutched the rock like greedy hands. Jayas looked at the black still water and murmured to Seyvyar "Tentacles or pincers?", then darted below. He came back on deck a minute or two later with a brick of dried fish.

Seyvyar looked at it. "It may be lunchtime, but you know I hate that stuff."

"It's bait," Jayas told him. They waited some more.

"I think this is meant to inspire awe and dread, but it's actually quite restful," remarked Jayas after a time.

"Not for me. I have a deadline," Seyvyar replied. There was a ripple in the surface, then a pair of claw-tipped tentacles emerged to grasp the rail.

"Why not both?" Jayas said, as a monstrous hybrid of squid and crab hauled its armoured bulk aboard. A dark carapace topped a fleshy bulb with bulging eyes, while suckered arms two fathoms long, each tipped with jagged pincers, surrounded a cruel beak. The ship tipped under its weight and a stay parted, whipping about. Jayas and Seyvyar retreated towards the stern and the creature followed, hauling itself along with its lower arms while the upper were poised to strike. Jayas waited for the next heave, then threw the block of fish at its head. An arm plucked the block from mid-air and stuffed it into its maw. The beak clamped down, the thing shuddered and collapsed, releasing a flood of black ink across the deck.

"There's your lunch," said Jayas as life faded from the black eyes. "Although whether to call it calamari or crab is a puzzle."

"Here's the main act," Seyvyar told him. A figure had strode on to the platform in a swirl of robes. They looked up, it looked down. On high, a tall man, glossy black hair spilling loose to the waist, framing a face set in a sneer. The robes were layers of diaphanous black material, weighted at the hem with silver beads. One out-flung arm held a staff topped with a fanged snakes-head.

"I might have spared your lives before, but now you have used vile poison on my creation," thundered the man.

"It was not poison," Jayas said.

"What?"

"It was not poison," repeated Jayas patiently. "Poison is expensive. It was the standard potion for dispatching animals. I can assure you it did not suffer."

"Enough with this quibbling," cried the man. "You have done me harm, and now you shall die!" He lifted the staff theatrically.

Seyvyar spoke Words that caused an oval shimmer to appear before him.

"Magic will not save you," cried the figure, conjuring his own oval. There was a pregnant pause, then Words sent a red streak down to shatter Seyvyar's Invisible Defence. This was immediately followed by a spell to cut off Seyvyar's air. Jayas wove his hands in the Dispelling Touch, Seyvyar drew a breath and uttered four short Words. Jayas' hand on his shoulder was pushed back and two silver spikes materialised, one above Seyvyar, the other above his opponent. They drove down, there was a small clang as one met Seyvyar's improvised headgear, a look of shock and surprise very briefly crossed the other man's face and he fell dead, pierced through from the nave of the skull to the neck.

"Magic may not save me, but cookware did," said Seyvyar. "Also, it did not save you."

"Nice," said Jayas, scrutinising the shore. When no further threat arrived, he continued "Where did you get that one?"

"The Association had me doing still-work in the basement. There were a few shelves of old spell-books in one of the store-rooms, so I went through them after hours. I couldn't afford to go out, and it passed the time. That one came from a guy called Tiemase; lived about a hundred years back and did a lot of fighting. Died when he met Donske Iron-head."

"Nice," repeated Jayas. "Let's see what Hole-in-the Head has."

They levered the crab-squid hybrid overboard, Jayas flung a grapnel over a root and they pulled the *Land Breeze* alongside the stairs. The sprawled figure on the platform was an ugly sight, if not a novel one to either. He lay face-up, red-tinged fluid leaking from a hole that gave them a good view of his brain. Jayas bent to lift a heavy gold medallion, raising the head by the hair to ease the chain over it. Seyvyar retrieved a dagger in a green leather sheath. The robes had lifted, showing pale legs decorated with tattoos of sea-creatures among kelp.

"He had an obsession with tentacles," observed Seyvyar, picking up the staff. He then asked "Why do magicians that live in the Wild so often fall off the pedestal?" Jayas took the question as rhetorical and suggested they explore the path. They cast a look at the pool, where bubbles and the odd gobbet told of an underwater contest over the crab-squid corpse, and went on. The path was uneven polygonal slabs of stone, tilted and sometimes fractured by invading roots, winding its way between the ancient trees. It was little cooler here than on the water, but Jayas did not loosen his helmet straps. It was only a short time before there was more light ahead, and they halted on the edge of a piece of open ground, flat, laced with raised paths between ponds. In the centre, behind three separate moats, tall trees supported a house hung on cables between the trunks. As they watched something with teeth flung itself into the air over a path, to land in a neighbouring pond. There was a short struggle, the surface reddened, a few belches and calm again.

"Let's come back tomorrow with Delfe, and we can fly over to that house," Seyvyar said firmly.

SKAEYRE, FACTOR FOR House Juleize in Haliek, was chewing her stylus, wondering just how to word a letter to Mer Ammery telling of the loss of the *Land Breeze* and the deaths of Jayas and Seyvyar. It would not be welcome news. There was little to offset it, as Diense continued to resist arbitration. There was a clap at the door, and Seyvyar came in, looking none the worse for wear. She dropped the stylus and surged forward to clasp his hand.

"You're back! The Powers are kind! Jayas?"

"Fine. He's minding the boat. I flew over. I'll need a ship and enough crew to bring the *Land Breeze* back. It's over by Siolnes, anchored just offshore. It's full of Juleize goods, by the way, as well as some other stuff." This was tossed off in a nonchalant manner.

Skaeyre was so irritated that she checked her enthusiasm, responding only with "That's good. I'll have someone round up a crew straight away."

Seyvyar gave her a grin that acknowledged his own play-acting and they both laughed.

The *Land Breeze* came back into harbour that very day, her cargo unloaded and carried to the warehouse in as conspicuous a manner as Skaeyre could contrive. Diense agreed to arbitration the following day.

"Job done," Jayas said. "Back to the delights of Mer Ammery, city of a thousand assassins."

8. Where to Now?

Tol and Serriet sat at an outside table of the Lonely Python restaurant in Uoka, each nursing a beer. They had to admit Uoka was pleasant enough: a mid-sized town clustered around a small harbour in south Reghen. Ship-building and the coastal trade kept it from semi-rural idiocy, and the climate was congenial. Yet it was not where they wanted to be. The boards by the harbour advertised nothing going to Mer Ammery for the next month. Should they wait, or take a coaster to Pelsie, where there was more hope of finding a ship bound for Mer Ammery? The next coastal ship was little better than a floating pig-pen. Tol pointed out that the trip only took two days, three at most. Serriet said that two days aboard that scow would seem like a month. Tol argued money. Serriet sulked. In the end she agreed, on condition that she got to kill the crew if it took more than three days.

It took two days, and they were very glad to get off the ship. It wallowed. It stank. The food was awful. The crew were surly, so much so that Tol almost wished they had been delayed two more days. It did get them to Pelsie, a larger, livelier version of Uoka. Alas, the boards posted nothing bound for Mer Ammery for several weeks, and Pelsie was more expensive. Serriet waxed sarcastic, until Tol spotted something on a broadsheet. They had both learned enough Merllan to get by, and could puzzle out the flowing script. Tol was passing through the lobby of the Association when the word 'Jayas' in bold print caught her eye. It helped that she was practising a spell that aided concentration and was thinking of Jayas. She crossed to the rack, pulled out the sheet and approached the desk.

"Can you tell me what this says?" she asked the clerk. "My Merllan is rather poor."

He glanced at the sheet and spread his hands apologetically. "Probably better than mine. We keep those for visitors from the archipelago." He added "The librarian speaks several languages and may be able to help."

The librarian could help. "It announces major changes in House rankings. House Juleize was on the brink of relegation after losing several contests with House Pens. A new duellist – one Jayas of the north – recently turned things around. Pens was defeated in a formal challenge, with the death of their leading champion."

Tol asked if there was any other news of this Jayas. The librarian rummaged through a pile of material from Mer Ammery, the latest no more than ten days old. Here were betting sheets going back three months, with the odds on House duellists ("some of our members like to have a little wager"). The oldest had the lone Juleize duellist rated at 90 to 1; then Juleize added Jayas at 60 to 1, then 30 to 1, then 10 to 1, then odds-on. Over the weeks the Juleize stable had gone from one to five, all with respectable ratings. Tol looked at the latest sheet; Jayas was not listed for Juleize. She checked other Houses, and could not find his name. It was dated three weeks previous. Had Jayas abandoned duelling, or left Mer Ammery? She asked the librarian, who was by now intrigued. All the material was laid out on the long table at the centre of the room, and the librarian cast a spell. Her eyes took on a distant sheen, and the words 'Jayas' and 'Seyvyar' sprang out in small star-bursts as she looked, with second-order associations traced in purple. Tol placed markers and they collated the results.

When Tol left her head was buzzing with calculation. It seemed Jayas had abandoned duelling, after a spectacular run of successes. A commercial bulletin mentioned him and Seyvyar in connection with the recovery of a ship and an agreement in arbitration in an outer island town. In the agreement House Diense agreed to pay compensation for the detention of a ship by one Telzin. The librarian's spell highlighted a connection to an Association notice of the disposal by sale of the papers and other effects of Telzin, magician emeritus, deceased, latterly resident near Haliek. Several pamphlets inveighed against foreign interlopers and one noted that exiles had often fled their home countries to avoid conviction for such vile crimes as piracy and maternal incest. It seemed Jayas was not popular.

Was it significant that two other non-Merllan duellists had disappeared from the lists around the same time? If, as seemed likely, Jayas and Seyvyar had recruited another group, where would they go? In this season, sailings from Mer Ammery to the south and east were less frequent. A Wild, was her guess. That ruled out Dravishi and the far northern ports. She was sure he would not return north. The Corillion Coast was one possibility, the Haghar League another. Some reading and a talk with the librarian made the first less probable: an abundance of sea-monsters kept regular shipping well off-shore on the Coast. They would check the Haghar League, starting with Dtlag. This might be their chance to get ahead of Jayas and Seyvyar, rather than continue to trail them across the world, finding in each new place that their quarry had moved on days or weeks before.

Serriet was sitting on the bed at their lodgings, crooning to her axe, when Tol walked in. Tol held up a hand to forestall any remarks and told her "I have several bits of news."

"Go on," Serriet said.

"First, at least one – probably both – of our targets have left Mer Ammery. My best guess is for the Haghar League. We should start looking in Dtlag."

Serriet unfolded herself from the bed in one easy movement. "Then let's go there." "Yes, after I write my report and we go to the bank. We'll need another advance, and then we can check the harbour.

"The second piece of news is that Jayas killed a very high-ranking duellist in Mer Ammery, and defeated several others."

"Guess I'll need to practice harder," said Serriet.

"Third is the two were involved in some affair that led to the death of a magician in an island Wild. They likely picked up some choice stuff."

"Guess we'll both have to practice harder," said Serriet. After a moment she added "And I'll get a crossbow. Great for ambushes."

TRAVEL ON THE PACKET *Wave-Bat* was very different from the voyage from Uoka to Pelsie. The ship swooped over the waves, the food was good and the company pleasant. The packet carried mail, small cargoes and eight passengers. The three members of a Brahnak martial order returning home were reserved but not unfriendly. Two men returning from a family visit to their oldest child were happy to pass the time in conversation. They were both mid-level officials in the complex Haghar bureaucracy; most of the talk was of their son, who had apprenticed as an iron-singer. He was now a junior partner, and they were happy to recount his path to success and their experiences as parents.

The remaining passenger was a dealer in magic Items, returning from a buying trip. Szien was a tall thin man in unremarkable clothing; the pale blotches of vitiligo across his face distracted from his features. He remarked to Tol that he could have this fixed but preferred not to. "People remember my skin more than they would my nose or eyebrows," he said.

Tol was interested in his wares, despite her shallow purse. Szien was happy to talk about the oddities he had picked up in the past, like the talisman that re-directed magic to the next person, or the gypsum tablet that, when broken, removed the holder a long day's walk away in a random direction. "Best not used near seas or lakes, I imagine, even if it does get you out of a tricky situation," Tol said. Then there were routine Items which went wrong, such as the Dust Bombs which caused nearby rodents to explode, or the Live Mops that could not abide small children. Tol outlined what she knew of advances in vegetable magics, mentioning the draught cabbages and spell-absorbing squash. She brought out one of the carrots she had bought in Kaber, which Szien examined with interest. He agreed that they were charged with etheric power, but to what effect he had no more idea than Tol.

When Szien asked after her own business, Tol merely said that she was an inquiry agent, currently engaged by a northerner to find someone. "With Serriet along to keep them safe when found," said Szien drily. Tol just smiled. When they were a day out from Dtlag, Szien did offer Tol two knowledge vials of Haghakin, the language of the League, in exchange for one of her three carrots. The vials were part of a set he had picked up, and not likely to find a buyer in Dtlag. The offer came with a suggestion that Tol keep an eye out for Items of interest and a scrawled note of introduction to a research magician near Dtlag, who had more knowledge of vegetable magics and might be interested in Tol's expertise. Tol accepted the trade as she was tired of fumbling through a limited vocabulary to get a meal.

Dtlag was an old city, a settled labyrinth of grey stone and weathered brick embracing a sheltered harbour. The Haghar folk led sedate lives for the most part, ordering their round with frequent rituals and a constant flow of small courtesies. Social life revolved around the many clubs and the bath-houses, where social station was set aside as all degrees mingled in the pools. The Saka, Brahnaks and other foreigners who routinely passed through were treated with polite reserve. Tol and Serriet disembarked after a few formalities, found the guest-house recommended by Szien without difficulty and settled in.

"Now what?" asked Serriet.

"I have portraits of both Jayas and Seyvyar Trist. I'll check with the Association on Seyvyar, and we ask around about Jayas. You tell people you're a cousin, trying to find him to tell him about a death and an inheritance. Now who would have seen him who would tell? He's a shady sort."

"Waterfront bars? Places like this, which cater to foreigners?" suggested Serriet. Tol gave her an approving look.

"We'll need some Copy Sheets, and I want to look up the magician Szien mentioned. He might have heard of Seyvyar; magicians are a gossipy lot. If those don't turn up a trace I'll use a finding spell, although that has some risk of alerting him."

Their new-found command of the language made routine tasks much easier. Portraits of the wanted pair in hand, they separated to cover as much ground as possible. Seyvyar had not been seen at the Association, and the gossip in the tea-room turned up little of interest. Tol sampled *liani,* a herbal infusion originally from the Saka uplands, now popular throughout the League and beyond, and found it insipid. She switched to light beer and watched the afternoon rain pour down outside, splashing off the cobbles and swirling into the deep drains. The folk of Dtlag wore wide hats, tucked their lower garments up and carried on. It was, Tol mused, not unlike an outdoor version of a Haghar bath-house, with only a little more water and you kept your clothes on. At least it wasn't the chill rain that swept off winter seas into Kaber city, sending people scurrying for shelter. She remembered the drops sliding down the window of her student garret and the way the damp cold seeped into the blankets. The students had taken each other to bed just to keep warm. Sometimes it had taken more than two.

Tol dragged her mind back to the present. Where were Jayas and Seyvyar? She went over her reasoning again. Shipping from Mer Ammery almost always called at Dtlag unless bound for the ports at the head of the gulf, such as Daruz Alman or the Rai Harbours. These seemed unlikely destinations for a crew on the make – and she was sure those two and anyone with them *were* on the make. The Eig Wild further up the coast was a narrow strip between the sea and the high ranges, with little to offer the adventurous. There was every chance the pair had either passed through Dtlag or were on their way.

There was no point in looking for traces with this rain washing everything every day. If Serriet's queries did not turn up something she was inclined to use a spell of finding. It might alert Seyvyar, but it would give some more certainty. Also, she thought to herself, she was sure she was not the only person looking for Seyvyar. He might almost be used to alerts.

What other avenues might there be? If Seyvyar was selling the papers of a dead magician, he might also be selling any Items he could not use. Dtlag boasted Feriol's, a long-established and well-known firm of dealers in magic Items. They would not disclose their clients of course, but people might hear things. A visit to that research magician Szien had mentioned might pay dividends. That led to another thought. She went to the desk and asked where the latest news from Mer Ammery could be found. The clerk was helpful, and gave directions to the streets where Merllan places of business congregated. She decided to go there next day, and went back to have another beer.

Serriet came back that evening a little tipsy, with no news of Jayas or Seyvyar. Three vessels from Mer Ammery had put in over the last week, none carrying passengers that matched their description. While no arrivals were expected over the next three days, there should be several in the week after. Tol decided their quarry was likely on the water, which meant a finding spell would be pointless. The domain of Selm of the Waters was not kind to such magics.

"If we have some spare days then we'll visit this man Szien recommended," Tol decided. "If he can tell us what the carrots do, that would be good. We'll need every edge we can get. I'll see what news from Mer Ammery I can gather tomorrow."

The Street of Seven Sons was near the commercial wharves and boasted two Merllan eateries, a tea-shop, the domicile of an exiled minor House and three saloons where the Merllan community gathered to exchange news and do business. Tol's approach was straightforward. She walked into the first saloon and asked where she might find the latest scandal sheets from Mer Ammery. She was told the tea-shop had a reading room, so went there.

The teashop was clean, quiet and, at this hour patronised only by a half-dozen older folk, chatting quietly in Merllan over their infusions. The dusty smell of snap-root mingled with the rich tangy odour of dried sea-pea. Tol ordered liani rather than try something unknown and took her cup over to a table near the rack of sheets. The latest was only a week old; she spread it out and tried the spell she had picked up in Pelsie to search for mentions of Jayas or Seyvyar, but achieved only a light purple overlay. Tol frowned, took note of the general interest her effort had sparked, cleared her throat and asked if there was anyone willing to scan the latest sheets for her. An older gentleman in a shabby tunic and worn sarong was very willing to oblige in return for a small sum, a drink and a meal. Tol listened over a second cup of liani as the gentleman translated headlines in between mouthfuls.

Houses Petition Syndics on Outlanders

"Maybe," noted Tol

Magicians Injured, Garden Destroyed in Hybrid Parsnip-Mouse Explosion

"Not that one," Told said

"Demon-beast attacks shoppers in Great Market; Outland Duellists Interrogated"

"Can I have the full report?" Told asked. The gentleman took a swig of sea-pea tea and read out the article.

> *Thanks to the prompt intervention of the Syndic Guard, there were no deaths or serious injuries resulting from a fight between a conjured demon-beast and the notorious outland duellist Jayas of House Juleize. Jayas' impressive run of luck has produced some winners – and many losers – in Mer Ammery, and it is probable that this event is one outcome. The beast – described by terrified shoppers as combining the worst features of an ape and a mantis – manifested in the colonnades of Well Street and immediately attacked Jayas. The duellist evaded its clutches until the Guard arrived and dispatched it with an accurate volley from their crossbows. Jayas was taken into custody together with an accomplice and questioned by the authorities.*
>
> *It is many years since a demon manifested in the city. Senior Fellrezk of House Taliere, the last person to have combated one, tells us that such creatures are summoned by name. We must ask, does Jayas the duellist know such names? Does he owe his success to these etheric monsters? Senior Fellrezk thinks it possible.*

Tol checked the date against her notes from Pelsie. Jayas had dropped from the duellist lists not more than a week later. It was clear his 'run of luck' had aroused serious enmities. Nevertheless, using a demon was surely extreme even by the standards of Mer Ammery. Was there some other actor in this? She listened to the rest of the article, which added no facts and a lot of innuendo about foreign duellists, with a particular focus on Jayas. What more she could glean strengthened her belief that Jayas had left Mer Ammery. She bought the gentleman another drink, pressed a gratuity into his willing hands and left. A trawl through the other Merllan establishments yielded no more news, so she went to collect Serriet, who was keen to try spiced fruit pudding. Tomorrow they would visit Szien's contact.

CHENIZEI THE MAGICIAN lived some distance out of Dtlag, south and a little inland from the coast. Tol saved the hire of transport by making Serriet weightless and then using a flight spell. They skimmed over the ordered countryside, above the tidy villages, the stone-walled fields and the manses of the gentry amid their ornamental gardens, keeping low to avoid the stronger winds high up. It was Serriet's first time flying, and she found it delightful, exclaiming over the views and the speed and waving to those who looked up. As they neared their destination she drew Tol's attention to the land ahead, where the gentle Haghar landscape abruptly gave way to jungle-covered hills. Tol was concentrating on landmarks, but found time to pass on that the jungle was the Hansippif, a notoriously hostile Wild. They dropped down, circled the squat tower that Chenizei had made his home and landed before the front door.

Serriet looked around. The tower stood atop a small hill with a fine view over a rolling countryside. To the east, a brighter sky told of the sea; to the south the Hansippif was a menacing dark line. The tower rose no more than three stories, and was capped with a conical roof. A lower stone outbuilding stretched behind. The green grass, the mellowed buff of the stonework, the light wind and play of sunlight all made for a pleasing scene. A vine growing beside the door unfurled to waft scents over them, sampled the air and opened the door. A waving tendril invited them to enter. Tol went first.

Within was a pleasantly rural hall, where wide floorboards gleamed with wax, plastered walls shone white and antique glowstones sat in patina'd brackets. A sideboard held a few mementos and an intricate confection of glass rods graced one wall. An older man, clad in country smock and loose trousers, came forward.

"Welcome to the home of the magician Chenizei. He is glad you have arrived and awaits you in his workroom. If you will follow me?"

He led the way down a stone-paved passage, up a flight of stairs and to a plain door. This he opened to announce them. Beyond was a large room, well-lit by skylights, windows along the wall facing the south and glowstones. The long bench under the window held trays of seedlings, an array of plants in tubs sat under the skylights and outside a vigorous garden flourished. Near at hand a short square fellow in stained clothes smiled at them from next to a table set with food and drink. He had the hooked nose and copper complexion Tol had learned were typical of the Saka people.

"Welcome. You must be Tol, and you Serriet. Welcome again. Szien's note interested me greatly, and I am gratified that you could come. He sent me the carrot you gave him, and I have had a preliminary look. But let us have some refreshments, and then we can talk as I show you around."

Tol and Serriet made small talk about their travels while sipping fruit beer and nibbling spiced rice wafers. When Tol mentioned the carriage-cabbages, Chenizei said that he would like to visit the north one day, to meet the colleagues he corresponded with and see what their work was producing. That led to a discussion of his current projects.

"Cabbages are all very well and I would like to know more of them," Chenizei said, "but what the Haghar League needs is a way to travel up the coast from island to island. If Selm of the Waters keeps us to using wind and tide, then we must take to the air."

Tol frowned. "Is not that, well, ambitious? In college, they went over some of the many different approaches so far, all failures. Some rather disastrous failures, like the try at harnessing clouds."

"True," conceded Chenizei, "The failure to take the clouds' feelings into consideration was not wise. I don't see a similar risk with my efforts. Have you seen cloud-plums?"

Tol said she had, in Pelsie. In her understanding they made a carriage lighter, so allowing it to be pulled by the large birds used for that purpose in Reghen.

"That's right," said Chenizei. "But cloud-plums lose their lift after a year, even if painted with Unrot. Also, you can't have more than thirteen together, which limits the lift. A light carriage is about all they can handle. I have a different direction in mind. May I?" he asked, offering her an arm as if to escort her into the next room. She laid her fingers on his arm and heard his voice in her mind, transmitted through the contact.

"I am happy to show you my progress, but I would also value your advice, possibly your assistance, in another matter. Szien mentioned that you are an inquiry agent, and I thought you might have some expertise in detecting surveillance. I have felt that someone was monitoring my house for some time, but my own knowledge in this area is scant."

"I am, of course, willing to do what I can," responded Tol. "I will need to ask some questions, so best to let Serriet know what's going on before she starts giving us weird looks."

They wandered arm in arm through Chenizei's workroom, while Serriet made random impressed noises. Tol listened while Chenizei outlined his concerns. He had noted minor perturbations in the ether, tried to locate the sources and found them elusive. The flavour was of something passive, disguised, listening. At first he thought it might be an emanation from the Hansippif – had Tol noticed the feel of the southern horizon? - yet it lacked the underlying hostility of that domain. There were persons interested in his research, so it was plausible someone had set devices to monitor him. Was Tol open to an exchange of services?

Tol told him that she had some experience in detecting eavesdropping and a number of spells that she could use. Such checks had made up part of her meagre income in Kaber City and she was quite good at them. Curiosity led her to ask why he had not consulted some specialist in Dtlag; Chenizei's reply was that he was not sure that rivals in Dtlag were not the eavesdroppers. Tol, as a newcomer and outsider, could have no conflicts of interest.

Tol agreed to do what she could. They kept to silent speech, now including Serriet, as Chenizei conducted them outside to the garden. At the back several enormous cucumbers rested on raised beds. Rested was not the word, Tol realised, as they were clear of the soil, straining upward against stout canvas covers attached to heavy stakes.

"These are my best results yet. They will rise to nearly four hundred paces in the Haghar measure, and each lift ninety Haghar stones weight. There remain issues with their useful life and their sensitivity to some provocations, and they need at least ten paces separation from any form of forward propulsion, but these can be overcome with more work. Indeed, your carrot has given me some useful ideas, and I hope the craft yonder will be ready within a few days."

The craft yonder was a graceful shell, lightly built, as broad and long as the bed of a wagon, equipped with anchor-points for lift and a ilot-stand at the front. Chenizei foresaw such vehicles plying the islands, if only he could raise the money needed to address some last few issues and then, of course, to fund the initial operating expenses. He went on to lament the greed and short-sightedness of the financial community of Dtlag, which blinded them to the riches that would accrue when his project came to fruition. Tol and Serriet offered appropriate words of agreement and commiseration.

After lunch Tol cast her quietest eavesdrop detection spell, a spell that listened intently while comparing backgrounds and responses to the most minor fluctuations in the surround. She was proud of the working, for even the most alert magician would be hard put to notice the effect, yet it showed intrusions in the same way the smallest grain of sand stood out to the fingers. When she was done she touched Chenizei's arm again, that they might have silent speech.

"Three passive listening devices have been placed in your home – one in the workroom, one in the study and one in the kitchen. If you want to deal with them you can remove them and drop them in a bucket, or I have a spell to cloak them so they hear nothing, or another that sends a painful squeal back." She hesitated, then added "I have a third spell which turns speech into small ether-pulses, which then accumulate in the parent device until it reacts. If the device is powerful, this takes time, but the reaction is often, well, excessive." Their speech was silent, but Chenizei could hear the note of glee in her voice. His annoyance that someone had dared to snoop on him for months crystallised into a determination to retaliate.

"Let's try that last," he said. "In return, I will scrutinise your carrots in detail. I think they can be imbued with at least two effects."

PERGOL, MASTER IN THE Order of Hidden Servants, was writing a letter in a secret language. The stylus made thick black marks on the paper, each stroke bold and clear. When he was done a simple spell would overlay the message with insipid guff about the doings of relatives and the health of children, all in a barely-literate hand. Pergol had composed the letter in his mind and now his hand moved fluently. The paper sat on a small lap-desk, the desk on Pergol's thighs as he sat cross-legged, and Pergol on a thick mat woven of fine straw. The room was small, the walls plain stone, the light from a single glowstone. Both doors were firmly closed. As Pergol wrote the last character the room shook slightly, there was a whistling noise and then a loud crack, bangs, a crunching sound and the wood of one door vibrated as something pounded on the other side.

Pergol's reaction was immediate. He was on his feet, fingers weaving as he drew on craft, before the first falling dust hit the floor. He stood, hands poised, facing the door, waiting. The noises passed on to a scraping and scrabbling, then stopped. Pergol still waited, the dust motes drifting through the air. His eyes flicked to a parchment square set in a frame next to the other door. Two touches, and underlings would come running. Running to his aid, or running to join the attack? One could not be sure, so best wait. If they had turned on him, they would arrive of their own accord. He waited. No-one came, and there was quiet next door. Perhaps this was not an attack. Perhaps there was another explanation?

Pergol gave it another minute, then moved to the door, quietly. He reached out with his mace, delicately flicked the latch up. The door eased back a little. Another wait. He nudged the door a little, enough to see into the room beyond. The floor was the same square black tiles, bare of mats, now with a scatter of blue beads and blue powder. The light from the single window shone on shards of glass, bent copper wire, a shelf lying broken. Pergol's mouth twisted in dismay. He gave the door another nudge, to reveal more breakage. There was no apparent cause, no movement. There was no other entrance, the window was closed and the bars intact. Pergol's head turned as he scanned the view, his nose twitched as he tested the air. Only when he was satisfied did he move forward, past the door. Something dropped from above and he was blind and suffocating.

Pergol grabbed at his head, only to have his hands slide off a smooth hard surface. He felt around, gripped, pushed up with all his strength. His hands slipped, and he could feel the top of his head being sucked upwards. In desperation he smashed his head sideways into the door-frame. There was no sound, but the impact was painful. He pushed again, to no result, smashed again. This time there was a faint cracking noise. Pergol remembered the mace dangling from his wrist, seized the familiar handle and whacked himself in the head. He had sometimes wondered how a mace-blow felt, mostly after dealing one. His imagination did not do it justice, but – sweet relief – there was a louder crack and a puff of air. He whacked himself again, trying to use enough force to break the hold on his head without spilling his brains out. There was a gush of air and sound, the hold loosened, he gripped the thing and heaved it off. He could feel himself stretch, then snap back, like toffee reluctant to leave the pan. Pergol staggered, the wall lent him support and he dropped his attacker, taking in great gulps of air. A bead crunched under his foot, and he did not care. His head felt awful, just as if it had been squeezed, pulled and then bashed several times.

When he slowly looked down – slowly because moving his neck hurt, he saw a broken horn lying on the tiles. Once it had a wide bell-mouth, tapering to a narrow neck that coiled around and under to provide a base. Once it was a glossy black, with neat lines of characters around the rim. Now a large piece was missing from the rim, the letters had wandered off or burned black holes, a crack ran down the side and the base had uncoiled to lie out like the tail of some dead beast. Pergol gave it a cautious kick. It did not stir, although a word glowed briefly red. Pergol cursed.

It took every ounce of concentration he had to perform the Rapid Recovery. Anything more complex was beyond him, but that eased the throbbing and allowed him to regain enough composure to face his subordinates. He touched the parchment twice, and was gratified when two faces suffused with suppressed curiosity showed at the outer door. He waved a hand at the next room.

"An Item has malfunctioned. Clean up. And take care to collect all the beads, without breaking any more. Understood?" They assented, eyes down, stepped carefully across the room and went to work. "I shall be in my retreat. Notify me when you are done," Pergol told them, and left. Every step jarred his neck and set his vision wobbling, but he held his back straight and his stride even. One could not show weakness. He kept a still face as he ascended the stairs, pressed his palm to the door and played his fingers in the only rhythm that opened it. It was not until the door had closed that he relaxed, and then only for an instant. For he saw himself in the large silver mirror standing in the corner. His hair! Decades of shaping and styling, nurturing with creams and oils, a sleek perfection. Now his head looked like a blasted landscape, pocked with bald patches, hair ripped out, tufted, discoloured, thinned, clumped and matted, teased into spikes. He moaned aloud and clutched his temples. The underlings had surely noticed, and were sniggering downstairs. Sniggering internally, because he had taught them the value of discretion, but still sniggering. He briefly considered some punishments but, no, that would only draw attention to his suffering. Better to maintain a dignified indifference. Also, he would buy a wig.

As he feared, a vial of Healing did nothing for his ruined coiffure. It did still the aches and pains enough to allow for some thinking. Some etheric sending had sent the Gathering Horn feral, while also destroying the dedicated partner devices. He presumed that a target of his spying had discovered his surveillance and taken counter-measures. Who, though? The Horn had monitored thirteen different targets, any one of whom might have resented intrusion. It was possible the remaining beads might offer a clue, but it would take time to process their contents. For now, a stiff drink and then some rest. He would shave his head after that.

When he went to inspect the room it was clean and bare. The Horn was gone, along with all the partner devices. A small basket sat forlorn on a repaired table. It held nineteen blue beads. Pergol inspected the room, turned a stern face to his subordinates.

"It is acceptable. We need to establish who caused this and, as we cannot use our usual method of listening to the beads, we will need to use you instead. You will each ingest the beads one by one and record what they tell you. You will be able to transcribe four beads each day. You will have the first report," he glanced out the window, "before the evening meal." Pergol watched as they gathered paper and stylus, then glumly swallowed a bead each. They both hiccuped, a strained look came over their faces and they began to scribble. Pergol swept out before the inevitable gastric upsets could manifest.

Three days later he sat before a sheaf of transcripts. The underlings knelt before him, hands clasped behind their backs, eyes cast down. They were both visibly thinner, pale and – he sniffed – still somewhat odorous. He thumbed through the papers.

"The writing on the last pages is atrocious, but I will let it pass this once. Piemiss, what is your analysis?"

The one addressed took a moment to compose her thoughts. "We have a complete record for two targets, and a partial record for another seven. It is possible the cause lies with the remaining four. What we have from Paghin Paail shows nothing out of the ordinary. Likewise for Toul and Dnangh in the League, although both are partial. There is a mention in the High Councils' record from last week of taking additional security measures, but nothing further in the one bead left from there. That's the political side. The full record of the courtesan Climbing Rose is talk about poetry, along with coupling noises. We have one bead from the magician Chenizei, which records some visitors chatting."

"A succinct summary," acknowledged Pergol. "I *asked* for an analysis."

"The only positive lead is the mention from the High Councils," Piemiss answered after a respectful pause.

"Then we shall return this favour there," Pergol told them. One must show decision. "Piemiss, you may leave." She rose, touched hands to her feet in obeisance and left. "Goern, you will prepare for a journey, after some study into the ways of shades."

Goern turned even paler, but said nothing. Obedience was the path to advancement; all others led to much worse places.

9. Hard Words

Delfe sat at the bar in Felisher's with a glass of white wine and a plate of vinegar mussels in front of him. His own provincial House was of little interest to the professionals in Mer Ammery. That suited him. It meant he could have a drink and engage in conversation without being sized up as a potential opponent or, worse, being dragged into any of the plots swirling about. He would take Jayas' advice and keep a low profile as long as possible. Just a harmless minor magician. He took a sip of wine, speared a mussel and listened, while feeling smug. His own abilities as a magician had grown, his spell-book would soon need more pages and, best of all, he and Seyvyar had flown over to Siolnes Island and spent a day rummaging through the dead weirdo's home. The Association would find a buyer for the volumes of research notes on how to stick different sea-creatures together and the curios would fetch a good price here in Mer Ammery. What with that and his take from their bets he could envisage a future of wealth and ease. Well, after a few more hauls, and some more time in the Wild. The sense of the ether there really was quite addictive.

The Items they had shared would come in handy. He had picked up an Absorbent Tear and a pair of Feather Shoes, while Seyvyar had Instant Gills and a Snake Staff. The latter was something of a show Item, but then Seyvyar liked show. He had spent a good bit on clothes. Jayas had chosen a Falling Charm and another Item. Jayas was a secretive sort, went on Delfe's thoughts. Seyvyar had described the encounter with the swamp magician and his creature. That man and his little bottles; it was a wonder Jayas didn't chink when he moved.

A phrase caught his ear. "Cheating foreign thieves." He took a moment to place the House colours - dark brown over light. House Kiayemse, an ally of Pens. His own bets had collected handsomely from them, and the House had lost standing. There were murmurs of agreement and some other ugly words used. Kiayemse were not the only losers.

"Us foreigners get the blame – again," commented the man next to Delfe. He too had a glass of wine in front of him, and wore no House colours. "They don't even make the wine cold for us." Delfe performed a cantrip and touched the other's glass with a finger, causing beads of moisture to form. The man took a sip and nodded appreciatively. He was a compact fellow, unobtrusively muscular, brown-haired, steady hazel eyes above high cheekbones. His Merllan was fluent but had a slight sibilance. Delfe could not place his origin.

"Yerech" the man said, flicking a finger at his own chest.

"Delfe," Delfe responded. "Magician, of course."

"I do this and that," Yerech said. "Most recently, a bit of duelling, but looks like it's time to move on. This Jayas fellow arrived like a crow at a pigeon party, and the pigeons are working themselves up to mob him."

"And you believe other foreigners will be targets of the mob?" asked Delfe.

Yerech nodded. "Feeling about foreigners coming in has been building for a while. We arrive with little or no prior form, which makes setting the odds difficult. Sometimes we bring unfamiliar Items or new spells, which makes things worse. Merllan pride leads them to bet on the locals. A decent fighter can make quite a bit before they wise up." He smiled reminiscently.

"I'm Merllan," pointed out Delfe.

"I noticed," said Yerech. "I also noticed you collecting handsomely on Jayas. I believe you spent time out in the provinces recently."

Delfe paused. Here was someone with a sharp eye.

Yerech gave him a twisted smile. "If the pigeons are looking to mob foreigners, some of the shit will land on their friends. And some people will use the excuse to recover their losses – or at least avenge them. You might be in both camps."

Delfe had not seen things in this light before. For outsiders, the competition between the major Houses of Mer Ammery was a game, a subject of interest or a contest where those so inclined could win or lose on wagers. He suddenly realised he had been thinking of it this way despite seeing the blood on the Mazere. It was not a game to the duellists of Mer Ammery, nor for their Houses. Could his association with Jayas and Seyvyar bring ruin down on his own house? It was too late to disavow them, even if such a course were honourable. Could he himself be imperilled? His command of magic was much improved, but he did not flatter himself that he was the equal of a veteran duellist-mage. He came out of his reverie to find that Yerech had ordered another two glasses of this excellent Pallender and a plate of shrimp marinated in a sea-fruit sauce. When thanked, Yerech said that he had won on Jayas too, and was glad to spend some of it on good wine, "For life is too short to drink bad wine, and more so in our trade." Delfe could drink to that.

NOW THEY HAD SOME REAL money, Seyvyar and Jayas could do more than look at the shops on the Mazere and in the Great Market. Today Seyvyar wore a fitted coat of fine cloth and an intricately-dyed sarong, both chosen after prolonged consideration of his now extensive wardrobe. Jayas stayed with a loose shirt and breeches of heavy twilled cotton, both in dull browns. He had no wish to stand out, and his investments had been in precaution, not display. The medallion at his chest would confuse spells of location, the tattoo on his wrist warn of noxious substances and an Absorbent Tear defend against offensive magics. They had wandered through the Great Market, stopping now and then to sample a new snack, and exited on to Scented Street. The afternoon rain had set in, and they stayed under the colonnades, moving slowly through the crowd towards Sharin's, Mer Ammery's premier seller of magic Items. While both had stocked up on the usual Items, but one never knew what might turn up among the uniques. Jayas side-stepped a stout man carrying two bags of groceries, gave way to a woman with a child on one hip and another in tow, moved aside for a figure in the voluminous robes of a devotee of the Silent Watch. Seyvyar was a pace or two behind. His eye caught the shift as the robed figure half-turned, the glint of dark metal and cried "Jayas, beware." Jayas reacted instantly, diving forward and to one side even as the blade thrust at his lower back. Cloth parted, and the fine mail underneath turned the edge aside. Jayas' hand slapped the paving, he twisted, his reach found the bracket supporting a statue of some Merllan civic benefactor of yore and he was up with his back against a pillar, knife out. Shoppers scattered amid a flurry of screams.

The robes collapsed, billowed up again and changed shape. Cries of surprise and shock were replaced by screams of terror as jointed arms ending in jagged blades emerged from the rending mound of cloth, along with a fanged head. Seyvyar saw a small human form wriggle from under the robes and scurry towards an opening in the wall. He grabbed it, it stabbed his hand and in sheer irritation he flicked the mannikin down and punted it. His foot made a good solid connection: the small form, arms waving wildly, sailed in a high arc across the street. His aim was off – instead of hitting a wall it crashed through a window. A moment later it flew back out to land in the roadway, where it was stepped on by a very large woman as she ran away. A dying squeak was lost in the general mayhem.

The thing ripping free from the robes was now revealed as a horrid combination of mantis and baboon, plated with chitin on chest and shoulders, red-faceted eyes glowing above a striped snout, buttocks flashing a luminescent purple. The hind legs were short, the arms long and held poised as it stalked towards Jayas. Jayas wondered how it fed itself with blades for hands, then dismissed the thought – demons did not eat. They did kill, and this one lashed out at his head. He ducked and scooted around the pillar. Chips sprayed from the stone where the blow landed. The creature hissed and advanced; Jayas retreated, keeping close to the pillar.

Seyvyar ran through the spells at his command. From Jayas he knew that demons were immune to etheric forces – it was the stuff of their being, so one might as well throw water at the ocean. The Winged Dagger would only scratch it (and turn its attention his way, one part of his mind added). The column shuddered under another blow. Before Seyvyar could find an effective spell, there came the distinctive thwock of a crossbow and a bolt sprouted from the creature's back. The Syndic Guard had arrived. A magician swooped down to land in the street, took in the situation and spewed Words. An etheric wreaking spun through the rain to hit the creature in the head, to no effect at all.

"Crossbows and spears, you idiots," shouted Jayas, dodging around the pillar. "No magics – they don't work." He ran into the road, snatched a spear from a guardsman and hurled it into the creature's chest. Another quarrel smacked into its hide. Jayas ran away, the beast lumbered after, and he led it into the open. A squad of the guard levelled their crossbows and released as one on command. The thing spun, wavered, dissolved into a purple mist that thinned to nothing.

"You!" said the guard commander. "You will come with us."

"I saw it all," said Seyvyar. And this one had something to do with it." He crossed to the trodden corpse, little larger than a one-month babe, and picked it up. A small rectangle of violet glass lay cracked on the cobbles. Seyvyar wrapped his hand in a cloth and picked that up too. The guard commander looked askance, but took him along too. As they left the guard were gathering up discarded shopping and tending to the few injured.

The senior Syndic in charge of the Great Market listened in grim silence to the commander's succinct description of events. At a lower table a scribe scratched away, recording. The Syndic asked a few sharp questions, then turned to Jayas and Seyvyar.

"First, what is *that*?" She pointed at the small body laid out on a side table.

"If I may, Honourable?" asked Jayas. At her nod he crossed to the table. The body was that of an adult man in proportions, clad in a muddy tunic and sarong of black cotton. The hair was dark, tied back in a queue, the small face set in its last agony. The limbs were crooked, reflecting the several violent impacts the man had suffered. Jayas borrowed a stylus and poked through the tunic pockets. One yielded a few shards of glass, stained with a purple fluid.

"This was the man in the garb of the Silent Watch, Honorable. When his stab failed, he released a demon using the glass tablet over there, then took a dose of the potion called Sizing. He was next to the demon, so this was his way of avoiding it, although no doubt the last instruction was to kill me. My colleague and an accident" - here he looked at the imprint of a large heel square on the body - "prevented his escape."

"Is he known to you?" demanded the Syndic. Jayas shook his head, then added a verbal negative for the benefit of the recorder.

The Syndic considered a moment, leaned aside to ask something of the guard commander, then straightened.

"You are that Jayas whose championship of Juleize has occasioned some remark?"

"I am," Jayas acknowledged.

"You are fortunate I do not gamble," she remarked, and left them standing while she read the latest reports from the scene. After a time she looked up. "It seems clear that you did not instigate this crime. You are free to go, although do not leave Mer Ammery. In fact, best if you do not leave your House. Shopping is excitement enough without demons. Commander, please have these gentlemen escorted to House Juleize."

OF COURSE THE HOUSE-Mother of Juleize wanted to know about the excitement, and sent Dekkes to ask questions. Their fellow duellists were also interested, so it was late before Jayas and Seyvyar could talk in private. They included Delfe, who had some gossip from Felisher's to add to the mix. Yerech had been unusually direct that evening, passing on that three major Houses had banded together in agreement that foreign duellists would not be tolerated. The Syndicate would be asked to pass a ban and, in the interim, there would be serial challenges.

Seyvyar was dismissive of this last threat. "They will be less eager after the first few defeats."

Jayas took a wider view. "There's luck in every fight. Besides, Juleize is stronger, but not strong enough to resist major Houses acting together. They will have to let us go, and what then? Today showed our enemies will go outside the code, so who knows if we are safe even here? No, time to take the swag and move on." He looked at Delfe. "Are you coming?"

Delfe was unhesitating. He wanted to feel the Wild again, and was tarred as an associate of Jayas and Seyvyar anyway. His House-Mother had given him leave for another year, merely asking that he bring no discredit to the House. He might return to be received with honours and position within the House, perhaps enough riches and skill to raise his House higher. That was worth a little risk.

"I am. I think Yerech is interested in leaving Mer Ammery too, as another outlander."

"Well then," Jayas said "Time to talk to Dekkes about how we go, and also about bank transfers."

"Isn't 'where' a consideration?" asked Delfe. Seyvar and Jayas shrugged at the same time.

"Away. Not where we came from."

Neither Jayas nor Seyvyar spoke much about their past, and Delfe knew it was fruitless to ask. Instead he continued on possible destinations.

"Dravishi?"

"Too hot, too many skulls, all the Wilds are swamp," was Seyvyar's terse summary.

"Hirre?"

"Too far, we don't speak the language and they eat bats."

What's wrong with eating bats? Smoked bat-wings are delicious, done right," said Delfe. "Alright, what about Reghen?"

"Weak Wilds, most a fair way inland."

"I take it the Brahnzhever is out?'

Seyvyar shuddered. "The only Wild is the Hansippif, and that *hates* people." He put a stop to the guessing game by saying "Jayas and I have talked to a few people. The only real possibilities are the Eig Wild and the Pia-Pia Wild, so we either head for Dtlag or for one of the ports on the Corillion side – Umma or Memberi or even Lagash, although I hear that's a dive."

Delfe put his bit in. "One of my House-cousins went into the Eig Wild. She said that side was mostly moors infested with huge flying things, at least until you are well up the Corillion Coast, and first you had to run past the sea-monsters."

"Then Dtlag it is," said Jayas, and no-one dissented.

DEKKES AGREED TO A meeting the next day. A page conducted Jayas to a small room looking out on to an enclosed garden, where the adviser sat watching the slow rain fall. He was dressed informally, in sarong and a loose shirt, both dyed in a traditional pattern of silver leaves against a green ground. The page brought tea and left them. Jayas took the first sip, as Merllan manners dictated. The thought crossed his mind that, were poison acceptable in duelling, he might have made even more money.

Dekkes was direct, "Your schemes and your skills have turned around the fortunes of Juleize. A few weeks ago we were on the brink of relegation; now we are restored in rank and wealth to a secure position. Juleize is grateful. Yet all such arcs have their apogee, and it seems ours has reached that point. If you stay here, descent is inevitable, for Juleize and yourselves. If we are both to keep rising, we must part."

Jayas nodded slowly. "Can I ask what tangible form Juleize' gratitude will take?"

Dekkes sipped his own tea. "I understand your own fortunes have improved along with that of the House."

"True. Also we garnered some interesting Items from our excursion to Haliek. Before this last excitement confined us we were about to see if Sharin's had anything that might aid a speedier departure. Anything we could afford, that is."

"I will have Sharin's send a list of their unusual Items. On more mundane means of transport, the House cannot provide one of its own ships, and I recommend you leave from a minor port. The harbour here is closely watched."

"Our removal from the roll is not enough?"

"For the Houses, yes. For those with a personal grievance, no. Their number includes Cremione. She declined to move on to the afterlife, and House Pens saw fit to provide her with the body of a Dravish male of impressive physique. Nor is she alone in desiring revenge."

After some more discussion of ways and means Jayas left, brooding on the unfairness of life. He had killed Cremione fair and square, so what right did she (or, now he) have to complain? He went upstairs to impart the news to Seyvyar and Delfe.

The list of uniques from Sharin's was sent over a day later. Seyvyar went over it with the other two, commenting as he went.

"A Warm Scarf. Keeps the wearer warm in all weathers. Useful if we go to the Frozen Wild, I suppose. Unfish Sauce? I'm not that sick of seafood – yet. A Quick Monument? Could come in handy when one of us dies. Assuming that they want a gravestone, and we can afford the time. Hmm, I see it writes the epitaph itself, and who wants to lie under a stone saying 'Complete Loser'? An Illusory Meal? Nobody here needs to lose weight? Skin-tones? Could indeed be useful. Easy Stilts? Crimson Beacon – really, no. A Mule-less Saddle. Possibly. Could save us sore backs. Why are there no Items of death or destruction?"

"The Syndics discourage the sale of such to ordinary people," Delfe told him.

"I'm not ordinary!" protested Seyvyar. He gained no sympathy, so went on. "Impervious Robe. Says it was made for a Hirrese noble, but he was assassinated before he could take delivery. Purple and gold, three capes and a hood. No? I take we'll pass on the Whimpering Sword."

"Dekkes says he can get us a Breaching Stick," put in Jayas.

"Don't forget the stuff we got over at Haliek, and that theatre in Gull Lane is selling off Stock Characters, the paper ones they use to cut costs. One of those could be useful," added Delfe. Jayas made a note to ask if Sharin's or the Archivists could supply any useful languages.

They went over the full tally of gear and began to toss ideas around.

CREMIONE WAS INCREASINGLY frustrated. Her own House-Mother had forbidden a direct assault on House Juleize. She would have to catch those conniving foreigners outside its walls, and so far they had not come out. Or at least she thought they had not come out. Servants had come and gone, as had visitors from other Houses, merchants and factors and the officers of Juleize ships. All had been closely scrutinised by vigilant watchers. Merllan etiquette condemned the examination of auras without consent, but being killed gave you a different view. She could see auras now. She could paint Jayas' to the last detail, burned as it was in her memory. At all times one of the watchers wore a brass headband that showed auras, and all knew what to look for. Those examined felt a slight nip at the ears and saw a green flash, but Cremione did not care. Let them know they were under the gaze. If they confronted the watcher, well she stood ready. It would be the worse for them.

Cremione stretched her new body, flexed powerful biceps, ran a hand through tight curly hair. She liked it. In her old body she would have admired this one, perhaps invited the person to spend a night with her. She smiled. She still liked men. It will only be the body that is different, she thought. Well, and a different preference on the other side, she supposed. Cremione put aside these musings as she arrived to question the watcher of the day. Alone, she noted. There should be two.

"Mostly the usual, Champion. Twenty-seven people have gone in, twenty-five come out. Mostly people of the House, but also a cart delivering spices, messengers from Houses Srosse and Temeling, three from their ships and four salespersons. Umm, there was an incident with a laundress, which is why Hainus is not here."

"Which was?"

The watcher searched for the right phrases, failed to find them and went on "She came over to Hainus as soon as she came out and challenged him. He started to draw, she whacked him with a stick, took his sword, broke it and threw the bits in the canal, kicked him in the stomach and then said to me if it happened again she'd be back with friends. That's why Hainus isn't here," he concluded lamely.

"Perhaps we should recruit laundresses instead of supposedly trained duellists," remarked Cremione, then paused. "What did she do afterwards?"

The watcher had to think. "I was helping Hainus. Yes, she went back to pick up the lead of her lift-pole and went away."

"And this lift-pole," pursued Cremione awfully, "Did it perchance have a basket or two under it?"

"It did," confessed the watcher.

"What laundry? What laundress?" demanded Cremione.

"She didn't give her name. Let me think. The baskets had a green stripe on the side. I haven't seen that mark before."

Cremione left the idiot on watch after a few choice words. The nearest laundry was two streets away; it was not the one she wanted, but her questions directed her to another on the west side of the city. Cremione walked briskly, sometimes breaking into a trot. Home-going passers-by gave her odd looks, and a few called out to ask what the hurry was about. She ignored them and kept to her course, stopping only to ask for directions, yet when at last she found the address the laundry was closed. Cremione bit back a curse and asked around for employees, looming first over a quivering seller of seaweed rolls and then confronting an older woman nursing a cat.

"Don't you go a-shouting at my poor Whiskers," she was told. Cremione moderated the urgency of her voice and asked again.

"I don't see why I should tell some Dravish about the neighbours. What's it to you?"

Cremione tried a winning smile. The woman recoiled and made motions to a child who had paused a hopping game to watch. Before Cremione could complete an entirely unconvincing story the child returned with a Syndic guard in tow. After a tangled three-way conversation Cremione took the guard aside and explained that she was looking for the notorious duellist Jayas Zrei. As it happened, the guard and her colleagues had lost money betting against Jayas. With her help Cremione was able to find a young man who worked at the laundry.

"Telsie's basket? Sure, that was a laugh. She gets back here, carrying on about some pervert checking her out, and then this man pops out of her basket, says thanks and is off before she can make out what's happening. Did we have a giggle? Sure we did!"

It was quickly established that the man had not looked at all like Jayas, either in face or figure. Cremione returned to her command post at a jog, pondering courses of action. Was the man in the basket Jayas in some elaborate disguise? Or another of his party? Was the location of the laundry a misdirection or a clue? She was sure her quarry was about to make a run for it, but in which direction? Cremione ground her teeth in frustration, then set out back towards House Juleize. She would send people to the most likely out-ports and herself keep watch that night. One had got away; the next would not escape.

JAYAS WENT TO TAKE a deep breath, remembered his situation and took a shallow one instead. The smell was still awful. Nothing to be done about that, so he checked the night sky. It was the usual

Mer Ammery haze, the stars dimmer here than in the cold clarity of the northern skies. Perhaps that would help, as there would be less contrast. One could hope. His hand made a circular sweep of his body, checking that his gear was in place. Time to move. He stepped up and out, onto the narrow walk, high above the streets, settled the corpse atop his head and quaffed the potion. As he shrank the gutted body of the possum settled over him, first a helmet, then a cape and finally a shell concealing him entire. He clipped his harness to the spine overhead, gripped ribs and started forward, an unwary marsupial out for a stroll, shuffling along.

Out to the end of the walk, a long pause, an awkward turn, back along the walk and a massive jolt. Curved talons, wickedly sharp, pierced skin and bone, stopping just short of impaling Jayas. Even as he twisted away from the points he was lofted into the night, up over the roofs of Houses and lesser dwellings, shops and markets, temples and the grand offices of the Syndics. The only noise was the rush of air as the owl pivoted soundlessly to glide towards the towers that divided the city from the fields beyond. The wall passed below, his transport banked as it turned back towards its roost and he hit the catch of the harness and dropped into the night. A hoot of annoyance above, a fluff of wings as it braked to search for the escaped prey, but Jayas was growing larger as he fell. He looked down, to see a dull glimmer. Two long bow-shots beyond the walls were kept clear of walls, buildings and trees, but did not go to waste. He was going to land in a rice-paddy, which meant muddy clothes and a squelching slog to the path. No help for it. As his shoes touched the first soft green stems there was a flash of blue light, his motion was absorbed and he fell no more than if he had stepped off a stool. It was as wet and muddy as he had expected. Jayas sloshed across to the dyke and along that to the path, changed his footwear, took his bearings and set out. First step accomplished: he was clear of Mer

Ammery. He made a mental note to clean the Feather Shoes before he returned them to Delfe.

CREMIONE GLANCED SIDEWAYS at her watch-fellow. Coming back from being killed was chancy: some people felt no essential change, some were afflicted with a weirdness, some gained a further sense. She might have come back unable to see the colour green, or a compulsion to stand in absolute still silence for an hour at sunrise and sunset, or eyes that glowed white when sighting bread. She had heard of all of these. Then there was poor Hebben, who could not eat without gagging, as all food tasted of rot. Seeing auras was not the worst thing that could have happened, although it made some people uncomfortable. Often deservedly so, she thought. As for instance, her fellow, whose aura was tinged with apathetic resignation and not illumined by any great degree of intelligence. His companion at the back entrance was of similar make; she had picked them because they were not easily bored and could be relied upon to follow orders. She arched her back and rolled her neck, loosening muscles tight with unrelieved waiting. A dot of colour sped across the patch of sky in her vision. A shooting star? No, it was small tangle of blue and green, teasingly familiar. Almost like a very small aura. She recalled Jayas' expertise with potions, burst into lurid cursing and sprinted for Changers' Way. That broad avenue might give her another sighting. Yes, there it was, a tiny spark just visible before it vanished behind the black bulk of the Shipwrights' Bank. Too far, too fast to make out any details, but she was morally sure it was Jayas. She sprinted back to clap the fellow on the shoulder.

"Rouse out our team, have all of them meet me at Pens as soon as may be. Run!"

10. A Ship or a Boat?

Jayas moved along briskly, keeping to a pace that would bring him to Hane Bay an hour after sunrise. He had been raised far from the sea, and knew little of maritime affairs, but he'd been assured that tides were important. He should be there at the tail of the flood, whatever that was, ready to run out on the ebb, whatever *that* was. Running out sounded good. In any event, an hour after sunrise was the appointed time, and he should make it easily. The ground under foot was firm, the starlight enough to keep to the road, the night made no more than the usual noises. Frogs croaked and whistled, nocturnal birds belled and hooted, small animals rustled and chirped. A thin scream came from somewhere to his left as a luckless beast met its fate. He was yet to become familiar with the wildlife of this land, and now he supposed he never would. It was enough that it left him alone. He took a drink of cool water from the flask at his hip and walked on.

The sun was just over the trees when he strolled into Hane Bay. To the residents it doubtless had its own character, but to his eye is it was just another Merllan small port. The bay offered shelter to a pair of wharves and a yard where the skeleton of a ship lay on the ways; warehouses, chandlers, drinking establishments and other necessities of the maritime life stretched along the strand, with houses behind or tucked in between. The smell of the first loaves leaving the oven reached him as he left the fields; his stomach rumbled, and thoughts of breakfast mingled with his native curiosity. The houses were small, plastered and painted in bright colours, thatched with long reeds varnished a glossy brown. A man sweeping his doorstep gave him an acknowledging nod, and he asked directions to Jikker's store. It was only a few minutes walk, and he was able to buy a warm roll on the way.

Jikker's fronted the strand with closed shutters and bamboo blinds drawn down over the porch railings. Jayas took a narrow alley at the side, pushed open a gate of salt-worn timber and called softly.

"Jayas? You are in good time." Seyvyar stepped out, followed by Delfe and Yerech. Yerech handed Jayas his pack, he shouldered the straps and they filed out the gate.

"Our ride is tied up at the southern wharf. You can have breakfast aboard, as they will be eager to cast off. You had no trouble leaving? You weren't spotted?"

"I don't believe so," Jayas said as they came on to the strand and turned towards the wharf. He could see a three-master lying alongside, sails bundled along the yards ready to let fall, the green pennant of imminent departure fluttering from the mast-head.

Yerech shaded his eyes to check the ripple of water in the bay. "Tide's on the turn," he told them. He turned his gaze on the craft awaiting them, checked, asked Jayas "Are you sure you were not seen? Someone carrying steel just ducked behind a bale over yonder."

Jayas knotted his fingers and bent sharpened eyes upon their goal. A crewman aloft and two officers on the poop of the ship were looking at the wharf rather than attending to their duties. There – the glint of steel as someone shifted behind a stack of cargo. A tiny movement gave away a pair of eyes watching them through a gap between barrels.

"They're waiting for us!" Jayas spun round. "They'll have others on the road."

"This way! Follow me," cried Yerech, and ran towards the other jetty. This was not the time to have a debate. They all ran after him, packs bumping against their backs, across the stones of the street, out on to the planks. From behind came shouts; an arrow plunked into the wood and others cut into the water. Their boots sounded loud on the hollow timbers. Jayas looked ahead to see the end of the jetty only twenty paces away. There was no cover; what did Yerech have in mind?

"That one" shouted Yerech and scrambled down into a boat. The others followed, first Jayas then Delfe. Seyvyar paused to utter a few Words and gesture at the planks before following.

"Here, take the oars with me," Yerech told Jayas. "Delfe, you steer. Seyvyar, do what you can to hold them off." He had jerked the lines free and shoved off with an oar. Now he fitted it deftly to the thole-pin, helped Jayas do the same and took up the stroke. Jayas pulled hard, nearly toppled backwards as his oar met little resistance, angled the blade and tried again. "Watch me," Yerech said, they matched strokes and began to make headway. Jayas concentrated on the motions for a dozen pulls until he had the rhythm, and only then looked up. Yerech had been right – as well as the group now pounding out on to the jetty, others had burst from behind the houses and were running to join the fray. The land-side group halted to loose more arrows, but both Delfe and Seyvyar had cast the Invisible Defence. The shafts that did not hit the water broke against magical barriers. A tall black figure led the charge. Cremione, out for revenge? Jayas' craft-enhanced vision showed a face set in furious determination. Out on the jetty she ran, long legs extending, spear in hand. Suddenly the confident stride turned into a wild dance as her foot went from under her. Jayas could only admire the athleticism which kept her upright, a hand flashing out to grab a piling and swing her round, out over the water and back on to the jetty. The woman behind was not so gifted; her feet went up, her body down and she skidded off into the sea. The man behind *her* made an heroic leap, straight into Cremione, and both went down in a cursing heap.

Seyvyar had picked up a green glass fishing float, Now he extended his arms, sighted between his raised thumbs, spoke a few Words and sent it hurtling across. It stuck a piling and shattered, sending out a spray of edged shards.

"Slitherslick," Seyvyar grinned. Jayas and Yerech pulled hard, putting more distance from the wrathful mob. Jayas risked a glance over his shoulder and another across, to see the ship that they should have been on standing out away from its mooring. His attention came back to the wharf, where the woman had been pulled from the water. Cremione was speaking to her urgently, pointing at their craft. He could see her mouth twist as she uttered Words. Seyvyar flung his precious coat aside and dropped his pouch, spewing Words of his own that hit Jayas' ears like soft mallets. "I'm not mad," he said and leapt over the side to swim away from the boat.

The magician, Cremione on her back, swooped into the air and sped towards them, the oval of the Defence shimmering before her. Cremione leaned out, spear thrust forward, the very spirit of vengeance hurtling from above to pin him to his seat. Down they came, and then Seyvyar uttered a last Word. Abruptly Cremione was in the water and Seyvyar on the magician's back, one arm around her, the other with a dagger to her throat.

"Keep on for the boat," Seyvyar demanded.

The magician uttered a frightened assent, then added indignantly "Get your hands off my tits!" Seyvyar shifted his arm, the woman tucked her head down, lifted her legs, twisted a shoulder and executed a neat roll. Seyvyar was thrown off and forwards. "Cunning bitch," he thought as he splashed head-first into the sea. When he surfaced the boat was already turning to collect him. A few strokes, a reaching arm and he was hauled over the side. He swivelled to look around. Where was the magician? Where was Cremione?

"Swimming in armour is really hard," Jayas answered his unspoken thought, even as he pulled his oar. There – the magician was hovering, then plummeted into the water. The ripples were still spreading when she burst into the air again, Cremione in her arms. Her return to the jetty was the laboured flight of an osprey with a too-large fish.

"Keep inshore," Yerech directed Delfe. "We want to round the point and be out of sight as soon as may be. Looks like our ride has abandoned us. They've spread their sails and are off to open water."

From what Jayas could see, the wharf was now in chaos. Cremione was spewing sea-water, a mob of fisher-folk were shouting at their pursuers and – yes – the town guard had arrived. He could see their sashes of office. He kept an eye out until they pulled around the horn of the bay and the scene vanished behind the land.

Rowing on the open sea was different. It called for short strokes, steeply-angled. It took Jayas a little time to adjust as they worked their way along. His hands and back were sore when Yerech handed his oar over to Delfe, set Seyvyar, still dripping, at the rudder, and set to hoisting the sail. The outriggers were swung out and locked, the ties along the booms unfastened, the halyard pulled, the peaks rose up, the control lines let out, the boat leaned as it gained way and he could change places with Seyvyar and take them out away from the coast. Jayas rolled his shoulders, flexed fingers and took stock of the situation.

The boat was not some calm-water dinghy, but a craft that could ride the waves in style. The front portion was decked, the back had a covered box on the centreline with thwarts either side. At the very back three lockers provided storage and seating, and space for Delfe to handle the steering oar. He eyed the lockers: perhaps there was something to eat in there? Water he could supply, drawing it from the air with craft. The single mast supported a triangular sail, two peaks above and point down, now urging them briskly over the sea. Jayas had no idea what the various ropes did, but Yerech seemed to have things in hand and no doubt would give them lessons. They had all their stuff and Cremione was left behind. He made a careful scrutiny of land, sea and sky back towards Hane Bay and descried a small dot hanging in mid-air. That Powers-please-blast magician was aloft again, taking note of their course. Seyvyar declined to chase her off, and they watched until she circled back towards land.

"We'll have no problem taking this lady all the way to Dtlag," Yerech said cheerfully. To Jayas this sounded appallingly optimistic. How many days in this thing, comfortless, hungry and damp? He checked a locker, to find a small sack of dry biscuits, a beaker of water and some fishing gear. What of the enclosed fore-deck? As he started forward the hatch was nudged open. A bleary voice called "Hand me a bun with pickles and glass of water, will you?" A tousled head emerged, blinked at Jayas with his mace, Delfe and Seyvyar and Yerech. Broad shoulders and deeply-tanned arms followed the head. Jayas saw the upper half of a woman in a worn blue sleeveless tunic, dark hair escaping a leather tie, brown eyes where crows-feet told of squinting against sea-glare, a wide nose and a full mouth.

"Who are you? Why are you on our boat? Where are my cousins? Where are we?"

Jayas swept her questions aside with a courtly salute. "We are a band of refugees who have unfortunately been compelled to make use of your vessel. It was empty – apart, obviously, from yourself – when we, ah, commandeered it. We will do our utmost to return the boat to you in good order but, for now, our need is greater than yours."

The woman gave him a sceptical look. "You mean you stole our boat, right? And kidnapped me to boot."

"I would not put that interpretation on it," Jayas said.

"Yeah, well, I would." She looked around, gauged the sun. "Where are you – we – headed anyway?"

Jayas saw no harm in telling her. "The Haghar lands. Dtlag probably."

The woman was evidently a pragmatist. She looked at the four men, shrugged, said "Guess that's where I'm going then. Now, I need to pee."

Bodily needs attended to, their unwilling crew-mate introduced herself. "I'm Attaiye. I have a two-fifths share in this boat; my cousins have the rest and they won't be happy. We'd be out gathering snap-clams, so you'll owe us for the lost days. Oh, and for the biscuits too. I'll keep a tally."

Jayas handed her a five-gull piece with a flourish. "Here's for the biscuits. We regret that we were not able to provision this fine vessel properly, as our departure was a little hurried. Could you advise of the best way to sustain ourselves on the voyage? One that does not involve stopping at a port?"

"Just how much trouble are you in? This does not involve the Syndics, does it?" Attaiye spoke of the Syndics with the typical Merllan respect and fear.

"Not at all. We are well with them," Jayas assured her. "Our issues are with a few Houses jealous of our success."

Attaiye considered the group again, her face clearing. "You would not be that outland duellist that has twisted the odds-makers' underwear into a knot, would you?"

"The very same."

She gave a broad grin. "My sister made a packet betting on you, and Juleize was going to sell the warehouse before you gave them a pickup. Guess you made enough to buy this boat five times over."

Do the Merllan never stop thinking about money? thought Jayas. Then he realised that it was never far from his own mind. He thrust that realisation aside irritably and invited Attaiye to join them in planning the voyage. Yerech took the lead here, as an experienced sailor. They had no charts or Locators (Attaiye's cousins were to bring those down, along with provisions), but Attaiye knew these waters. Seyvyar and Delfe both knew a cantrip that would give them the direction of true north. Today would be biscuits and water.

They reached the Hundred Islands, a scatter of islets, reefs and lagoons, before noon the next day. As Attaiye had predicted there were several fishing craft busy with line and net, only too happy to sell fish fresh and dried, fruit and greens preserved with Unrot, and yet more biscuit. At exorbitant prices, of course. Jayas did not haggle too hard, for the sooner they were clear of the archipelago the better. They stowed their purchases and shaped a course that would take them out past Pious Point on the long Brahnzhever peninsula and then up the Gulf of Reghen to Dtlag.

FOR THE NEXT DAY JAYAS had little to do but stay out of the way. He drew water, helped with meals and listened as Atteiye, Yerech and Delfe talked of seas, boats and rigs. When he asked about pursuit Atteiye laughed. The *Sea-Spider*, she told him, was the fastest boat in Hane, for the snap-clams had to be delivered to the steeping-tubs within a few hours of harvesting. They were kept fresh in the box amidships, which opened to the sea. Jayas still kept an eye out, and indeed the trip had points of interest. This was a much-travelled stretch of water, as all the trade of Frouan and Dravishi, the Corillion Coast and far southern Hirre came together at the Saske Channel, bound for Mer Ammery, Brahnker City, the Haghar lands, great Daruz Alman, Reghen and the Rai Harbours. Broad-beamed merchanters wallowed along deep-laden, coasters in all their varieties tacked upwind towards the archipelago or ran down to ports in the Brahnzhever, packet-boats skimmed the waves and once a swift naval galley went past, the long blue pennant of the Brahnak fleet streaming from the mast-head. So far nothing they passed seemed interested in them. So he tended his gear, made idle plans with Seyvyar and worked on his tan.

He did have time to muse on this latest adventure. It had proved profitable enough in monetary terms; he and Seyvyar were no longer paupers, if not as wealthy as they desired. It brought him no closer to less tangible goals, if only because he did not know what they were. There was Atteiye: she would return to a life of fishing and sailing, no doubt find a partner and raise children in time and consider her life well-spent if she could look out over Hane Bay from some comfortable spot in old age in the company of family and friends. All ambitions achieved by most people and, Jayas supposed, satisfying for them. Seyvyar had his art, Delfe a place in his House. He and Yerech had, what? An endless quest for the unknown?

Jayas knew that addictions - even to something as tempting as money - enslaved the mind as surely as chains did the body, and he hated being chained. For him, wealth was a means, and he had yet to find the right end. He would know it when he came across it, he supposed. On this thought he went back to tanning.

They rounded Pious Point close inshore in the early morning. Jayas took in the towering cliffs lit by the sun, the red beacon-light flashing on the heights above, the white smudge that marked the statue of Sebres Brahn, arm upraised as he preached to this new land. Impressive, but more welcome as it marked the turn into the Reghen Gulf. From here it was a straight run up to Dtlag. Far out to sea a flash of white marked a ship making up the Gulf. Closer in, another vessel, larger than their own, was making more sail. As he watched it hoisted a string of signal flags and sent a blue light soaring aloft. He looked around, to see an answering signal astern.

"Attaiye, do we have a scrying ring?" She gave a firmly negative dip of the head.

"Yerech," asked Jayas in a disinterested tone "What would you do if you commanded the resources of several Houses in Mer Ammery and wanted to capture a boat bound for Dtlag?"

Yerech brought to mind a chart of the Reghen Gulf and surrounds. "I would send to any ships in Brahnker or thereabouts to lie off Pious Point and watch for it. If none, I would send to any ships in Dtlag to stand out to sea and head south, staying maybe five leagues off shore with boats out."

"Thank you. Do you suppose that that vessel out to sea there and the other behind us might have been given just such instructions?"

Yerech gave a startled oath, scrambled up and shaded his eyes to scan the craft out to seaward. "That's a pinnace. A lot of Houses use them for fast freight or passengers. I can't make out the ensign. Seyvyar?"

Seyvyar gave out a few Words and peered across the water. "Gold stripes on green. A lot of people on deck."

"House Taliere," Delfe told them. Seyvyar turned his gaze astern, to descry another similar vessel coming up from the south.

"They won't catch us," declared Atteiye confidently, and let out a control line to spread the sail wider. The chuckle of water from the bow grew louder.

Yerech and Jayas exchanged glances. One pursuer behind, another to seaward and ahead. If they turned away from the coast they would be caught between the two as they converged. If they kept their course, they might out-run both. Yet what if their enemies had foreseen this?

"Can we fight?" asked Seyvyar, causing Attaiye to make a noise of alarmed protest. Jayas looked at Yerech, caught his grimace of doubt, considered the odds and shook his head.

"They will have learned the lessons from Mer Ammery and Hane Bay. There will be a dozen with craft and several mages on each vessel. Can we get a closer look, and a look ahead?"

Seyvyar considered. Flight was the simplest choice, but then he would be visible. He did not fancy another swim. Worse, some magician yonder might try the same spell he had used on Cremione, and he would find himself on a hostile deck, no doubt bristling with sharp objects. The Roving Eye, that would work. He consulted his spell-book, ran through the conjuration in his mind twice (a high-order spell, but nothing *he* could not handle), then spoke the Words. His view of the boat and the sea vanished, replaced by a wheeling survey of the sky. He steadied himself, carefully moved his point of view until he was looking down at their frail craft from high above, a speck on the blue expanse. Another shift, a few Words to give him an eagle's vision, and he was peering at the deck of a pinnace, seen as a soaring frigate-bird would do, looking down that it might snatch a fish. Jayas was right; the deck was crowded with arms, and several magicians were staring across, hands fidgeting with their spell-books and Items. A dart-thrower stood ready, crew clustered about and a shaft in the slot.

A little effort brought the second chaser under his gaze. It was much the same as the first, only the red pennant of Pens flew, not the green and gold of Taliere. Seyvyar took his Eye higher yet, to throw his view north. Dots resolved into a merchanter making north, a cluster of fishing craft and then, a little out from the coast, two sharp-prowed vessels, sails angled as they worked against the wind, one flying the red pennant, the other a bright yellow. A swooping pass and yes, both were ready for a fight. Here was the trap they were being herded towards. He let the spell lapse, kept his eyes closed against the dizzying rush of transition to normal sight, and relayed his findings.

Attaiye had a face of dismay, while Jayas and Yerech had brought out armour and weapons. Yerech had pulled on a padded arming coat and was unhappily regarding a suit of mail. "Spear-thrust or drowning," he muttered. "What choices must we make." Delfe was checking spells, chewing the tail of his moustache as he concentrated.

Attaiye roused herself to protest - could they not talk to these people? Jayas was brisk. "They want us dead, and no witnesses. That includes you."

"What did you *do* to them?" wailed Attaiye.

Jayas was again succinct. "Made them look silly, and cost them a lot of money. Pens lost standing. Cremione died, although she seems to have gotten better."

Attaiye stood and shaded her eyes. "I can outrun that one upwind on a reach. We could bring her across and be out into the Gulf before the other can do much. Be touch and go, but if they take a moment to notice we could head them by, oh two-three cables, maybe more."

Seyvyar made a sceptical noise. "At that distance I could disable – maybe sink – this craft in four different ways. The fellows over there will have at least two. Then there is the dart-thrower." Attaiye's shoulders slumped.

It was plain that if they kept on they were sailing to their doom. Their chances of escape to seaward were small. What of the land? Jayas put the question and Attaiye was again aghast.

"That's the Hansippif, a Wild that hates humans. To be wrecked there is to disappear, never to be seen again." Delfe was similarly opposed; the Hansippif was the land of nightmares in Mer Ammery. Jayas and Seyvyar had both journeyed through hostile lands before, and emerged mostly intact. Yerech weighed their chances against the surrounding armada against the unknown dangers of a Wild, and supported Jayas and Seyvyar. Attaiye at first thought to throw herself over the side, then refused to relinquish the steering oar. Seyvyar laid the Binding Will on her and bade her lie down. She was trussed and laid out on the foredeck, while Yerech took control. Lines were brought in, the sail shifted, the oar moved in a smooth sweep and they were heading briskly west towards the looming coast. Attaiye made muffled noises of despair. The pinnace to the south brought the wind on the quarter and packed on sail, while the sails on the one ahead shifted as she angled in towards the coast. Yerech changed course a little to keep their own craft on her best point of sailing.

One outrigger dug deep, sending up spray to shower them where they crouched by the rail. Closer came the land and closer, with all watching for some place they might run ashore. Here the wind was weaker, shifting as it curled around hill and headland, and the party cast many an anxious glance backwards as their pursuer gradually made up the distance. Steep-to headlands, fringed with surf over rocks, offered no harbour; nor did rock shelves running out from jungled hillsides. Delfe's sharp eyes spotted a reef closing off a tiny cove and they ran on. There – a stretch of shingle behind a small hook of land. Yerech brought them closer in, closer yet, around the point into the calm, Jayas and Delfe dug oars in and they ran the prow up onto the land with a crunch of shells and sand. Their gear was already on deck, to be hastily tossed ashore. Delfe leapt into the water, Attaiye was handed down and they trotted with their burdens across the strand to where a cluster of boulders offered cover. From there they watched as first one, then the other pinnace came up, to back their sails and lie two bow-shots offshore.

Jayas peered through a small gap, watching as their enemies rocked easily on the swell. A sail shifted, the ship turned slightly, a flat whack echoed across the water and a bolt the length of his outstretched arms was hurled across, to open a great breach in the hull of their craft. Another followed, to shatter planking and part stays. A third overshot, plunging into the forest. Before a fourth could follow, the land retaliated. A palm swayed back, whipped forward to throw a volley of hard nuts. Some splashed into the sea, sending up gouts of water, others rang off the hull and a few ploughed bloodily across the crowded deck. The ship wheeled for the open sea, pursued by another volley that ripped through sails. The partner ship hastily followed as another palm took up the fight, sending a volley down-range that straddled the fleeing vessel. Jayas kept watching as they retreated to a safe distance and then laid to.

They all stayed still for some time, not wishing to incur the wrath of the palms. When the agitated swaying had subsided Jayas cautiously stood up to survey the scene. Someone had untied Attaiye, for now she ran out, crying aloud, to run her hands over the maimed boat.

"Our *Sea-Spider*! What have you done to her! Now I will be eaten by the land, and my cousins will blame me!"

Practical Jayas asked if the damage was repairable, and she rounded on him. Did he have planks? Glue? Saws, chisels, a rebating plane? A wright's hands and skills? Jayas admitted to deficiencies in all of these. He felt impelled to add that the damage had been done by Pens and Taliere, not by himself. This did not mollify Attaiye.

"You robbing, useless hypocrite! Who stole the *Sea-Spider* from her moorings? Who has dragged this feud across the waters?" And in a blind rage she beat at him with her fists. Attaiye was strong, and not unskilled at fighting, but Jayas was in armour. Mail and padding absorbed the blows, while he fended off those aimed at his face. He had no desire to harm Attaiye. He was intent on protecting himself while uttering calming words, and her sudden elevation and removal into the greenery took him by surprise. A vine had crept up on them, and now it seized her and whisked her away. Her last cry was "Thieving outland slug!"

Not just obsessed with money, but vilely prejudiced to boot, thought Jayas.

11. Dtlag and the Hansippif

One by one the others joined Jayas by the wrecked *Sea-Spider*, all keeping one wary eye on the vegetation and another on the ships hovering out to sea. Yerech knew the most about boats, and he confirmed Attaiye's judgement with a rueful shake of the head. Two large holes, a broken rib and a toppled mast were beyond his competence to fix, the more so as cutting wood did not look like a survivable option. In all this time there had been no sign of Attaiye, not even a dying scream. The shrubs and vines had been quiet, with only an occasional twitch or shiver. No animals had assailed them, nor the ground swallowed them. Perhaps, Delfe ventured, Attaiye had been particularly irritating? If they went quietly, all might be well.

They all agreed to be quiet and meek as worms in their going, but which way to go? That was the question. The shingle of their little bay gave way to cliffs where the waves washed over fallen rocks slippery with weed. They were burdened with armour, arms, food and the possessions they had lugged from Mer Ammery. How would the land react if Jayas drew water from the air? Seyvyar said that the etheric surround felt so hostile that he was reluctant to attempt even the most minor working of magic, a judgement Delfe agreed with, shivering. Perhaps if they swam well off-shore, he might then cast a spell which transformed one into a spiny sea-creature. With this, a pair could travel up the coast over a few days and bring back a boat.

The idea had many negatives, not least the eager harpoons awaiting any such swim. The two ships that were to have closed the trap on the *Sea-Spider* were now visible to the north, working their way down to join the watching pair. Their enemies could take turns loitering there, gleefully observing their slow demise. They gloomily trooped back to the shelter of the boulders and ate a thoughtful lunch.

CREMIONE LOWERED THE scrying ring and demanded to know why Jayas was still alive. The captain, the senior magician and the squad commander gave explanations, all of which boiled down to the inadvisability of arousing the Hansippif Wild. Cremione dismissed these as craven excuses, but the captain refused to bring her ship closer in, and the magician refused, in colourful language, to send a fearful wreaking at Jayas. Cremione ground her teeth. What of a message, she demanded. Was that beyond the magician's competence? Would the Wild extract their bones one by one if they sent a short message? The magician allowed that this much was probably safe, and a simple spell would send a short message to another magician.

"Then tell that Mother-abandoned pimp Seyvyar that I challenge Jayas to a duel here, on this deck. He and his companions to have safe passage to Dtlag afterwards, should he survive."

The message, somewhat edited, was duly sent. The reply was not long in coming. The magician's face reddened; he did not repeat it verbatim but only said that the offer was emphatically rejected. Cremione's tooth-grinding was audible. When she prised her hands from the rail it was to state flatly that they would stay here until Jayas death was evident, however it occurred. The captain did not agree; there was dirty weather coming in, and they could linger here this close to shore until no later than mid-morning of the next day.

Shouting and threats did not move her, and Cremione flung herself aloft in a rage. She spent the remainder of the day and the whole night there, and was awake when the sun rose over the Gulf to illumine the shore. There was no sign of Jayas and his friends. The closest scrutiny showed only the wrecked *Sea-Spider* and a cluster of crabs dancing a quadrille on the strand below the waving palms.

"The Hansippif has taken them, and it leaves no remains," she was told when she descended.

Cremione made a chopping gesture. "That weaseling fraud would choke even the Hansippif, if he did not cozen it into providing him a path paved with pearls. Let us to Dtlag, for the news will come there first."

TOL PUSHED OPEN THE door to Enner's Bar. Serriet would meet her here at the fifth bell; it was now just past the fourth, but she had cut her walk through the harbour district short when the afternoon rain started. Tol had not yet adjusted to the regular downpours of this season. Serriet had recommended Enner's – the beer was good, the food good, the prices reasonable and the atmosphere quiet. Tol was therefore surprised to see a dead wasp on the floor before the bar. The wasp was nearly the size of a small child, with a sharp curved stinger as long as her hand. As she halted the stinger twitched and a drop of venom oozed out. One wing lay out-flung, broken struts leaking fluids over the translucent surfaces; the other was crumpled beneath the body. A knife protruded from each faceted eye, another from the back of the head. A purple line along the torso told Tol of a hit from the Malevolent Streak. Three people were arguing over the corpse, while a worker stood by with bucket and mop. Tol sidled past, gained the attention of the bartender and ordered a beer. A woman next to her tilted her head at the arguers and rolled her eyes.

"What are they arguing about?" asked Tol.

"Idiots. One wants the price of his knife, because it's no longer virgin steel. The other two are arguing over who gets the body."

Tol frowned. "I was told this was a quiet bar. Why is this thing here anyway?"

The woman tossed her head towards the back of the bar, where two booths were full of folk engaged in animated talk. "They were all paid out today, and don't know whether to be relieved or annoyed. Relieved because it means a trip into the Hansippif is off the menu, annoyed because they thought the job would last another week or more. One decided to show off the wasp. It was going to be his secret weapon." She quirked her eyebrows.

"Four hits and it's a mess. Probably would not have done him any good," judged Tol.

The woman nodded. "My money would have been on the other guy." She sighed. "It's all moot. Once again, Jayas escapes."

It took an effort for Tol to keep her tone casual. "Did you say Jayas? The duellist of Mer Ammery?"

"The very one. It's no secret. He and his band stole a boat and made for Dtlag. That obsessed cretin Cremione put a crew together to trap them. Rather than be taken they wrecked themselves on the shore of the Hansippif and when morning came – they were not there. Cremione paid off the crew and has gone to find some other way to get Jayas. She won't rest until she has his stuffed body to use as a footstool. With his soul trapped inside. She's off on some mad quest for something that will let her trespass on the Hansippif."

Tol was gratified that she had been right about Jayas's intended destination, but miffed that he had again diverted course. Before she could probe for more, a hand fell on her shoulder. It was Serriet, wringing water from her braid with one hand while holding two fingers up to the barman. Tol added a third for her companion, then pulled Serriet forward.

" Serriet, this is – oh, sorry, my name is Tol, Tol Henze .. " The other gave her name. Tol resumed, "Lussein has been telling me about Jayas the duellist. He and his company cast themselves away on the Hansippif."

Serriet was clearly big with news, but quick to take the hint. She just nodded and said that she had heard something of this along the waterfront. Was the Hansippif really so dire? Lussein gave a sober account. The Hansippif was indeed averse to a human presence, although some few cast on its shores had survived by keeping within a few paces of the sea. Of those who entered on the inland side, most were never seen again, but the odd one had staggered out hideously transformed, in one case endowed with the back legs of one animal and the front ones of another, in another case with poisonous shrubs in place of ears. Perhaps the Wild left them their lives that they might be an awful warning.

Tol asked her if Jayas was alone. No, some three or four others were with him, including a fellow duellist and the magician Seyvyar Trist. His probable death had been reported to the Association. At this point the group at the back became rowdy and Lussein left to quiet them. Tol and Serriet ordered food and took their own seats in a quieter corner. Serriet imparted her news between slurps of spiced squid with noodles. The manager of the local branch of Green Sea Mercantile had also heard of Jayas' and Seyvyar's probable demise. In accord with her instructions, their allowance was suspended. If either of the pair turned up alive, then their commission could be re-activated. The manager asked that they submit their expenses as soon as possible.

Serriet picked out the last piece of ginger and chewed. "So this job ends here. Could be worse places. I have enough to tide me over until I find something else. You?"

"Same. Pity we'll never see the two thousand, but I was looking forward to meeting Jayas in person. Although I still had not worked out what to do when we did."

Serriet let that one slide. "We can start looking for work tomorrow. For now, let's try the desserts."

JAYAS SLUMPED AGAINST the sheltering boulder and gave himself over to a moment of self-pity. All he wanted was to be rich. What was so wrong with that? Why did so many of his attempts end in flight, pursued by the irrationally vengeful? This was – he stopped to count – the fifth or maybe the sixth time his plans had been thwarted by fate just as he was on the brink of success. He had been poisoned, hurled into a lake, felled with a poker and now menaced with piracy. *What was wrong with these people?* Surely the Powers had better things to do than stoke every petty grievance until it resulted in manic persecution of poor Jayas. He glanced around. Delfe was nervous (this was the first real excitement in the poor lad's life), Yerech was stoically calm, Seyvyar had laid his Snake Staff across his lap and was thumbing through his spell-book. It was hot and still here, and the shingle was damp under his haunches. A small bird landed on a nearby branch and regarded the group with one beady eye. A spy for the land? It plucked a caterpillar from a leaf and flew off. Probably not.

Fight Cremione on her own deck, surrounded by her partisans? The proposal was insulting; surely she did not believe him that naive, to think he would swim into the monster's mouth?

"Are they still there?" he asked Delfe, who had his eye to a crack between two rocks. Delfe grunted and added that Cremione had climbed a mast and had her eyes fastened on their hide-out. Jayas' mouth twisted. Why was Cremione so upset? She had a new body, didn't she? A better one than she had before. Jayas would really like a body like that, and yet she blamed him! Jayas let himself brood on the injustices of life while the afternoon wore away. Birds and bugs came and went, their enemies stayed obstinately off-shore, the shadows crept out from the jungle. What to do when night came? It would be perilous to clamber along the sea's edge, never knowing when you might annoy some random plant or misstep into deep water. Yet they could hardly stay here for days. They talked desultorily among themselves in low voices, to no conclusion. In the afternoon the rain swept in from the gulf, for a moment blotting out their nemeses afloat. They huddled under their capes and dripped gloomily.

Night came and they sat there, unable to come up with a good reason to move. Jayas shifted sideways and Seyvyar's staff, propped against the rock, fell on his shoulder. He pushed it back up, careful to keep his fingers away from the head. It fell again and he made an irritated noise. When his hand met the staff it flowed up his arm to lie across his shoulder. Jayas froze, then very slowly turned his head. That faint green glow was from the snake's eyes, a hand-span from his cheek. It let him see the glittering fangs beneath. Jayas knew how deadly was the venom coating them, for he had brewed it himself. The snake's tail tapped him on the leg, then pointed inland.

"People, we are being invited to move," Jayas called in a low voice. There was a round of muffled exclamations.

"We, or just you?" asked Yerech. The head shifted slightly, to bring its lambent gaze upon him. "Alright, alright. It's we," Yerech conceded. Mindful, despite this latest turn, of the watchers offshore, they gathered their gear as quietly as they could and followed Jayas. The bushes parted before him, to make an opening just visible in the starlight and one by one they entered the dreaded Hansippif.

For the next hour Jayas scrambled uphill, guided only by the plants opening before him. The way made few concessions to the terrain, leaving him to haul himself up sloping rock faces, bruise his shins on logs and stub his toes on stones, scrape his hands as he clambered up some leaf-deep bank. From the grunts and occasional curses behind the others suffered the same pains. Yet the snake kept him moving, swaying close when he faltered, tapping his ribs when he slowed, as a rider might dig heels into a reluctant horse. At last Jayas and his companions staggered into a small clearing where the trees showed no break. As Yerech came in the way closed behind, the snake dropped to the grass and slithered away and they stood, knees trembling with weariness, in the night. Doubt and the dark had weighed heavily on body and mind.

Delfe's young voice broke the silence. "Well, on the bright side, the Hansippif has not killed us." Jayas could hear the quaver under the bravado.

"Yet," added Seyvyar.

"If the Wild wants our lives, it can take them at any time," put in Yerech. "It has not, so it wants something else."

"Maybe our kidneys for its favourite tree," speculated Seyvyar. *Not helping, Seyvyar*, thought Jayas. He put forward a distraction, calculated to engage Seyvyar's tendency to the didactic.

"Does this Wild think, then? Has it intelligence? A mind?"

"It has wants, and the means to obtain them. It can make palms, vines and a wooden staff move, as we have seen," replied Seyvyar. "That makes it alive, I suppose. Intelligence? That is a matter of debate. Qaresmei writes in his *One-Eyed Inversions* that, just as demons arise from curdles in the etheric flows, so the land and the ether interact to produce land-spirits, and these spirits in turn enliven the land, giving rise to the Powers. Demons, spirits and Powers all display something we might call intelligence, so Qaresmei sees mind as an inherent property of the interplay of ether and matter. Jurek disagrees; she sees mind as the moving force, a property of the world as a whole which manifests in Powers, spirits and people alike. Sebres Brahn drew on her arguments in formulating his own doctrine..."

Seyvyar's lecture drew Delfe in, and the two lost themselves in argument and counter-argument on theories of the ether. Yerech gave Jayas a pat of approval and they set about preparing for the night. A cape would keep them from the damp ground, a folded coat make a pillow and their one blanket each cover them. Yerech asked Jayas if they should take turns on watch; Jayas could see no point – either the Wild would leave them alone or it would not, and the outcome would be the same waking or sleeping. On that comforting note he went to sleep, lulled by Seyvyar's disquisition on intentionality.

The following days were blurred in his recollection. They would wake, eat a meagre meal and a path would open before them. The Hansippif was a country of steep ridges and fast streams, and of rain, rain every afternoon and dripping damp day and night. Often it took a full day to descend a long slope, sometimes looping rope around a tree to avoid sliding helplessly towards some ravine, then crossing rushing waters by clambering over debris trapped between boulders, the whole shifting underfoot and soaked with spray, only to toil up another rain-slick hillside, hauling themselves up from branch to branch, slipping and cursing. They were caked with mud, pricked with thorns, scraped with rocks, chafed everywhere as wet clothes rubbed against skin. Food grew mould and their bellies ached from hunger. The Hansippif did not provide – it drove.

After the first day Jayas went barefoot, both to keep his boots whole and for better grip on the earth. By the third Seyvyar was so distressed at the state of his clothing that he risked spells of cleansing and protection. When these evoked no reaction Delfe tried the Circle of Shelter that evening. Instead of a translucent blue dome he achieved a wobbling ovoid of suspicious and sickly colours, but it was at least dry. They argued various courses as they lay there, exhausted and sore, and in the end it all came down to the brute fact that the land would have its way. There was no contesting the power that had them in its grip. Seyvyar was familiar with the surrounds of the Wilds, with their faster, more complex, more challenging rhythms. The surrounds here in the midst of the Hansippif did not challenge; they confronted. Here the ether was heavy, thick with suspicion and menace, quick to take affront at the least whisper of non-compliance. Seyvyar felt choked. Delfe drew on experience with the hostile nature of the Fever Coast to wring a limited degree of freedom, modulating minor spells with tones of soothing deference to ease their pains and hungers. Jayas laboured on, seething inside at being so coerced. Yerech was careful in his movements, lest a tug on a vine or a broken branch lead to punishment. They saw no animals, and birds were few. In most Wilds the ether manifested in harmless oddities, such as inverse waterfalls or flowers spelling out archaic runes. Here, any oddities emanated watchful enmity. A flock of eyes followed them from tree to tree, each time arranged in vaguely ominous patterns. Their shadows were not their own, but at one moment spindly creatures with burning eyes and at another geometries that contorted space. The very air was cloudy, limiting sight to a few paces, keeping the Hansippif's secrets from view and threatening ambush by some lurking monstrosity.

So it went, with the presence of the land ever weighing on their minds. After a time the rains lessened, the slopes were less steep, the trees more widely-spaced, the mists lighter, the views to the west and more open county. This vista of a land beyond the reach of the Hansippif barely registered, so worn were they. It was a numb Jayas who halted mid-afternoon, staggering like a sleep-walker suddenly awakened. He stood in a grassy hollow, shaded by three enormous trees rising from the leaf-mould like towers. No menacing thorns penned the band in, yet they all knew that here they must wait. For what they did not know, but the imperative was clear. They pulled their last scraps of food from their packs and ate, drank deeply from the water-bottles Jayas had refilled each evening. Some tickle at the back of Jayas' mind had him stretching and twisting, doing the breathing exercises and finger movements that had become second nature in his first years schooling in craft. Years ago now, but still ingrained. Looking around, he saw Yerech had been smitten by the same impulse; he was going over his armour and weapons with care, checking laces and straps and airing his quilted arming coat. Seyvyar was leafing through spells, and Delfe had brought out the knives that would fly as directed when he uttered the Words. *We have been brought here as gladiators or champions, to fight as the Wild wills, for its pleasure or profit*, thought Jayas. What did the Wild fear or want, that it must send them out as its slave-warriors?

The shadows crept across the ground and one by one the stars glimmered into being. Jayas rolled his shoulders, once more clad in the comforting weight of mail, and stood at rest, a conscript awaiting orders. Jayas had rebelled against authority in his youth, and ever since lived by his own code. This coercion struck at the core of his being, the more so as it could not be defied.

The orders came in the form of Attaiye, who strode out from the trees. It was not the Attaiye of Hane Bay, the practical fisher-woman and capable sailor, but an Attaiye of the Wild. Her eyes were patches of dark moss, her hair a coiling mass that waved in the still air. Green lines snaked over her arms and torso, shifting in patterns whose meaning he could not guess at. Her voice was dark, sepulchral, binding.

"Over the hill and down, a distance you will walk as the star Henebre moves a hand-span across the sky. There, there is a tower, and on the tower a light. The light must come down and be broken before this night ends. It is guarded. Let that not prevent you. Do this thing and the Hansippif will shelter you from pursuit for five days. For this night nothing enters or leaves that place but yourselves, and yourselves only if the light is gone."

With that, Attaiye wheeled about and was gone into the trees. Jayas' eye swept his fellows. "Well, let's go check the lay of the land." He picked up his pack and started up the hill.

12. Western Light

Jayas, Seyvyar, Yerech, and Delfe made their way up the slope, winding through the scattered trees. Stars winked above, and as they neared the top a soft glow was visible along the skyline. They slowed, moved with caution, worked their way over the crest and down. The glow emanated from a tower standing alone on a patch of level ground below them and, as its light came on their faces the grip of the Hansippif faded, to leave their minds clear. Still, Jayas led them further down, to where they had a clearer view. A small cluster of buildings stood not far from the tower, with a stable-block adjacent and gardens about. A road away to the west was a pale line.

Jayas did not want to do as the Hansippif commanded. Should he defy it? It was a Power in its domain, and might reach well beyond that. Moreover the threat was open. His mind was free of the Hanippif's yoke for now, and he dreaded its suffocating clasp.

Seyvyar voiced his thought. "What if we just stay here until dawn and then go down the road?"

"The Hansippif held us by night and day. If we have not done as it wishes by dawn, it will reach for us again, and I have no mind to find out how long its reach is. More – guards mean something someone is worried about. So we get interrogated, maybe imprisoned, perhaps sent back to Mer Ammery. The Brahnaks are keen on the letter of the law, I believe."

"But we didn't do anything wrong!" protested Delfe. After a moment he added "Well, apart from steal a boat. And I suppose it could be said we kidnapped Attaiye. But we aren't pirates!"

"So you won't go to auction, then," observed Yerech. "I for one am not anxious to defy the Hansippif."

Jayas took the silence that followed for grudging assent. He did add "Just in case we find ourselves before Brahnak justice, let's try not to kill anyone."

It was in a sober mood they divested themselves of their packs and made ready for combat. On an impulse Jayas slipped the folded Stock Character into his belt. They might need all the help they could get, illusory or real. Then it was a slow, careful slither from cover to cover, angling across the hill until the tower was the closest building. Jayas touched Seyvyar's arm, he in turn reached back, and they all halted. After a few minutes Jayas' voice came soft in Seyvyar's ear. "One on watch on this side, there to the left of the entrance. He walks to the corner, looks, walks back. Well-trained, for he does not keep a set pattern. Probably another on the other side. Can you take him? Preferably when he's at the entrance. I'll go forward as soon as he's down."

Seyvyar ran through the spells at his command, nodded. Jayas tensed, Seyvyar uttered the Words, low and swift. The ether was no longer the jagged menace of the Hansippif, where the lightest Word had to tip-toe between obsidian shards and ease past coiled snakes. Here the surround was fresh, and the Words slipped from his lips like honeyed kisses. The patrolling figure, dark against the white stone of the tower, paused in its steady walk, then slumped to the ground. Jayas sprinted forward in a crouch, to kneel, roll the body into shadow. When he stood, it was in the blue and white cape and crested helmet of the unfortunate guard. He marched to the corner, looked, marched back past the entrance, turned. This time he disappeared around the corner, to return with a second guard over his shoulder. He waved and others came forward. The two victims were bound and gagged, and Jayas sidled up to the door. Polished wood, each side carved with the broad arrow that was the symbol of the Brahnak faith. He played his fingers, glad for the free play of the ether, approached his hand to the surface, then tested the handle. Locked, and neither guard had a key. He bit his lip and beckoned Seyvyar.

"Locked, and proofed. Possibly alarmed."

Seyvyar considered. "Breaching Stick?"

Jayas shook his head. "Too noisy." Seyvyar squinched his eyes in thought, uttered some low-voiced Words and pressed his hand to the door. After a moment he gave a feral grin.

"This is old-time stuff. No problem." More Words produced a ghostly blue hand, which disappeared through the door. Seyvyar made arm movements, clearly feeling around for something, there was a click and one leaf eased back a trifle. "There you are."

They signalled to Delfe and Yerech, now posing as guards, and slipped inside. Jayas had been in many strange buildings, often uninvited, yet it took him a moment to take in this interior. The tower was empty, a great tube rising to a dome and cupola far above, from which shone down a white light that rebounded from the white walls. A spiralling stair was a slash of shadow turning up and up, like a vine seeking the sun. The floor was again that bleak white, broken only where a ramp continuing the stair cut into the tiles, descending to some mystery below. Jayas had the feeling that any noise would be amplified, as it might be by some huge flute, to whistle down to the plains. When he spoke to Seyvyar it was in hushed tones."You go up, see what you can do with the light. I'll check the ramp."

Seyvyar stepped as noiselessly as possible over to the narrow stair, eyed the steep treads and the flimsy hand-rail, then began climbing. Jayas moved slowly down the ramp, alert for traps. The cool stone slid under his soft steps, the harsh light did not waver. The walls rose and the ramp ended in two leaves of stout wood closing an arch. As before, the door was locked. A thin probe showed no bar. Jayas knew of protections that would destroy fingers – or worse – if tested. He was warily confident that no such had been laid on this door, and went to work with his picks. Some small movements, a feel around, a twist, a click and the left-hand leaf eased back. On the other side the ramp continued, sloping down gently, lit by small glow-stones in brackets on the walls. Like the above room, it was plain and bare, without ornament. Somewhere below a brighter light suggested a wider room.

Jayas left the door to check on Seyvyar. He had climbed nearly to the top, a small dark figure moving steadily upwards. A peek outside gained a reassuring hand-signal from Delfe; all was quiet and the night dark. The star Henebre had moved another hand-span. Still some hours to midnight, thought Jayas. That was the usual change of watch. Plenty of time to put that light out and get away, so might was well see what was here. He returned to the ramp and door. He would take a quick look at the room below and then return.

The ramp surface was not quite smooth. The stone had been scored with countless tiny grooves so that feet did not slip. By contrast, the walls and ceiling were as smooth as dwarf-work. Jayas kept close to one wall, kept his steps soft. Twenty paces, twenty-five, and the passage was marked by a line of black running across the floor, up the wall and around in a great loop. Jayas eased up to it, knotted fingers as he drew on craft and gently extended his hand. It met resistance; when he pushed a little harder, it was pushed back, as if by an invisible hand. Jayas studied the back of his hand, tested the resistance with his other hand, then made the twining gesture that ended the spell. This time his hand met no resistance. Interesting. No active etheric force could cross the line. What of Items? Jayas had a number of useful ones about his person. A test showed these to be unaffected, and he went on down.

At the bottom was a light grille. Once again the picks went to work, and this was soon open. Jayas eased through, to find himself in a large room, brightly lit by hanging glow-stones. Numbered alcoves around the walls each held small chests, and of course Jayas had to check the contents. What he found after opening three sent him back up the ramp at a rapid pace.

JAYAS ARRIVED AT THE top of the ramp just in time to see Seyvyar plummet from the roof. He did it in style, scarcely screaming, one hand clutching a short length of chain attached to a glowing white ball. Jayas could only watch as the ball hurtled down. At what seemed the very last moment, Seyvyar let go the ball and brought his feet under him. When he hit the floor there was a blue flash that seared Jayas' eyeballs. The ball hit the floor a moment later with a crash that sent out an etheric pulse that reverberated through every bone and tooth in Jayas' body. For a brief moment his eyes turned around, seeing every major organ clear and distinct. Before he had time to worry about his pancreas normal vision returned. It was not a comfort. The tower was vibrating slightly, shadows rippled across the floor and the stair was re-making itself as a spider-web far above.

Seyvyar grinned apologetically. "Sorry. It was heavier than I thought."

The door was shoved open and Delfe ran in. "There is shouting and lights over yonder. What in your Mother's name did you do?"

"There's no way out until dawn, and we still have to put that light out," Jayas told them. "Also, there is a bank's worth of riches below, so the guards will be upset."

"Riches?" asked Seyvyar.

"No way out?" said Delfe. Yerech ran in, slammed the door shut and wedged it with a dagger.

"Visitors on the way," he told them.

Jayas tossed him a vial of Stickfast. "Run that around the edges of the door and keep your dagger. You might need it." It would buy a few minutes at most, but they might be important minutes. He took rapid stock of the interior and decided the best place to defend was the room at the bottom of the ramp. Also, he added to himself, if they died there, at least they died rich. A few words, and they were all heading down, Delfe dragging the ball. When they came to the band the ball would not cross. Jayas hissed in annoyance.

"Delfe, Seyvyar, can we destroy this thing here?"

Seyvyar shook his head. Delfe spoke Words, cast blue-glowing eyes upon the ball, bent to peer at a spot, pulled at his lip. "I saw something very like this in the Fire Islands, and there is a some work on encapsulation that applies." After a brief exchange with Seyvyar he went on "There's a small crack from the fall. If we could get some copper in there, and then..." Jayas just managed to pick two words out of the technical jargon that followed.

"Ether-flare? And how long will it take?"

Delfe shrugged. "I can't say how long. There will be a flare, but how powerful that also I cannot say. Probably sufficient that the results will be extensively strange."

"Then we fix it here and take our stand below," decided Jayas. Yerech went on down to start on a barricade, Delfe whittled an edge on a coin, hammered it into the crack, pulled out his spell-book and uttered Words that went through Jayas' ears like the whine of the world's largest and most aggressive mosquito. He and Seyvyar worked to fix the chain to the floor as immovably as alchemy and two kinds of magic could contrive. They had just finished when a boom shook the doors above. Delfe clapped his book closed and they ran for it.

Below, Yerech had dragged boxes out to make a low wall behind the grille. Seyvyar and Delfe hurdled this and dropped, Jayas dragged the grille closed, Yerech stacked a last box and took up his bow. Jayas spanned his crossbow, dropped a quarrel in the slot and squinted up the ramp. The glare of the ball was hard to see past. From above came the shuffle and clank of armoured foes assembling. A voice echoed down from above, a query first in one tongue, then another, finally in Merllan.

"Those below! You have entered and broken, but not yet killed. Before the Highest I guarantee your lives and fair justice if you come forth unarmed." They looked at each other. Seyvyar shook his head, Yerech shrugged.

"We cannot do that right now. Sorry. Can you give us an hour?" Jayas yelled back. There was no reply, but the stamp and ring of people forming for combat.

Jayas tried again. "Please. There have been no deaths yet, and we would like to keep it that way. We are under orders and must resist if attacked."

"Who commands you?" the voice demanded.

"We act for a Power," Jayas replied.

Seyvyar gave him a side-eye. "Do you think to talk us out of here?"

"The Hansippif wants that light doused. It did not demand blood, and I see no reason to give it any. Ours or theirs."

"If we walk up it will be ours," muttered Yerech.

"The Highest rules all Powers," proclaimed the voice. "Yield now to the Highest."

"The Power rules us, for now," shot back Jayas.

Seyvyar snorted. "Great. We can argue theology over the spear-points."

"Then the Highest's servants must teach you otherwise," boomed the voice, and there came the stamp of feet.

Figures appeared beyond the ball, tall and dim, a close line of shields filling the passage from wall to wall. They tramped steadily down, dividing to pass the ball, closing up again. A tall man in bright mail stood at the centre, long blade poised, shield with blue blazon steady; to his side other figures bore spear and sword. Jayas and Yerech loosed and a figure went down. Another stepped forward and the line came on. When it reached the grille there was a short furious melee, spear and sword stabbing through the bars, Jayas and Yerech hacking at shafts and the hands trying to pull the grille open, knives flying as Delfe and Seyvyar cast. The defence had the best of it, protected by the grille and the boxes. For all his strength and dexterity, the tall man could not break through; he called out and the line fell back, leaving three bodies behind. Jayas had caught glimpses of others hammering away to free the ball, but it was still there when the retreat passed it.

He and Yerech leaned back against the wall, heaving in breaths. His ribs were bruised where a spear-thrust had met his mail, his shield-arm ached, blood from a small cut on his jaw dribbled down his neck. Yerech was also marked by combat. Jayas looked at the bodies. One had a knife through the eye, another a purpled face, the third a ragged wound in the neck. All wore the surcoats of some order, Brahnak blue with white markings. There was more noise from above, and he moved into what cover the corner afforded. Why were they so desperate to recover the ball? Why not wait them out? The Hansippif could not reach them, else they would not be here. These deaths were not of his wishing.

Yet desperate they were. Here they came again, and now the tall man bore a heavy axe. They passed the ball and the hammering resumed, levelled spears and drove on down. The tall man crashed the axe into the lock, a ringing stroke, struck again, hooked the bars and pulled. The jabbing points kept Jayas away, while a hail of small missiles distracted Seyvyar. One leaf of the grille opened with a screech of bent metal, the man and his companion sprang forward and in the corridor behind the ball disintegrated, sending a monstrous pulse of etheric force boiling down the ramp to spend itself in the bodies of the rearmost. Flesh contorted, eldritch screams assailed the mind, wisps of angry mist speared through bodies. Delfe shouted Words and green rays dispersed the tendrils that reached into the room, but the ruin behind was complete.

The tall man was undaunted. He leapt down, driving Yerech back, and his loyal companion followed hard, thrusting at Jayas. Each fell into their private duel. Jayas ignored the clash of arms to his left. That was Yerech's problem. His own problem faced him square, shield up and sword angled. Jayas's experience summed the other up with a quick cast of the eyes: well-trained, by the way he stood; not his first combat but not his tenth; young, determined. He tried a feint, met a fast response that shook his shield-arm. Jayas fell back, feigning fear and the other followed, too eagerly. A crouching spring forward, a twist, a sweeping blow, the thud of the flanged head against a knee and the youth staggered back. Jayas shoved, the injured leg gave way and the youth fell to his knees. His face showed only defiance as the mace came down on his shoulder and the sword fell from his hand. He said something in his own tongue, voice clear if creaking with pain, his fingers flickered as he drew on craft. In pure reflex at the threat, Jayas' mace crashed into his temple, a killing blow regretted even as it was made.

Yerech did not face a youth but a man full grown, well-skilled and old in the trade of arms. The long blade danced in his hand, the shield met every thrust and cut precisely angled. Seyvyar's winged dagger swooped in, only to fall to the floor before it could meet flesh, while a deft step sideways and a flick of the blade sent the magician reeling away with a deep cut on the arm. Nor did the loss of his comrade cause the man to falter. Rather he came forward boldly, seeking to cut Yerech down before Jayas could join against him.

Yerech fell back, Jayas snatched up the crossbow he had made ready earlier, gauged his moment and put a deliberate bolt into the man. The tall body jerked under the impact, the shield dropped, Yerech lunged and it was over.

Jayas did not feel triumph. He had been compelled to this fight, and the last look of that youth lingered in his mind. The tinkle of glass on stone recalled him to the immediate. Seyvyar's arm was half-healed, the vial drained and lying on the floor, Yerech was battered but mostly whole, Delfe leaning against a crate, eyes shut as he fought off the after-effects of the ether-flare.

"Hey, we're alive! And rich!" Seyvyar's voice cut through the air.

Yerech surveyed the bodies at their feet and the tangled mess up the ramp. "Well, 'Let's not kill anybody' did not work out."

Jayas drew breath. Yes, they had won. These others had paid the price, and it was pointless to abandon the riches around them. Snatch a few ingots and flee? They could, but better to make an effort.

"We are rich if we can carry it – and keep it. I'll see if there are any pack animals. Yerech – you're with me. Delfe, Seyvyar, gather up what you can that's worth it and start moving boxes upstairs." He picked his way up past the gruesome wreckage on the ramp. Where the ball had been was only a patch where the floor had taken the shape of the ridged back of a marine creature and around it a pile of bodies twisted beyond recognition as human. The band that had prevented the ball from moving was now a chain of roses. Curious, Jayas made the same test as before, to find it no longer active. It must have absorbed much of the energy, he thought, else we would all – his mind shuddered – look like these poor fellows. Even what had reached below had done enough. He climbed on, out the broken door, to find the same cool night.

Henebre was not much lower in the sky. Fights are always longer in the mind, reflected Jayas. He and Yerech approached the buildings with caution, keeping to the shadows until close. There, under an arcade, a small crowd milled about, most peering anxiously in the dark towards the tower. Light from the windows showed no-one armed, but only old folk and striplings, some in night attire. *I have no mind to kill any more children* thought Jayas. A muttered conference, and then he strode out of the dark, Yerech at his shoulder, causing the crowd to gasp and cry out. Yerech spoke, a harsh command, and the noise redoubled. Yerech spoke again, imposing silence. At his gesture most of the group sat, although an elderly pair stayed on their feet, the man uttering urgent queries. Yerech cut him off, lifted his bloody blade and the pair joined the others on the floor.

"I have told them their lives are safe if they stay quiet, forfeit to the last if but one moves," Yerech passed to Jayas. Jayas faded back, watched as the crowd stirred a little, came forward into the light in as menacing a pose as he could contrive. The muttering subsided. He prowled about, stepped back into the dark, took out the paper figure of the Stock Character, spat on it, added a hair from his head and unfolded it. His own semblance stood before him.

"Second Guard, keeping watch on the prisoners," Jayas told it. The figure's skin lightened, it added a fierce moustache, a hooked nose, a red coat and a spear, then marched to the edge of the light and took up a vigilant pose, glaring at the huddled troop with narrowed eyes.

After a quick inspection of the stables he returned to the tower. Delfe was towing a line of spell-lifted boxes to the door, to add to the pile already there. Seyvyar went to join Yerech while he and Delfe made the animals ready and so it went for two frantic hours, two and the paper soldier on guard while two hauled and loaded. When their pack-train was ready Yerech had a last few menacing words for the servants, Jayas folded up the Stock Character and they made their way back towards the Hansippif, harnesses creaking and hooves thudding on the turf. The trees parted, the animals baulked but were urged on and they passed back into the Wild. The sun would rise before long, on death and a tower that no longer lit up the land around.

THE HANSIPPIF KEPT its promise, closing behind them and opening before as they moved along. If it did not harry them, it was yet impatient, a householder ushering unwanted guests to the door. Rest it would allow, and grazing for the horses, even short halts to snatch a meal, yet the urge was always there. It wanted them gone, and they were not inclined to argue. There was still time for talk as they walked, the more so as they were moving along the grain of the land rather than across it. As they wound their way along the ridges Yerech, Delfe and Seyvyar tossed about ideas on their course. They had a great fortune and had stirred up a great enmity; now they had to keep the one and avoid the other. Where should they go? Yerech had one answer.

"I am from the city of Ysmir, in the next link of the Necklace. If we can get to the passage, we will be beyond the reach of the Brahnaks – and anyone else. It is a while since I have seen my home."

So Yerech was from another world. He had not mentioned this before, but then neither Jayas nor Seyvyar had been exactly forthcoming about their pasts. Delfe was full of questions.

"What do you call that world?"

"The World," was Yerech's dry answer.

"Then what do you call this world?"

"The world beyond the Frarziara Gate."

"And the one on the other side – the link of Necklace opposite to ours from yours?"

Yerech untangled this. "The world of the Inutuk Gate. What do you call your two links in the Necklace?"

"We learned that in cosmography," Delfe told him. "Yours is the Sunrise World, and the other is the Sunset World. The passage to the Sunset World is far away to the east and south. So what's the Sunrise World like?"

Jayas listened to Yerech's description of this next world while musing on his own desires. Once again he was within reach of a fortune, and this time it would not escape his grasp. Or so he hoped; the Brahnaks would undoubtedly pursue, and be joined by every greedy venturer as soon as word spread. What would he do with it? Buy a country tavern? Ha! He had enough – if he could keep it – to buy the Oberis or the Old Palace in Azbai. Not that he would want to, as he had too many enemies in both places. If he wanted to settle down, it would have to be in some new country, one where Jayas Zrei was unknown, and could be free of his past.

Well, first get the dragon to talk ... Jayas returned his full attention to the conversation. It appeared the passage to the next link – Yerech's home-world, was up beyond Frouan, at the northern end of that body of water variously known as the Dravish Sea and the Corillion Gulf. That meant finding their way across the Saka country and then up the coast. It would be a long and anxious journey.

Delfe and Seyvyar found the notion of travel to another world attractive. Jayas did not object, for the imperative was to get clear of Brahnak pursuit, and that meant heading for the Saka country. From what he had been told, the Saka and the Brahnaks had been at war more often than not over the last two centuries, and were wary of each other even at times of peace. All that left was keeping the Saka from peeking into their packs, staying ahead of bounty-hunters, and avoiding the usual hazards of travel.

Jayas was not a talkative man, and now he fell silent for long stretches. This last fight had given him much to think about. So much death, none of his desire, and two of them heroic by any measure. If Brahnak justice caught up with him he would attest to their unfailing devotion to their faith and their duty – not that it would do them or him much good. The death of the youth by his hand kept coming back before his mind's eye. The faith the young man had in his leader and his cause had been written in his face. His calm defiance of death felt like a slur to Jayas. What was it he had cried out? Jayas asked Yerech if he had understood those last words.

"'Loyal Service', I think" Yerech told him.

"He did give that," Jayas acknowledged.

"He used the nominal prefix, so it is someone's name. The Brahnak name themselves after the virtues they aspire to. Perhaps it was the name of the man who nearly killed me."

Jayas let that go for the moment and brooded on the way he had been driven to this fight, like an animal in some base sport. It was not *his* fight, it was the Hansippif's. All knew that there was no resisting the land, even if this land in its ill-will to humans had demanded blood. It nevertheless felt wrong to Jayas. What else could they have done? Defied the Hansippif and died? Would it then have found other hands ready to its wants? So what? That had always seemed a fragile argument to Jayas. If someone else had done the things Jayas had, then that alternate not-Jayas would be the object of vengeance, and not himself. At this point Jayas realised he was indulging in philosophy, and resolutely concentrated on leading his pack-horse.

THEY HAD SO FAR ALL avoided talking about their loot, for fear of the ill-luck that comes of counting gains before they are secured. Yerech cheerfully breached the taboo, as one who had only the smallest glimpse of the load burdening their pack-horses.

"How much do you think we have, then?' he asked as they plodded along a ridge soon after dawn. The hostile attitude of the land had muted a little as they approached the northern boundary, or it might be that they had become accustomed to the atmosphere.

Yerech's question was addressed to the air, and it was Seyvyar who answered.

"Twelve chests of etherically-pure silver? I hardly dare guess. Then a chest of gems and three of silver coin. What the gems are worth only a jeweller could say, but the coin is many thousands, and that would be less worth than a single bar of the pure silver."

Yerech rubbed his nose. "Why keep so much? And in that form?"

Again Seyvyar responded. "It was all packaged for transport, and in a form that kept weight as low as possible. My thought is that it was meant to be delivered by a magician, one using a spell of instant transport. So long as the magician is trustworthy it is a rapid and totally secure means; indeed, it is what the banks use when they adjust their balances. Two of my class-mates went into the profession," he added.

"Did you consider it as a possible career?" asked Delfe.

Seyvyar shook his head, vehemently. "The banks don't take the caster's word on trust, or rely on their reputation. You are name-bound, geas-wound and they have some way of finding you anywhere, no matter what Items or spells of denial you might have."

Jayas could understand Seyvyar's choice. He too would hate to be shackled, and the mere thought of being able to be located wherever in the world he might be made his nerves twitch. The list of people who would pay to find him was not short.

He was mentally ranking the names from worst to least-worst when Delfe gave a low call and pointed. They had reached the end of the ridge and now had a long view to the north. Through the trees Jayas could see open country, one marked by many small patches of pasture and sown, one where hedgerows made lines and paths were pale threads and the trees were clumped in tidy copses. The Hansippif had an end, and they were within reach of it.

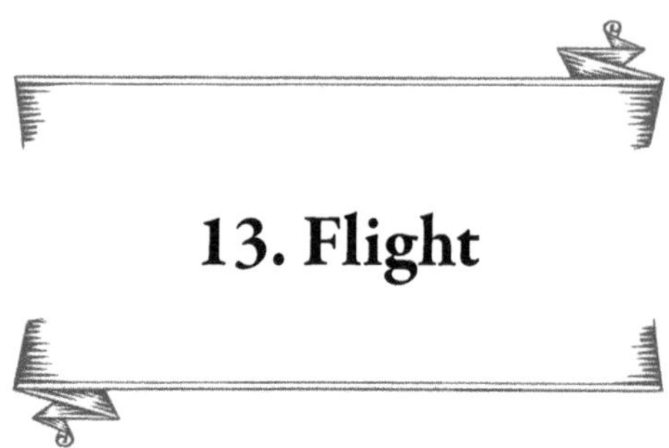

13. Flight

Tol kept low on the flight south, partly to avoid the strong head-winds higher up, and also because Serriet enjoyed the view. Not so low as to alarm animals or allow some teenager with his father's crossbow an easy shot. *Why is it always the boys?* thought Tol. They left early enough that they could return before the afternoon rains, unless Chenizei offered them lunch. In that event, a minor cantrip would keep Tol dry, and Serriet had a hooded cape.

The same spell that had enabled silent speech with Chenizei allowed Tol and Serriet to chat as they flew, without shouting over the wind. Serriet kept up a running commentary on the landscape, interspersed with speculation on yesterday's news. Rumour had it that a small army had descended on a Brahnak stronghold on the edge of the Hansippif and wreaked enormous destruction. The defenders had been slain to a man, the buildings demolished and all valuables carried off. Whose was this army? Where had it come from? Had the Hansippif, brooding on past Brahnak attempts to tame it, spawned a horde of monsters? Would they next descend on the peaceful Haghar lands? These questions and more gave the folk of Dtlag topics for endless discussion.

As they neared Chenizei's home Serriet suggested a quick loop further south, a short patrol of the northern border of the Hansippif. After all, if an army of monsters were marshalling to invade the Haghar lands, they would gain kudos for reporting it. Tol obligingly lifted higher and kept on past the tower, heading towards that dark line of forest and miasma to the south. She was wary, though, of coming too close. A tilt, a turn and they were running above the rough pastures that bordered the Wild. There were no monsters visible and no signs of the passage of an army. The few homesteads were a little back from the Hansippif, and none were on fire, under siege or in desolate ruin. Tol turned back north.

Serriet pointed below. "What are those people doing?" Tol looked down and to her left, to see a group waving arms in debate around a clump of horses. A sale, perhaps? A pack-train assembling? An investigator's curiosity sent her swooping lower, to circle and hover at roof height above the argument. The debaters were clearly Haghar country-folk, olive-skinned men and women in bright tunics, wide hats slung back across the shoulders. The horses were four sturdy cobs, hard-used these past few days but not starved or lame and a fifth, a fine riding animal with a high-cantled cavalry saddle. All were marked with the arrow blazon of the Brahnaks. One of the women looked up as Tol's shadow fell across the ground. The debate trailed off as the pair found themselves the focus of a circle of upturned faces.

Tol gave her a wave. "We heard of odd happenings near the Hansippif, so dropped down to ask if you had seen anything," she offered in explanation.

The woman waved her hand in negation. "We don't trouble the Wild, and it don't trouble us. Been nothing out of the ordinary way around here."

"Yet I cannot help but notice that these animals bear a Brahnak mark, and the Hansippif lies between Brahnak land and here," observed Tol. The woman remarked that anyone could sell animals where they pleased and, by the same token, others might buy where they pleased. Was Tol in the market for a horse?

"I might be," Tol said cautiously, "if I could be assured of the provenance of the animal."

"Bought fair and square," the woman insisted.

"The Wild washes away all claims," a man in a lemon-yellow smock chimed in. The woman gave him a dirty look.

"Indeed it does," agreed Tol. "These came from the Wild, then? The dreaded Hansippif?"

"Not so dread. It's Brahnaks it hates, not us honest folk what respect the Powers," Yellow Smock told her. The woman endorsed this, and added that they had much to discuss. Perhaps Tol could call by later, at her house? Tol took the hint and lifted away after getting directions, parting with a courteous farewell.

"What do you make of that?" asked Serriet.

Tol took her time to reply. The animals were Brahnak and had come from the Hansippif, presumably led by a lone rider. Jayas came to mind, but there could be other explanations. The animals were sold (with what they carried?) to the locals. Perhaps smuggling? By all accounts the Hansippif did not allow the gathering of herbs and other alchemical ingredients, so where had the cargoes come from? Where had the seller gone? She would go back later and try to find out, but they had an appointment. She passed her thoughts to Serriet and took a last scan of the south. The Hansippif lay quiet and dark under the morning sun, the only sign of life a large bird riding the winds. As she watched it banked and turned, slipping sideways as it lost height to investigate some possible prey below. Tol turned her head north, where Chenizei's tower nicked the skyline.

CHENIZEI HIMSELF BUSTLED out into the courtyard to greet them. He was in the best of moods, cheerful, even excited, embracing them both as old friends.

"Great news, great for you and even better for myself. Come with me and rejoice in our good fortune!" Chenizei urged them in the door and through his laboratory to the garden. There, resting on raised beds, were their carrots, grown until they were as round as barrels and twice as long as Serriet. Each had been fitted with a harness of leather woven through with copper wire, and a saddle with extra straps.

"It is as I told you," Chenizei said proudly. "They were receptive to two properties, and amenable to flight. So I imbued response as the second, and the ether added the usual tangent third. It varied, of course: this one" – here he slapped the red flank, causing it to quiver – "yodels at dawn and sunset. Its pair insists on absorbing a dead mouse once each two days. You will note I have added a pouch for the mice on the near-side. They are yours, in celebration of my good fortune."

"And the third carrot?" asked Serriet, fascinated.

Chenizei clapped his hands. "Wants to lie in contact with earth for an hour each day. Hmm, did I mention that to that young man? No matter. You will recall my issue with forward motion? Carrots are the answer! With my cucumbers for lift and carrots pulling, the sky-service is about to be realised. Why, in time people will be conveyed to Daruz Alman or even beyond, as regularly as they now fare to the market at Tenle! These are faster than the carriage, but it can carry at least ten people, with luggage. I was out with it early this morning and it was perfectly steady. I have already written to Szien asking him to obtain at least a dozen more carrots, that I might try a team."

Tol noticed that the sky-wagon was gone from its cradle, and that the cucumber bed now held a few only half-grown vegetables. "You have tested the whole machine?" she asked.

Chenizei clapped her on the back. "Even better! I have sold it for a sum that will not only recover my expenses to date but provide for all the costs of operation for the first year or more. It is more than I hoped for, and I need not talk to a banker ever again, except to deposit my profits."

"That is good news, and I congratulate you with all my heart. Such a stroke of luck! You must tell me how it came about."

Chenizei was only too ready to do so. That very morning, only an hour after he had returned from his early flight, a stranger had come to the door. He had been told that Chenizei had built a sky-carriage, and asked if it were for sale. Chenizei was at first reluctant, for he had planned to use the vehicle to demonstrate his project. The stranger had offered a large sum, and then a larger yet, a preposterous amount, and Chenizei had yielded. The carriage was simple to operate, and the man had departed as soon as possible, winging his way south.

"Is it not strange that he had so large a sum on his person?" asked Tol, just as Serriet asked what this stranger had looked like. Chenizei answered Serriet first.

"He was a fellow magician, from one of those north-eastern countries by the look of him – very fair of skin and hair. Quite well-spoken, introduced himself as Seifie, graduated in the art at Azbai, a place that has quite a good reputation."

"Seyvyar?" asked Serriet.

Chenizei blinked. "Yes, that could be it. We spoke in Dzai of course, as he had no local tongue."

Tol repeated her query. Chenizei frowned, then shrugged. Yes it had been odd, but then, odd things happened, especially here on the fringes of a Wild. He had tested the metal, of course. Etherically-pure silver of the highest quality. Would they like to take the carrots for a test-flight? The second one had been fed its mouse today. Tol and Serriet accepted the offer at once, and Chenizei showed them how the straps went.

THE FLIGHT BACK SOUTH was short, if enlivened by Serriet's aerobatics. Her whoops of delight as she looped over and turned into a dive echoed across the landscape. Tol was more sedate, and concentrated on finding the right place. This was a small house with a long shed to one side and a field at the back where the five horses were busy head down, cropping the grass. When she called from the front the reply came from the shed, so she tethered her carrot and walked over as Serriet skidded in to a breathless landing.

The shed was a workshop. Racks down one side held pots and plates ready for firing, slabs of clay and jars of pigments lined another wall, a crate stood open on the floor half-full of finished pieces packed in straw. The woman was putting the last touches to a bowl on the wheel; as they came in she left off humming to let the wheel slow and stood up in her split potter's apron.

"Come for a horse?"

"Not quite, as the magician Chenizei has gifted us two flying steeds. The riding saddle might come in useful, though," replied Tol.

"Ah, Chenizei. We've seen a lot of his flying carriage in the last few days. Silly idea – who is going to trust such a contraption?"

The saddle was by the rear door. It was fine work: the leather highly polished, the buckles bright steel, lovingly engraved with vines and flowers twining around the Brahnak mark, the looping initials 'GD' and the sigil of some order. With practiced skill Tol led the woman to tell the story. Two strangers had come to the village with a tale of a trading journey from the Brahnak lands to the coast gone wrong, leaving them no choice but to sell their horses and return on foot. They had not bargained too hard, and had taken some of the price in provisions. Had Chenizei been mentioned? Why yes - his carriage had been out and about that morning. They had just come from Chenizei, so Tol wondered if these were the people he had mentioned as calling on him. She cast a cantrip that sketched Jayas and Seyvyar on a plate, drawn from her memory. Certainly - that dark fellow on the left was one of the two. The other had done all the talking, a nice young man with a Merllan accent.

Tol idly put a few more questions while they settled for the saddle, buckled it on to a carrot and changed the straps over. The price was very reasonable, but then it was a distinctive item, one that might well be traced. Chenizei's sky-carriage had been busy that morning? Yes. It had been out in the morning, and again after the strangers left. It was risky of Chenizei to take it so near the Hansippif, but then magicians never *listened*, did they. Anyway, he had taken it off on a long ride, because he had headed north-west instead of straight back home. It must be a nasty wind up there, and she hoped he did not capsize.

Serriet carefully packed away a small jug that had caught her eye, one of elegant shape and bright blue glaze, they thanked the potter and left her to her clay-shaping.

"Where to?" shouted Tol as they rose into the sky.

"After them, of course," replied Serriet. "They have only a few hours on us, and we are faster. Chenizei, then Dtlag to pick up our gear, and then west and north, at speed!"

Tol laid a hand on the saddle and cast her most subtle spell of detection, focusing on material associations. Her head at first wanted to turn to the south and west, over the Hansippif, but then swung north and west. Her chin rose and fell five times. North and west, and no more than fifty leagues distant. She bent forward and urged her carrot to greater speed.

JAYAS SAT SIDEWAYS on the bench and leaned out to watch the land passing below. This was better than walking, better than riding and, best yet, safe from pursuit. They had seen nothing more threatening than a curious eagle and two swallows that had hitched a ride on the rail until shooed away. His back still ached from the frantic haste of unloading the horses and loading this fine carriage, it had cost an amount that made Yerech grumble, and it was all worth it. He twisted to look smugly at the cargo in the centre of the wagon, covered and lashed down tight, then secured to the wagon with all the rope they could find. No sudden shift of the wind was going to lose them this treasure. Delfe was steering from the pilot-stand, hands on the reins leading out to the carrot ahead as it dragged the carriage through the air. Above, cucumbers strained the canvas roof, keeping them aloft. All working well. Seyvyar and Yerech lounged on the bench opposite, chatting amiably between bites of pickled vegetable on black bread.

He turned back to the land below. For the first while it had been the homely Haghar countryside, settled and peaceful in incongruous contrast to the hated Hansippif. How glad he was to see the last of that place! To their left (*or should that be 'to port'?* he wondered) the woods of the Saka hill-country had crept closer and closer, and now they slid below. A cluster of brightly-painted Saka long-houses drifted past, set back from a small lake. A patch of fields in light green contrasted with the dark of the forest. Pigs, nuts and fruit were the staples of the Saka diet, he recalled being told.

The afternoon rains had come and gone, spattering on the canvas roof and gusting into the carriage, obscuring the view with mist. It was clear now, clear enough to see the patches of rock and snow on Qiam Shan, last upthrust of the Frozen Wild. As he watched, a block of snow and ice loosened by the sun detached from a steep face and slid in a lengthening plume downwards until it vanished in shadow. It was some time before the faintest rumble reached his ears.

Delfe pulled on a rein and the carriage turned to bear more westerly. Another pull, and they were headed – Jayas checked the sun – south of west. He raised an eyebrow at Seyvyar.

"The wind is taking us north, so we must go against it or else we crash into Qiam Shan. We'll turn north again once we're clear of the high mountains," explained Seyvyar. Jayas could accept this. He had gleaned that travel by air was nearly as difficult navigationally as by sea. Their carriage had no wheels or feet to keep it from being pushed about by the currents of the air, and their course must be by guess. They had no maps, and the pointers at the pilot-stand showed only north and the direction of Chenizei's home. No matter; all they had to do was keep the Corillion Gulf on their left (*port?*) and the mountains on their right (*some nautical word*), and they would come to Frouan and the Gate. He rummaged around until he found a sack of rednuts, cracked a few and popped the meat in his mouth.

The carriage turned yet more southerly and began to descend. Seyvyar went forward to talk to Delfe, then came back.

"The wind is too strong up here. We have to go lower and head south, then west."

Jayas squinted at Qiam Shan and its neighbouring peaks. They did seem closer. A look over the side showed the forest maybe two long bow-shots below. A comfortable distance, to his mind. The carriage levelled out, then went into a dive. Delfe gave a shout and Seyvyar ran forward. They hauled on the reins together, but the carrot kept on, to come to a stop in the yard of a cottage below a cluster of bright longhouses. It buried itself point down in the earth, wriggled about until only the top showed and went still. Saka faces showed at the windows and then two adults appeared at the back door. They were clearly agitated; there was much waving of hands and shouting, but none of the four spoke Saka. After a few trials communication was established in broken Haghakin.

"The onions! And the garlic! Your cart is on my plants!"

"All right. We move." With some effort, and under close direction lest they step on the young plants, the carriage was hauled sideways to a more suitable patch. Delfe examined the carrot-top, conferred with Seyvyar and said he thought this was the usual tangent-property of a powerful Item. It would unearth itself when ready to fly. In the meantime, perhaps these fine people would be willing to share a meal? They would, for a silver coin, and the four enjoyed a hearty soup thick with dumplings. People drifted down from the houses up the hill to gawk at the carriage and the visitors. A senior with good Haghakin and even a little Brahnak arrived, but not before Seyvyar had time to concoct a story about delivering the vehicle as a gift from one senior magician to another, with hints of high political connections. It was near dusk when the carrot unwound itself, shook the dirt off and would again take to the air.

They boarded, rose into the air and headed west, found a tall tree and tethered the carriage for the night. As they floated in the dark above the treetops, Jayas' mind returned again to the experience of the Hansippif. He hated that he had been compelled, and re-thought his rejection of an offer to surrender and face justice. There was no law in the Wild, but was the tower actually in the Wild? Did the Hansippif have the reach it threatened? He put that aside, for his companions would not have accepted surrender, and he owed them his loyalty.

That brought to mind the boy he had killed below the tower. *His* devotion and loyalty were unquestionable, for all that they had led him only to death. In that other tower in another Wild, Jayas had killed poor Rudrin, who had been the most innocent of them all. What did that death say about this one?

And what *was* he going to do with all this wealth? At one time he had dreamed of owning a manse in the hills of his own country, living at ease like the gentry. He was not welcome there, of course, but did he want a manse in some other clime? One where he was not known for dark deeds? He rubbed a hand along the polished wood of the rail, restless, and listened to the hoots and rustles below. The others snored quietly and the stars wheeled. He sat alone until it was time for Yerech to watch, then tried to sleep.

THE FOLK OF DTLAG ARE used to magicians coming and going, often by odd means. A courier speeding across the rooftops is not an uncommon sight, and people have been known to appear out of nowhere, luggage in hand, on the steps of the Association. Nevertheless, the sudden descent of two carrots on the street before a modest lodging-house in Old Town was treated as something out of the ordinary. A sturdy young woman leapt from one, threw the reins to the other rider and called out to wait, as she would be quick. A man trundling a barrow of fresh-cut sweetgrass stopped to rest his load and watch, two children playing with a stick in a patch of dirt gave up their game to run over and ask if they could pet the carrots and an older woman commented loudly that riding animals were not allowed on the streets of Old Town. Before an official could arrive to adjudicate on this the first woman hurried out with two bulging packs and a clutter of weaponry. As the last were disposed on the carrots the proprietor of the lodging came out on the steps, waving her hands. "Keep the three days' rent we've paid," shouted the rider, the other mounted and they rose steeply into the sky.

"I don't know about these vegetable magics," commented the barrow-trundler. "Next thing will be huge great eggplants rolling down the streets, squashing everybody in their path."

Above the rooftops, and once away from the inquisitive fellow who rose to ask their business, Tol and Serriet made good progress. At first the road up through Tach was their guide then, once over the crest of the first range, their course followed the Tal River as it threaded the hills towards the high lake country. A map of the country behind Dtlag had been among Tol's first purchases, and now a sketch copy was tied on her thigh, available to a quick glance. A quick late lunch at a hill village had allowed for some reorganisation and planning, and added two bags of food to their burdened steeds. When they skimmed down to a small island in a lake to spend the night, Serriet stretched, patted her carrot fondly and wondered if horses would soon be more for pleasure than use. Should they give these names? Tol's carrot gave a yodel that bounced across the lake and echoed off the hills.

"Screamer and Mouser?" Tol suggested. That reminded Serriet, and she went to hunt mice for her mount's breakfast.

That night they lay under the blue dome of the Circle of Shelter, just as they had those many months ago on the road between Kaber and Zyich. Tol remembered that Brahnak missionary, who had talked of giving law to the Wild, when all knew that the surest way to anger the Wild was to set up as a judge. Were she and Serriet pursuing a judgement upon Jayas and Seyvyar? As she had learned more of Jayas in her long pursuit the unwisdom of challenging him to a fight had become more evident. The man was endlessly resourceful. He and his fellows had survived the dreaded Hansippif, something that no-one in Dtlag had believed possible. They had offered Chenizei a small fortune, so they had even kept their winnings from Mer Ammery. She was out here chasing Jayas because she was an inquirer and he was the key to any number of puzzles; what was Serriet's aim?

From her breathing Serriet was not asleep, so Tol asked "What do we do if we catch up with them? They are four to our two, and Seyvyar is likely a more capable magician than I."

Serriet snorted. "We hit the carriage. Chenizei said the lift-cucumbers are sensitive - we let them feel a few arrows and watch the thing fall. That cuts the odds to two on two, and we have our carrots, while they have spells of flying. Can they keep those up indefinitely?"

"No," Tol conceded. "They will be unable to renew the spell more than a few times."

"So," Serriet pursued, "we wait until they land and then take them one by one."

The plan was very Serriet - direct, violent, tactically clever. Tol could see her landing at the front door of Green Sea Mercantile, heads dangling from her carrot-saddle like some Rai nomad chieftain fresh from victory. She put this image to Serriet, who laughed.

"Green Sea Mercantile? They had their chance. No, there's more than a paltry 2,000 aboard that carriage, and I want my share." After a moment of uncharacteristic reflection she went on "Three voyages, so many new places, a strange Wild. This is not just a job, it's a *quest*. What sort of warrior abandons a quest? Not I."

Tol could accept this. She fell asleep before she could decide what the goal of this quest might be.

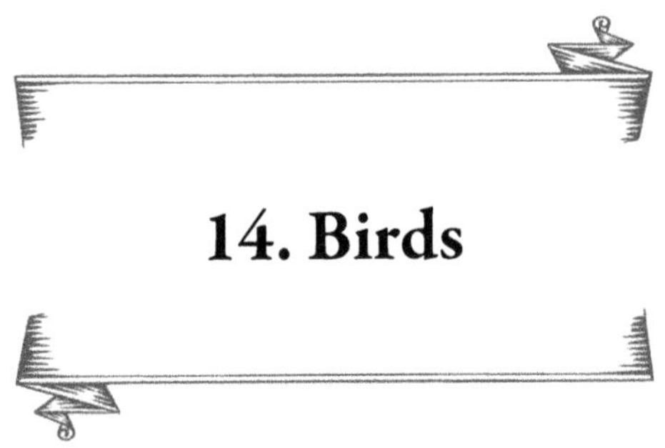

14. Birds

Jayas woke to the welcome noise of birds squabbling. He twisted and stretched, working the kinks out of his back. The floor of the wagon was not the worst place to sleep, but not a soft bed either. Around, the others yawned into wakefulness. Yerech opened a jar of eggs in spiced oil and observed that he was looking forward to a hot meal in Frouan. Seyvyar stared out at the morning haze, as if willing it to clear. Delfe was glumly sorting socks, finally giving a pair a few whacks before pulling them on. *A hot meal and a laundry*, thought Jayas. *And a bath-house*. He ate a frugal breakfast and wondered if he should put his armour on. It was not that there was any threat up here, it was just,well, he felt more comfortable in it. He was not in a boat, where armour would weigh him down if he fell overboard. From this height he was dead, whether armoured, clothed or stark naked. In the end he settled it on. Yerech gave him a look, then did likewise. Then they sat there until the air cleared, Delfe flicked the reins and the carrot stirred into motion, pulling the sky-carriage up and up.

Seyvyar had the best recollection of the maps they had glanced at in Mer Ammery. Now he stood beside the pilot-stand, hands behind his back, frowning over the landscape in the pose of the noble explorer. The impulse to give him a brisk push flitted through Jayas' mind, rejected even as it arrived. This was no time to fool around. Besides, they were not that high. Seyvyar might hit the ground before Words could save him. Seyvyar spoke to Delfe, the carriage swung around and they settled on their course. Jayas surveyed the land below, a rumpled canvas of hill and moor, dotted with small lakes, laced with twisting rivers, the whole rising to the higher mountains. Before long they should be able to round the end of the range and turn north. He contemplated the weary weeks of travel by horse or foot it would take to come so far and patted the stout rope securing the roof. How far to Frouan? He had no real idea. Not more than a week, surely. He hoped they could stop in some decent town along the way, even if only for an hour or two.

"What will you do when we reach your world?" he asked Yerech, who was lounging by the rail.

The answer was a lifted shoulder. "Take it as it comes. Put the money somewhere safe and then see what offers."

"Not buy an estate and settle down?" persisted Jayas.

Yerech was startled. "What would I do with an estate? Servants, workers, taxes, formal dinner with the neighbours, go into the draw for office every year and then fork out for the poetry recital? Why would I want that?"

Jayas had to agree that this was not the life he would like for himself.

Yerech was curious. "Why do you ask?"

Jayas struggled to answer. It somehow did not feel right to have great wealth and yet live as a wandering vagabond. Yerech had a different view; he pointed out that wealth was freedom, freedom to live as one wished, vagabond or lord as one chose. They tossed the issue back and forth until Seyvyar reminded them that they had yet to get their treasure home. Jayas took another scan of the landscape. Settled areas were now well behind them, the land below unbroken by field or pasture. The mountains were now on his right hand, falling from frozen heights through bands of rock and forest to wide upland moors. The warm seas of the Corillion Coast were presumably somewhere to the west; ahead and a little west lay Frouan, if his reckoning was correct.

Jayas flexed his fingers as he drew on craft to sharpen his eyes and took a closer look at the ground. There had been something mentioned about these moors. What was it? His eyes passed over tors poking up here and there like the gravestones in some abandoned cemetery, over the gleam of water in marsh and pond, over straggly trees leaning away from the wind. A movement resolved into a pig making its furtive way along a gully. Nothing joggled his memory, so he brought his gaze up, to sweep around from mountain to moor ahead, over to the sea and around back to the mountains. To the south a large bird was labouring along, perhaps on some seasonal migration. To the south-east, back the way they had come, the sky was empty but for two dots. He focused on them, checked, looked again. Two red dots, not birds.

His call brought Seyvyar over, to add his spell-enhanced sight. Seyvyar shaded his eyes with a pale hand and then swore. "Blind Powers! Your uncle's arse! Why us? Why me?"

"What is it?" asked Yerech.

"Two people on flying Items of some kind. Why else would they be out here except to chase us?"

Yerech checked his armour laces, strung his bow and arranged his helmet and quiver to hand. "We keep running. When they catch up, then we'll see."

Delfe had twisted around from his post at the front. "Could they be travellers bound for Frouan, as we are?" Both Seyvyar and Jayas dismissed this notion, Seyvyar pointing out that they had been alone except for birds (such as that vulture over there) up to now. This was not an aerial highway.

"Well, except for that thing up ahead. Is it a bird?" asked Yerech. Seyvyar leaned out to look and swore even more luridly.

"Some kind of big bird-lizard. Really big!"

"Sierlak," said Delfe.

"That's what I was trying to remember!" exclaimed Jayas. "Delfe's cousin mentioned them."

"That's right. She said they eat people," added Delfe helpfully.

"Is this the time for senile reminiscence?' screamed Seyvyar. Practical Yerech strapped on his helmet, took up his bow and told Jayas he would cover the port side and ahead if Jayas would look after the starboard and rear. Jayas spanned his crossbow, dropped a quarrel in the slot and took his station. The carriage sped on, held steady by Delfe at the reins. Seyvyar flipped through his spell-book, mouth twisted.

"Can you use that spike spell again? I'll lend you my helmet," offered Jayas.

"On something that big? And it has a crest too. I would need a stone slab on my head. No, I'll try something else," and he went back to his study.

Jayas's head swivelled as he looked back and forth between the two dots and the sierlak circling as it climbed higher, somewhat ahead. Would the beast decide their pursuers were tastier prey?

"There is a second one," called Delfe, and turned the carriage west. "We need to get out of their range."

Another good idea a day late, thought Jayas. The sierlak spiralled higher. *It's going to dive on us, like a hawk on the world's fattest, slowest pigeon.* He looked at the cucumbers straining against the canvas roof, keeping them aloft, then looped a rope around himself and the thick guy-rope and leaned out over the void, feet on the rail. Perhaps he would get a clear shot. The sierlak above screamed and dove, clawed feet to the fore, hurtling down, larger and larger in his vision. Jayas raised his crossbow, snuggled the stock against his shoulder, waited, waited. At the last moment the vast shape shifted a wing and plunged ahead to sink its talons into the carrot. Jayas' shot went wide. The carriage tilted forward abruptly, throwing Seyvyar out, then the front lifted as the beast pulled out of the dive. Yerech whipped his sword out and slashed through the traces, leaving the sierlak to bear off the carrot in triumph. As the rocking carriage settled, coasting to a stop in mid-air, they saw the beak dip to take a bite. The sierlak screamed again, tore the hapless carrot in half and wheeled in the air.

"I don't think it's vegetarian," Yerech yelled. Jayas had swung inboard and was frantically spanning his crossbow. As the sierlak barrelled in Seyvyar shot up in front of it, spewing Words. A black rod came down on the sierlak's head, splitting its crest and staggering it. It screeched, a sound to shatter the eardrums, and veered off. Yerech's bow sang and a shaft sprouted from its side. Jayas slammed a quarrel home and lifted his bow, but the beast had dropped away, crying out as it went.

Delfe peered out. "The second is keeping its distance, but now we are going with the wind."

Seyvyar turned back and the carriage shied away as he came close. Delfe called out to remind him of Chenizei's warning: the cucumbers did not like any form of propulsion nearer than ten paces. Seyvyar was thrown a rope and set to pulling them west, slowly, with complaint. If the wounded sierlak had left, flapping slowly off to some mountain lair to recover, the other was still there, a hovering presence.

"LOOKS LIKE THAT BLOODY bird-lizard did half our work for us," yelled Serriet. Their quarry was now in plain view, lurching along under single tow. In another handful of minutes they would be alongside. The other bird-lizard circled above, and how many more might turn up? They plainly had no taste for carrots, but would see Tol and Serriet as excellent snacks.

"If we drop the carriage into that jungle below, we may never find it," yelled Tol back. She came to a decision: if this was her quest, it would be a rescue, not a robbery. "What say we offer to get them out of this for full shares?"

Serriet gave a sideways look, then shrugged. "Your call." A few more words and they separated, Serriet climbing to cover Tol's approach. The carriage grew larger, a shape like some bizarre flying turtle, with its rounded roof and broad shallow hull. That would make the straining wizard out ahead the neck, she supposed. She uttered the Words that brought the Invisible Defence shimmering into existence before her as she came within bowshot, for this turtle could snap.

Tol saw a figure at the rear raise a crossbow, then lower it. She held a palm up in token of peaceful intent, and the figure made shooing motions, as if asking her to go away. Surely they could talk first? She slowed, but kept on, and the shooing motions became more urgent. Did they have a plague aboard? She would be within hail in moments. The features of the man became clear; it was Jayas, a little more haggard than her portrait, but unmistakable. The same dark complexion, wide face and flat nose, even if the beard was now a tangle, not a neat fringe. After five months and a thousand leagues, here they were, high in the air above a Wild.

Jayas cupped his hands around his mouth, but what came out was a startled shout. A winged shape had swept in behind him, transforming as it came, so that human feet slapped the deck, human arms grabbed Jayas and hurled him over the side. Tol reflexively put her mount into a dive after the plummeting figure, even as her brain realised that she could not hope to catch him. Above, her vision just caught the assailant diving off the carriage, changing as it went until broad wings took it away.

Jayas fell, his hand went to his chest, and the fall turned into a spiral, slowing as he turned in great circles. Tol overshot, pulled up, matched his curving descent, reached out a hand and pulled him over. Strong arms went around her waist as she set the carrot to climbing after the wagon.

"I don't know who you are, but you have my most profound thanks. That Item is only good for a fall much shorter than that," came a voice in her ear. The voice was not what she had imagined, neither deep nor harsh but light, even, without a tremor. There was not a tremble in the arms encircling her, kept prudently low.

"Good for you I did not depart when you waved me away," Tol told him.

"Ah, the cucumbers that keep the carriage aloft do not like any kind of propulsion spell within ten paces. They get nervous and start rolling around."

"Then they won't like *that*," said Tol.

The great bird had swooped around and now alighted on the carriage roof. Once again it blurred into a man, and now it raised a short spear and jabbed downwards. A cucumber gave a thin scream and jerked backwards, causing the carriage to tip and sway. The man jabbed again, the cucumber recoiled, slipped from under the canvas and shot skywards, crying as it went. The carriage tilted, began to lose height, to alarmed shouts. Seyvyar rose into view, but the man did not stay to contest against his spells. He threw himself from the roof and was again a vulture gliding away. Tol hurled the Malevolent Streak as he passed, sending feathers flying from one wing. The vulture tumbled, flapped wildly and twisted off in lopsided flight.

"It's that obsessed bitch Cremione!" exclaimed Jayas. "The maniac has gone were!"

"Old friend? Ex-lover?" asked Tol.

"I killed her once, and she can't get over it," Jayas told her. He could not keep a note of indignation from his voice. "I dropped my crossbow, so I did not get the chance to make it permanent."

Seyvyar had retrieved his rope and was now above the wounded carriage, adding lift. It was not enough to keep its bulk aloft and moving forward. Above the bird-lizard had dived at Serriet and the two were now swirling about, twisting and turning. Tol was on her own with Jayas, but he did not seem bent on taking advantage. She kept on with her plan, climbing up until she was level with the straining Seyvyar..

"Do you need a tow? Salvage rates will apply," she called.

""This is the Wild," called back Seyvyar, turning his head back over the rope over his shoulder.

"Then salvage *and* guard rates apply," replied Tol. "You have one obsessed vulture," she glanced upwards, to where Serriet and the sierlak were dancing through the air, "one presently distracted bird-lizard, a long way to go and some rough country below. Oh, and, if this wind holds, not only will you fall, but it will likely be into a monster-infested sea. You can see the first hint of water over yonder. Does this thing float?"

"We'll manage," ground out Seyvyar. Behind Tol, Jayas waved a calming hand at Yerech.

"We could lighten your load for you," offered Tol. Behind her she felt Jayas flinch. The pieces fell into place in her mind. A missing Brahnak treasure, on the edges of the Hansippif. Not a small army, but Jayas and friends. Just how much did they have? And how many people were looking for them - and would keep looking?

"Keep an eye out for Cremione," she told Jayas.

"Don't worry, I will. If she's come this far she is not going to give up."

"Could she bring friends?"

The question gave Jayas pause. Tol used the interval to follow Serriet's contest. The sierlak was the more experienced flyer, naturally at home in the air. Serriet matched it with a warrior's instincts, cavalry training, a tighter turning circle and archery. As they watched the sierlak dived, Serriet skidded out from under, rolled up and over and loosed a shaft. The sierlak tilted a wing and fled, dropping away to speed off north. Serriet did a victory roll and glided down towards them.

Tol could practically hear the wheels of calculation turning in Jayas' head. The carriage was damaged and vulnerable, Tol and Serriet commanded the air, Cremione was still at large and who knew what further dangers awaited over the long Wilds? If he put a knife to her throat, she might blow a hole in him with a Word, or Serriet put an arrow through him. And what would it gain? They would still be wallowing ever lower to their doom, with no possibility of help and at least one more enemy.

"I suggest we deal," Jayas called to Seyvyar. Yerech nodded and let his hand fall from the string. Delfe was soothing the remaining cucumbers, and now added his voice in assent.

"Fine," agreed Seyvyar through gritted teeth.

"Then we'll rig a line and try to keep you airborne," Tol said.

"THE CUCUMBERS WORK as a team, and the ones remaining miss their mate. The left one is already going soft, and I don't know how long it will last," reported Delfe, worried.

Jayas looked down. The ground was closer, and their progress was interrupted by odd jerks. This despite support from Serriet's mount above and Tol's carrot pulling away to the front. At least they had left the moors. The land below was a mass of thick greenery, with never a break. On their forward quarter the waters of the Corillion Coast glittered in the afternoon sun, a coast fretted with bays and islands, rocks and reefs. They had passed above a village, walled off on a headland, and seen the towers of a lonely hold crowning an islet. More alarmingly, the waters were broken here and there by the cruising snouts, arching necks and jagged fins of monstrous denizens.

"We pick an island – one with cliffs – and bring us in to land," Yerech decided.

"Then what?" asked Seyvyar

"Then we make another way to travel," Yerech told him. Delfe leaned out and shouted to Tol and Serriet, who turned due west. The carriage stuttered again and dropped lower. Jayas watched anxiously as they made their slow way over the trees and then out over a narrow inlet, to scrape over the spine of a rocky peninsula.

"There, the second one," shouted Yerech, pointing to a large rock thrusting up from the sea. Tol turned her carrot, urged it to greater speed and the cucumbers made thin keening noises. Out over the water they floated, where a monster hooted excitedly below, around a first island and grated to a stop on the chosen islet, a pillar no more than fifty yards across. A cucumber sighed and gave up, letting the roof collapse. Serriet dropped the line and landed as they struggled out from under the canvas.

"Do we set up camp first or say hello to the neighbours?"

"Neighbours?" queried Seyvyar as his head emerged.

"There is someone on the next island," Serriet told him. Tol looked across the strait. She could see rock, and clinging greenery, and birds strutting on ledges. On a rock shelf below a seal basked among the boulders. She could see no building or other sign of habitation.

"Spotted a face in an opening as we passed," Serriet said as Delfe, Yerech and Jayas joined Seyvyar, all rumpled. Behind them the canvas quivered as the last cucumber expired.

Jayas surveyed their landing place. A small patch of bare rock, roughly level (the Powers were kind!), surrounded by eroded stone out to steep drops to a monster-infested sea. Hardy shrubs had taken root in pockets of wind-blown soil, and a lone tree angled out from a cleft, stunted but clinging to life and hope. As was he, reflected Jayas. Well, life, hope and fortune. Perhaps it was a *rich* tree.

Yerech scratched his head. "How do you catch monsters? And are they edible? Because Jayas can give us water, but we are going to be hungry in a few more days. That is, unless you two came laden with food?" Tol shook her head. They had enough cheese, hard bread and dried fruit for a few days at most, on half-rations.

"If there is anyone out here they are likely an emeritus magician, the sort that goes off to a Wild to hone their art to a sharper edge. They are usually a little mad, and often a lot mad," Seyvyar told them.

"Good thing we did not land there then. They might be cross if we came down on their roof," observed Yerech.

"Best not to disturb them for now," Jayas decided, and they set about preparing for the night. There was little to do, and Jayas and Tol ended sitting on the seaward side, watching the sun set over the Gulf. Below a long serpent-shape was winding along the reef edge, poking a horned head above the waves from time to time.

"Those carrots you have are handy," Jayas said after a while.

"They are," Tol agreed. "So much so I have put protections around them to prevent theft."

Jayas sighed and laid back. "I have no mind to that, although you probably find that hard to believe."

"Your record is not reassuring," Tol remarked.

Jayas sat up. "Just how did you find us, and why were you looking?"

"I'm an investigator. Finding people is my trade. I was hired to find you." Tol added "Don't worry. The commission lapsed before we left Dtlag, for you were reported lost in the Hansippif."

Jayas was still worried. Were the Items he wore against spells of detection useless? Against all those but the highly-skilled, Tol told him, looking smug. How long had she been looking for him? *That* long? *Really*? He had hoped that all that northern bother had been left behind. He laid back down again, disheartened, only to be jolted upright by a piercing ululation.

"By the book! I forgot the carrot's evening yodel." Explanations were made and Jayas settled back down, now worried about the neighbour's reaction. Why was it, he wondered, that each escape from one enemy seemed to generate two more? And why had they not brought something to drink? He could draw water from the air through his hands, but not rum.

The deepening dusk made it easier to ask the next question. "We're grateful for your help, of course, but I wonder why, if your commission has lapsed, you're here at all. Why pursue us then?"

"Serriet is here for the adventure. And money - your money."

Jayas nodded. "I can understand that. I trust she will settle for an equal share?"

"She will. It's a better deal than she ever got from a caravan captain."

Jayas probed. "If you do the finding, what's Serriet's role?"

Tol shifted. "Well, the commission was to find you and Seyvyar and then ... what were the words '*visit upon them a punishment appropriate to their crimes*.' I've never done much more than restrain people, so Serriet seemed necessary."

"If she wants to spank Seyvyar, I won't object. Possibly he won't either. That still leaves you out here, a long way from home."

"Originally, it was another trace and locate, if a bit longer and more complicated than my usual 'find the debtor' job. It became something more. After so many months I did not feel I could just let go. Serriet says it's a quest, and I think that's right. Plus I wanted to meet you, if only to sort out which of the stories I heard were true and which false. "

"Really?" said Jayas. "I'm flattered. What did you want to know?"

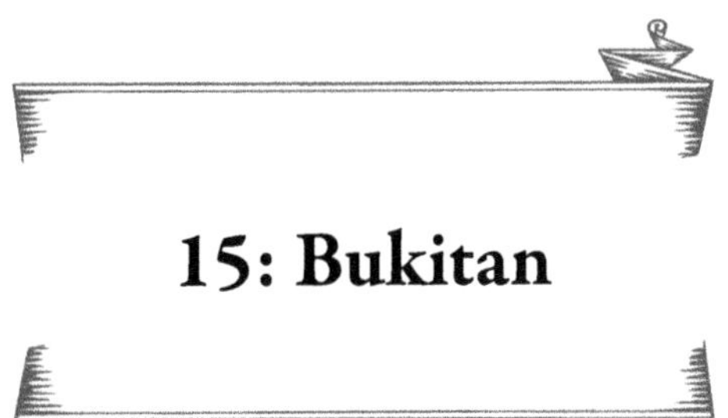

15: Bukitan

"They are still there, you know," the pot-plant in the corner remarked to Jamassein. "Ferka says they are making noises together, and Jieryn thinks the one with yellow leaves is nice. She peed on her and Kuel, and it tasted wonderful."

Jamassein sighed. Having plants keep an eye on the outside had seemed like a good idea at the time. They were not easily detected, excellent weather forecasters and surprisingly knowledgeable about rocks. She had not counted on their tendency to chatter, their intense interest in faeces and the endless squabbles between the perennials and the annuals. The arrival of the flying carrots had sparked a heated debate. The shrubs were shocked by the saddles (allow humans to sit on you!) and the weeds green with envy. The few trees were sternly judgemental: in their view root vegetables should be in the ground, not floating around like dandelion seeds. She would have to do something or she would get no peace.

As she selected bangles Jamassein kept an ear on the visitors' talk, as relayed by the mosses to a fern in a window opening. Their conversation was that of a crew shipwrecked on a perilous strand, far from their destination. Yet it seemed their concern was as much for what they carried as for their own bodies.

"Right now we don't even know where we are," exclaimed the pale magician.

That's as good an entrance line as I'm going to get thought Jamassein, and launched herself out the window.

JAYAS WAS JOLTED FROM sleep by another vigorous yodel as Tol's carrot greeted the dawn. He cursed, rubbed his face and went to piss off the rock. That done, he took stock of their situation, re-visiting the impressions of the evening. Current abode: a pillar of rock, no more than fifty paces across, separated from a larger fellow by a narrow tide-race, and that from the main by a wider strait. Both teeming with monsters, of course. Their carriage was defunct, so for transport they had three magicians and two carrots. This would not suffice to carry forty stones weight of gear and treasure except bit by bit. He was not inclined to leave a large part here with the unknown neighbour, or split the group as they ferried their haul by painful stages through a dangerous Wild. What to do? The Falling Charm that had saved him earlier would see him safe to the bottom of the cliff, but he could not walk on water. And if he could, something would bite his legs off.

He walked over to where the others were talking between bites of bread and cheese. They had made the same calculations, and arrived at the same dispiriting results. Jayas listened while keeping an eye on the skies, for Cremione was surely out there. Perhaps that dot over the jungle was her?

The conversation went around and around, until Seyvyar cut short speculation on methods of travel with " Right now we don't even know where we are."

"I can tell you that," said a voice. Rising from the neighbouring rock was a woman. For an instant she reminded Jayas of vanished Attaiye: the same broad shoulders, muscular arms and strong legs, wide nose and narrow eyes. But this women was darker of skin, a glossy black, deep-chested, hair a giant mass of tight curls. Silver bangles adorned her forearms, laced sandals her feet, a bright red wrap her body. Seyvyar and Tol were on the alert, Serriet and Delfe neutral and Jayas was amused to see Yerech struggling with a mix of admiration, desire and wariness. The woman clearly fitted all the contours of his imagination.

Two bangles shifted against each other. The woman ran her eyes over each of the group, a deliberate searching stare. Jayas noted an appreciative twitch of the eyebrows as she inspected Yerech's torso, and his own lower half got a nod. When her gaze shifted to the canvas covering their loot there was a moment of incredulity, a second look and then she turned to face them.

"You flew here?"

Seyvyar assented.

"Up around the mountains? From somewhere well south?"

Again Seyvyar agreed.

"You have a Power watching over you."

"We fought off two sierlak and a were-bird," Seyvyar told her. The woman waved a hand. "Hardly a challenge, although you obviously did not leave unscathed. No," she went on, "You have a shipload of Pure Silver, and you dragged it past several dragon eyries, and would have skirted more if you had kept north."

Seyvyar paled. The others looked very thoughtful. A sierlak, even two sierlaks, was one thing, a dragon quite another. Dragons *ate* sierlak, often teasing them first. Jayas looked at their desolate rock with new eyes; it seemed it had saved them from a worse fate. The awful Hansippif had led them to silver, if others to death; and now a near-disaster was a merciful escape.

"Well, aside from dragging fresh meat past dire-cat dens, what *were* you doing?" asked Jamassein.

"We hoped to get to Frouan," replied Yerech. The others were still contemplating their certain fate at the claws and teeth of dragons. Worse, they might have been forced to guess at riddles or engage in some other contest of wits, and only then be eaten.

“Frouan? That is a week by sea from here. By land? Months, if you survive,” Jamassein stated, and watched their faces fall in dismay. “To be clear, I have no interest in your gains,” she went on. “I prefer that you leave as soon as may be, before you bring ill-luck upon me. The town of Bukitan is less than an hour’s flight up the coast and I have a trusted friend there. He may give you a place to stay and help you arrange for a ship if I ask. What say you to my offer?”

“May I ask your name. And will you accompany us to Bukitan?” asked Yerech.

The magician smiled. “I am called Jamassein, and I will take you there. I may even stay a day or two.”

BUKITAN WAS A PLEASANTLY bucolic town, perched on a hill above a harbour kept monster-free by a bar passable only at high tide. The few monsters that became trapped were quickly turned into dried meat, sausage, powdered bone and alchemical ingredients. The houses were lime-washed in pastel shades of green, yellow, orange and blue, sported balconies overhanging shaded streets, wide eaves against sun and rain, window screens of fretted wood. The Corillionese went about their days in leisurely fashion. The streets were deserted from noon to late afternoon, purchases meant a conversation over many small cups of tea, work was done at a comfortable pace. Meals were an array of tiny dishes, sampled at the diner’s whim. Men and women dressed simply, in a loose jacket over a sarong, both dyed in intricate patterns. They seemed an easy folk to get along with, but Jamassein had warned that Corillion life was not as simple as it appeared. An intricate code underlaid social interactions and, while the Corillionese were forgiving of foreigners up to a point, they tended to extremes when some invisible line was crossed. Jamassein had witnessed a beheading and been told the victim had failed to use the correct hand in greeting for a fourth time. “So mind your manners,” she told Tol and Jayas. The trio had flown ahead to introduce themselves to Jamassein’s friend.

The friend lived above the town, in a rambling house which seemed at first sight to be made up of verandahs. Wide, railed, of several levels, they entirely obscured the building. Jamassein stopped to call to a bushy-tailed animal dozing under an ornamental shrub. It woke with a start, groomed its whiskers, darted across the lawn and up the steps and vanished within. They waited, standing in the morning sunshine, until a hale elderly man bounded out to clasp Jamassein in his arms. It was a long reach for him, and her return hug lifted him off the ground

“Jamassein! ... ” The rest was a blur of Corillionese. When he turned to Jayas and Tol, he spoke a courteous old-fashioned form of Dzai.

“I am Wiradiryo Heis, but please call me Heis. Any friends of Jamassein are welcome. Please come into my house.” As Tol turned to Jayas to translate, he replied in the same language.

“We are honoured to be so welcomed. We are at your service as guests.” Tol gave Jayas a quizzical look, but did not comment. She came back to the subject later, as they sat on a verandah overlooking the terraced fields around the town. Every second terrace was covered with the purple and white of fang-flowers. They watched a lone worker move slowly along the terrace edge, plucking petals with long-handled tongs. The sound of countless tiny teeth hitting armoured legs and feet carried to their ears as a metallic hum.

“Bad place to fall over,” observed Jayas. Tol nodded. One would not last long prone, the more so as the plants had a soporific venom. Death by innumerable small bites would not be good at all. In response to a question Jayas told her that the petals were a base ingredient in both a common anaesthetic and Instant Death, the potion used to give animals a swift and painless end.

“It’s unusual for a non-magician to know Dzai,” Tol said.

"Languages are a useful skill."

"You do know it is a dangerous tongue?"

"So I was taught," assented Jayas. "I listen more than I talk, for that reason."

Tol gave him a look that said that he had his warning, then went on. "Do you talk to Seyvyar and Delfe in Dzai?"

Jayas gave her a slight smile. "I don't think they yet know."

"Then why reveal your knowledge to me?"

Jayas gave a huff of breath. "I grow tired of keeping secrets. They burden me."

Tol digested this, then said "I checked your aura."

Jayas accepted this calmly. Had he that art, he would have done the same.

"By repute, you are an unprincipled rogue. Your aura showed something more complex," pursued Tol.

"You have met a lot of rogues?"

"I have been an investigator for five years now. I've met a lot of rogues. Sent a few to court, recovered stuff from others. Also thugs, brutes, sneaks, spies, swindlers, thieves and missing persons. Lost pets if I was feeling nice, or poor."

At one time or another he had been all of those, reflected Jayas. Well, not a lost pet. Yet.

"Your life has not marked your aura with malice or treachery. Odd. And there was a streak of, hmm, remorse? No, too strong. Regret? Reconsideration? Auras are not very precise."

"Good to know. I am not a philosopher, to examine my own soul so closely."

"I'm an investigator, not a mind-guide. You could get a closer reading, together with life advice, for a couple of silvers."

Below the worker climbed down from the terrace, squirming sack over one shoulder. Even at this distance the sheen of venom from the knee down was visible.

"Good thing those plants don't grow taller," Jayas said, to fill in the silence. Did he want to have his inner essence scrutinised? This conversation was difficult enough. That 'odd' had been a very back-handed compliment, if a compliment at all.

"How long have you been following us?" Jayas asked.

Tol thought. "I was first engaged in the middle of the Month of the Polecat. So that's six months ago. You have led us a long way. Not that I mind," she added. "I was getting sick of Kaber, and didn't know where else to go, other than 'not home'." She waved a hand at the landscape, the enclave of Bukitan, surrounded on all sides but the sea by the Eig Wild. "I would never have thought to come here and see this."

She fell silent. Jayas felt the absence of words weigh on him, and cast about for another neutral topic. She was good at this, he thought. Her silences were comfortable, inviting a confidence. He had none to give her, for she knew enough of his past that very little would surprise her. The face of that boy in the tower came to his mind, again.

"I have two deaths I regret," he said abruptly. Tol just sat there, receptive.

Jayas went on, low-voiced. "The group I was with was riven with tension. They were all planning to turn on each other. So I made a pact with Seyvyar, that we two would stick together. When the moment came, I killed Rudrin. He was the most trusting, the least happy with the rivalries. But he had to go first, for he was the other magician."

"Get the magician first," Tol nodded. Jayas gave her a wry smile. Now she was one of the magicians.

"The second was at Western Light – the tower at the edge of the Hansippif we were compelled to destroy. There was a youth, full of faith, determined to do his utmost even as those around him fell. He fought me and I won. Yet I take no triumph in it. His death in the right cause meant more to him than my life did to me."

"Did your death mean so little?"

"I was driven to that fight!" said Jayas with emphasis. "Duelling in Mer Ammery? That was my choice. Killing that child? That was not."

Tol absorbed this. "Just so you know," added Jayas defensively, "I have never killed anyone outside the law. Duellists take their chances and the rest? They were in the Wild."

"Where law does not run," said Tol. After a moment she added "I met a man who preached the doctrine of Sebres Brahn, that there is a source of truth and justice above all Powers, even those that rule the Wild. It would be nice to think so."

"Do not you magicians talk to the ether?"

"We do, but it does not tell us truth, nor guide us to justice. The ether flows through your hands. Does it guide them to do right?"

Jayas turned a palm up. "No, it does not. Who then will judge our deeds if we do not do so ourselves?"

Tol glanced at him sideways. "How do you judge yourself, then?"

Jayas pursed his lips. "More harshly than I would have a month ago."

Again Tol let her silence answer. After a time she slapped her thigh. "Seyvyar should be arriving with the first load soon. We should have the boxes ready."

SERRIET LIFTED THE last box on to the stack, stood back and dusted her hands. "There. All done and labelled." Heis had given them the use of a shed, and now it held a stack of stout boxes, all labelled 'Best Double-Refined Essences and Oils'. Each was stamped with the red star for hazardous content and the broken rod that marked fragile cargo. Delfe made a last count and they left. Delfe turned the key, Heis' protections flared briefly and it was time for dinner. Four nights of flying to and fro had transferred all their goods, leaving the wrecked carriage a forlorn shell. Their last act had been to push it over the cliff, for Jamassein did not want attention drawn to her home. The fragments would drift away.

Delfe and Serriet walked down to the town, chatting amiably. Serriet found Delfe an easy companion. He was not patronising (like Seyvyar), or darkly moody (like Jayas). They shared a common amusement in watching the normally self-contained Yerech go shy and nervous around Jamassein. She had stayed on, and the two had been spending time together, so Yerech was now nervously happy. The romance could not last, for they had arranged passage on a ship leaving in another two days.

16: All At Sea

One by one the heavy chests were handed down into the hold of the *Weaselfish* and there stowed securely. Hatches were covered, booms re-rigged, personal gear stuffed into lockers and under narrow bunks. Jamassein gave Yerech a kiss and soared off, the gangplank was swung in, ropes cast off and they drifted away from the dock. A pause, then a jib ran up, the bow came around and the vessel moved slowly on the still tide across the harbour, over the protecting rock shelf uneasily visible through clear water and met the first waves of the Gulf. The skipper gave the order, sails were let fall and she urged on, weaving through the passages that would take her out to the open sea.

Delfe stood at the mainmast cross-trees with Yerech, one with spells ready, the other with bow strung. Sea monsters infested these inshore waters, and passengers as well as crew must help defend the ship. Every few minutes the lookout at the foremast top called 'All clear forward', a cry echoed by the other lookouts, each for their quarter. At noon the pair were relieved by Seyvyar and Jayas. The routine calls continued, the coast slid past and by mid afternoon Jayas was getting bored. Then the starboard lookout called out, "'Ware Monster! Two cables starboard and ahead," and they saw a green bulk show briefly above the surface. Long spears were snatched up, helmets hastily fastened, bolts slotted into place.

"Pleriano's Fail," cursed the sailor next to Jayas. "It's a hull-breaker!" Then, to Jayas "Can you swim?"

"It's not getting *my* stuff!" said Jayas and dived off the platform, fingers knotting in a craft-spell as he fell. He hit the water in a clean dive, felt the gills open in his back, twisted and kicked to face the monster. It was big, blunt-headed, wide-jawed and coming on fast. *This may have been a mistake* flashed through Jayas' mind; what could he do against something so huge? He kicked off straight at it, flipped aside and sunk his knife into a flipper, stabbing hard and pulling back. Blood spiralled out into the water and the thing turned violently, the flipper smacking him away. Well, at least he had its attention.

It continued to turn, and Jayas desperately tried to turn with it, to stay out of reach of those jaws. It did not work, for this was the creature's domain and, while he could breathe water, his shape remained the same. *It should be Seyvyar down here, with his noxious, spiny sea-thing spell*, and Jayas kicked hard and vaulted over the bony plate of the nose, pulling his feet up. As he slid off he was briefly eye to irritated eye with the thing. He ducked under a massive fluke, fingers moving, and let the edge slap his hand. The beast circled, came in again, then slowed, its mouth gaped and it barfed a half-digested seal into Jayas' face. It smelled horrible, even in the water, and he flinched away. The creature retched again, and Jayas was brushed aside by a shark rushing in to collect a free meal.

If the sea was going to be swarming with scavengers Jayas' place was on the ship. He surfaced, looked around and stroked after the vessel. There it was, drawing away at a speed he could not hope to match. He waved desperately, saw Seyvyar launch off the mast to swoop down over the waves.

"Need a lift?"

"Just get us out of here before the thing recovers," Jayas snarled, and he was hauled out of the fetid water, leaving the nauseated monster amid a swarm of opportunist sea-life. He went on "Drop me alongside with a rope. This form is fixed for two hours."

"What did you do to it?" asked Sevyar, glancing back at the patch of discoloured water.

"The Nauseous Touch. I did not know if it would affect so large a creature, so I gave it a double dose."

"Well, it will be in no mood to be eating for a while," Seyvar said as they reached the ship. Jayas spent a resigned time being ignominiously towed from the starboard cathead. At least no sharks came calling. When he finally came aboard the *Weaselfish* had cleared the land, the lookouts had gone to dinner and they were running up the gulf. Jayas stomped below to change his clothes.

"YOU'RE MIGHTY ATTACHED to your cargo. Worth more than your life, is it?" remarked the mate to Jayas that evening. Jayas looked at him sideways. Was he fishing?

"Some of my friends are poor swimmers."

"Lucky for them you aren't, then," the mate said.

"And for you and the crew," Jayas reminded him. The mate gave a sober nod.

"True enough. Hull-breakers are trouble. Not easy to get at, as they don't surface, and they'll hit again and again until a plank gives. If they were as plentiful as whales then no-one would sail the seas at all, but Selm keeps them few, even on this coast! Yet one came for us."

"Bird-shit has to land somewhere, and hull-breakers find hulls as they will," was Jayas' take on the matter. The mate looked unconvinced, but turned the talk to what the cook would serve for dinner. When the time came, Jayas took his turn at the galley hatch, ate his bowl of fish porridge and greens without complaint and went forward to watch the sun set over far Dravishi. The breeze was steady, the sea only playful, the first stars glimmering in the east. It was as peaceful a scene as Jayas could wish. Yerech joined him for a time, silent if still glum from parting with Jamassein, then turned in, leaving Jayas to enjoy the last glimmers. The afterglow lingered when a seaman brought him a nightcap of spiced rum in warm water.

"Drink it wishing for a fair run tomorrow, sir."

"Thanks, lad. I will," replied Jayas amiably. As he lifted the cup the worm tattoo on his inner wrist gave a small squirm. Jayas inhaled the aroma, enjoying the spicy scent while his trained nose identified the ingredients. A cheap rum, cinnamon, allspice, nutmeg, waxroot and easyflower. That last was a mild soporific, often used to calm the nerves and induce a good night's sleep. A thoughtful gesture on the part of the cook, after his heroic exertions earlier? Perhaps. He drained the cup in a few swallows, handed it back to the crewman and settled himself in a sheltered corner.

"The night is so lovely I'll stay on deck a little longer," he remarked, and let himself slouch. His fingers were twining as the man left, setting his body to neutralising the draught. Jayas gradually drooped, than lolled sideways and began to breathe deeply. Snoring would be, well, *theatrical*, so he did not do that. Through half-closed eyes he watched the skipper, mate and three crewmen gather around the fore-hatch.

"Is he out of it?" with a jerk of the head.

"Looks like it. Teio says the others are all well under too." A grunt.

"So we take a look?" This from the mate.

The skipper scratched his beard. "Still not sure. That 'un did us a favour, and then they all have the hazard star. Could be nasty stuff, or just bluff. We don't know. Jaerke will get shirty if he thinks we tried to cheat on his share."

The mate snorted. "The star's for show. 'Oils' that don't smell, and the chests are too heavy. No, they have something else in those boxes, and best to know what it is before Jaerke sees them. He's not above a bit of cheating himself, and blind men get no bargains."

The skipper considered this, then decided. "Right. We look at two or three, no more, and put all back to rights." A seaman bent to unfasten the lashings. It was time to act. Jayas groaned, shifted, rolled over and wobbled to his feet. The group below had whirled at the first sound and now regarded him with expressions ranging from hostile to puzzled. Some had hands on knives.

"What's toward?" asked Jayas, rubbing his eyes. The group had been speaking Corillionese, and now Jayas used the Merllan that was the lingua franca of the southern Green Sea.

"Hatch cover needed a bit of attention is all," the skipper told him. "Could be a blow tomorrow."

Jayas put on a worried face. "The hatches are tight, no? Those vials are triple-wrapped and the chests sealed, but Heis warned us to keep it away from seawater, or even salt spray. We are paying hazard rates because that's dangerous stuff. I knew someone who turned half-snail when he dropped a bottle and it splashed on him."

The sailors backed away and the skipper hastened to assure Jayas that it was just a check. He accepted this and settled back down with the air of someone happily prepared to watch others work. The mate muttered something to the skipper, who shook his head. They fiddled with the lashings for a time and then dispersed. Jayas went below, to find Seyvyar, Yerech and Delfe all deeply asleep.

JAYAS HAD A QUICK WORD with Seyvyar the next morning. The promised blow had not materialised, and the *Weaselfish* was still scudding nor-nor-west under all plain sail. The pair had taken their breakfast mugs of strong tea to the foredeck and were leaning on the windward rail. For added security they spoke in Kabinese, a language no crewman was likely to know. Seyvyar's first thought was to kill the captain and mate, and then compel the crew to sail to Frouan. Jayas was not minded to be arrested for murder on the high seas within hours of setting foot ashore. The sea was the domain of Selm of the Waters, not some Wild where law did not run. Moreover, Frouan was no desolate beach but a great port, sure to swarm with customs officers, inspectors, harbour-masters and other officials. Arriving without a skipper or mate would invite questions. Seyvyar yielded with a few flings about Jayas' respect for the law.

"We lost the last haul to a lawyer, albeit one with a poker," Jayas reminded him. "I've no mind to lose this to a parcel of lawyers with writs."

In the end they could only warn Yerech and Delfe, and wait. Seyvyar went below; Jayas stayed, brooding on the way so much wealth weighed upon him. Perhaps the pursuit was better than the capture? He scanned the sky, wondering if any of the specks crossing the blue were Cremione. Most were winging their way north on some avian migration, and a vulture would not plummet down into the water, or at least not bob back up. Jayas could not believe that she had given up. No, she was out there, biding her time. She had been a canny duellist, and would be a canny hunter, as vulture or person.

They docked at Frouan two days later. As Jayas had forecast, official formalities were not lacking. The *Weaselfish's* arrival was registered, it was given clearance, conducted by a pilot to a berth in the East Harbour, and customs came aboard as soon as the mooring ropes were fast. Delfe, trained in these matters by his House, dealt with them while Jayas contemplated Frouan. He was no stranger to large cities; his wandering life had taken him to Azbai and Chiran in the Four Kingdoms, to northern Kaber and to Mer Ammery. Still, Frouan was daunting. The *Weaselfish* had entered the harbour by a long and winding passage, guarded by bleak fortresses whose loop-holed walls and strong towers promised destruction to intruders. Behind the wharves the city rose in tier after tier of gaunt stone, crowded and close, dark and dripping in this misty morning. It looked no more welcoming than the guarding walls. The buildings were square and blocky, their mass relieved by tall towers poking up, like dismal decorations in a dank pudding.

Jayas dredged through his mind for what he had been told of Frouan. It was prosperous, commercially-minded, ruled by a secretive oligarchy, foggy and the locals were reputed to be more familiar with the dark arts than was seemly (perhaps he could give them tips?). If it had inns and banks and people willing to buy what they had brought, the rest was of no importance. Yerech had a few contacts here, and Jayas was sure he could find people who would do business with him. Mer Ammery had been depressing in that regard, as even the criminals went in awe and fear of the Syndics.

Behind him, Delfe was signing papers and taking notes. An official in severe black came over, checked his name against a list and stamped the back of his left hand in green ink. The stamp would fade in ten days, he was told. Until then he was free of the city so long as he conducted himself within the law. He could renew for a further ten days if his departure was delayed, or apply for residence. Jayas accepted the stamp and conditions with resignation. There was never any point in arguing with bureaucracy.

Seyvyar joined him at the rail, and then Delfe came over. “All the paperwork is done, and we are free to go ashore. Our cargo will be held in bond until the duty and other charges are paid. The skipper transferred the papers to Jaerke’s Bond and General. That’s the dark brick building at the end of the wharf.”

“How do we get our stuff from them?” asked Seyvyar.

“We establish our credentials with the Shipwright’s Bank, have enough transferred to cover the costs and get a draft made out to Frouan Customs. We present that with the papers at the Customs House – the building with the pillared portico and the green dome over there, they give us a release and we take that to Jaerke’s. It will take at least two days, probably more.”

Seyvyar observed that matters were much simpler in the Wild. You took the stuff and ran. Delfe looked nervous at the mere suggestion that they might try to evade the Customs regulations – smugglers ranked second only to pirates in the Merllan index of criminality. Jayas simply said "We have an hour before they unload. I will find a suitable bag. Delfe, can you come with me?" and the two crossed the gangplank to the wharf.

JAERKE'S WAREHOUSE was stoutly constructed, the doors solid and well-secured, the windows small and barred. The interior was constantly lit by large glowstones, so that no corner lay in shadow. Crates, bales and barrels were stacked neatly, leaving wide aisles between each consignment. A pair of trained striped langurs moved around on a web of ropes stretched near the ceiling, ready to raise the alarm at any untoward sound or scent. The office was suspended in the centre of the room, so that from its windows the whole floor was visible. Jaerke himself assured Seyvyar that he and his trusted guards were mere seconds away at all times, in the house just across the street.

The most valuable cargoes were kept in a strongroom behind an iron door. The roof of this was a mesh of iron bars, so that the interior was visible to watchers. Seyvyar and Yerech had overseen the transfer of their boxes and sacks to this room, steadying the lift-poles with anxious reminders of the fragility and hazardous nature of the contents, making sure to count each item and then tallying the pile twice before signing. They insisted on inspecting the strongroom, asked about the security and leaving other possessions there and generally got in the way. They did not leave until they had seen the strongroom door locked. They were ushered out, and set off to their lodgings with many a backward glance. One by one the doors of the warehouses were closed, the last barrows, carts and lift-poles trailed off, ships alongside hoisted glowstones into the rigging to cast a pale light on the wharves and the district was left to the strays and the odd watch-fellow.

Yerech wriggled his shoulders slightly, twitched his toes and worked his fingers. These quarters were cramped and the surface under his back hard. Delfe had been unconvinced of the need for him to be here at all, and maybe he was right. Seyvyar and Jayas had been insistent. Delfe had doubted a licensed customs broker and bonded warehouse operator would break the law. Such a thing was unheard of in Mer Ammery. Well, rarely heard of, as the punishment was fourteen laps of the shark pool, done with a raw leg of lamb tied about the neck. Applicants for a license were required to witness the fate of a goat carcass towed on a line. Delfe could not imagine that the rulers of Frouan were any less stringent. Yerech breathed deeply, keeping his mouth open and wondered if he would get any sleep tonight.

In the end he did doze off despite the uncomfortable conditions. He was awakened by the clank of a heavy lock and a creak of hinges. A thin ribbon of light seeped into his hiding place. Was Jaerke making a conscientious late check? Yerech strained his ears.

"Right. Let's be careful with the seals. If the *Weaselfish* is wrong and the manifest is right, we don't want any questions. We'll check two in each row."

Seyvyar and Jayas had been right. Yerech drained the vial, then hastily thrust up with his dagger. The cloth ripped, he shot up and, to the startled Jaerke and associates, an armed warrior sprang from a small bag.

"I am told that interfering with bonded cargo is a serious offence," Yerech said.

Jaerke recovered quickly, glancing from side to side to assure himself that his accomplices were ready. One was a woman, a magician in loose trousers and a long coat, the linked chain belt at her waist probably an Item, as she carried the usual several knives in sheaths sewn to a baldric. It emphasised her figure, but Yerech was not distracted. She would be the danger, for the other two were merely your standard hench-persons, two burly men in thick shirts and leather waistcoats, each with a short heavy blade by their side. One carried a pry-bar, the other a full bag. Armoured Yerech was confident he could deal with both in short order. And unless Jaerke, who carried only a belt-knife, was high in craft he too would be no problem. The woman was the threat, and the focus of his attention.

"You are in my warehouse without permission, likely a thief, so I think we will kill you," replied Jaerke.

"You forgot to lock the door," said a voice behind Jaerke, and he spun around to see Seyvyar and Jayas standing there.

"I did not! I definitely locked it!" said one hench-person indignantly.

Out of the corner of his eye Yerech saw the langurs settle into a hammock with a good view of the room. One had a cup full of nuts. His attention came back to the stand-off before him in time to catch a flicker of motion in the outer warehouse. 'Beware, ' he cried, and Jayas threw himself one way as Seyvyar went the other. A crossbow bolt hissed through the space Jayas had occupied, missed a hench-person by a whisker and struck sparks from the wall. A familiar howl of rage resonated through the cavernous space.

Jayas caromed off stacked bales wrapped in stout hessian, whirled and charged for the door. He was not letting Cremione trap him in this room, where the mesh roof would have them all snakes in a basket. Behind him, Jaerke belatedly dived for cover, dragging his magician with him. A hench-person muttered "They left the door open too" as he scurried to hide – too slowly. The winged dagger that had been speeding for Seyvyar's unprotected back slowed as he vanished from view, wavered in mid-air, then plunged for the nearest body. The unfortunate man screamed as the blade bit into his side and he fell writhing to the floor. Yerech's flying leap carried him over the body as he followed Jayas, while Seyvyar spewed Words before running out.

Jayas whipped low through the door and scooted behind a stack of bales. From here he could play hide and seek through the aisles. The plan failed when Cremione found him straight away, looming up tall and dark even as he came out of his crouch. He barely fended off a smashing overhand blow, reeled back from follow-up thrusts and desperately dodged an off-hand dagger strike. He had no space to draw on craft, and the seconds needed to reach one of his little bottles would be his death. He had been hard-pressed by Cremione in her first body; he was over-matched by her in this one and she knew it. He backed away and she followed, flipping the dagger into the air to free a hand to cast a length of rope to the floor. As the dagger was deftly caught, she uttered a word and the rope sprang forward, binding about Jayas' ankles. He fell, her blade smashed through mail to pierce his shoulder and then the tip bloody with his own blood was at his throat.

Jayas whispered a Name, felt it send a tremor through the ether, whispered it again, and then again. Please let the called one come. Please let it hate me enough.

"Praying, Jayas? To whom do such as you pray? Vorë of the rats?"

Jayas kept still. Cremione pressed the sword a little harder, just enough to break the skin. She laughed. "You are mine, and when your followers are dead you will live. Until I decide to kill you. And then bring you back, and kill you again. And again. You are mine."

"Actually, he's mine," said a voice behind her. Cremione reacted on the first syllable, leaping forward to spin and land poised, blade at guard, to face the voice. She saw herself, her own body, the one slain by Jayas, in the colours of House Pens, just as she had died in that duel. Cremione-that-was held her own sword ready, eyes flicking between prone Jayas and the one facing her.

"You are not real. That body was given to the sea," cried Cremione-that–is.

The other laughed. "As real as you, in that borrowed body. I have come to claim my prize, but I will at the least give you pretty thanks for wrapping the gift."

"He is mine," insisted Cremione. At her feet Jayas drew on craft as discreetly as he might. The motion caught her eye and she kicked him in the wounded shoulder, sending a wave of pain through his body. Still, he had managed to staunch the wound. At least he would not bleed to death while they argued possession.

Cremione suddenly lunged, one leg extended behind, point shooting forward. The other merely twisted aside, equally fast, and brought her blade down, to point at Jayas' leg.

"I can carve a bit off, if you really need a memento."

Cremione's snarl of outrage was followed by a cry of "run!". A flying figure crossed Jayas' vision, rising fast towards the roof. A cast, a beam of force and a skylight burst, raining shards of glass down. Jayas used the moment's distraction to again draw on craft. Cremione stabbed down at his throat, he caught her blade in his strengthened hand and directed the point into the floor. Cremione dragged it out in time to deflect a blow from Yerech as he skidded around the corner, she leapt on to the stacked bales and threw herself upwards in vulture form, vanishing through the shattered skylight into the black night. Yerech nearly tripped on Jayas and then lunged at Cremione-that-was. From below, Jayas judged his form to be on a par with Cremione's.

The blade met air, causing Yerech to overbalance. His knee came down on Jayas' chest, he recovered and stepped forward, ignoring Jayas' spasms.

"Foolish, foolish," the other chided. "I am immune to your steel. But you are not immune to mine," and she cut low at Yerech's leg. He skipped back, to take up a wary guard. Jayas drew a painful breath and wheezed "This is air. Look for a buzzing thing."

"Liar," proclaimed Cremione-that-was, and stabbed at his leg. Shockingly, Jayas felt a sharp pain, and then another, worse, in his lower back. He threw his heavy mace, and if his arm was weak his aim was true. The head hit chitin with a crunch, the figure of Cremione vanished and an insectile form crouching there gave a thin scream. Yerech's heavy steel came down, it was split and withdrew into the ether with a hiss and a whirl of green vapour. Jayas gave a groan of thanks and the monkeys above hooted in appreciation.

"Cremione brought five with her. Four are dead and the magician fled when our carrot friends arrived," Yerech told Jayas , reaching down to help him up. The pain in his back was excruciating, an agony that radiated through his whole body.

"That demon bit me. *Hurts*," he managed, and passed out.

17. Dealings under Bond

When Jayas was next aware of himself, he could not feel pain. He could not feel anything at all, not even his own breath in his nostrils. Nothing. He realised he had no nostrils, nor anything else. No arms or legs or face. Was he dead? Or worse, had Cremione captured his soul, that she might put him to death again and again? This bodiless existence was not like any version of the afterlife he had heard of. If he was a ghost, would he not be hanging around his own corpse?

Jayas extended his awareness, cautiously. He gained an impression of being contained, of being within something. Was he confined? He pushed his awareness outwards, to find three auras nearby. All were a steady bright green, a colour associated with intelligent self-awareness. One felt vaguely familiar, and he extended a tendril of thought that way. The aura swirled at the contact, a gold flash illuminated it and a voice spoke in his mind.

"Jayas! You're awake. This is Tol."

"Great. Where am I?"

"In a jar. The venom was dissolving your internal organs, starting with your kidneys, so the quickest save was to put you in a jar while the healers worked on your body."

"I guess a jar is better than the alternative. Do I get a new body? If so, can I have one like Cremione's? She beat me like I was a novice."

"You did manage to hold her off until Yerech arrived. We don't have a spare body lying around, although I would not be surprised if some of the places we passed had a couple of dozen stored in the basement. So you go back into your current one once it's fixed.."

"That's a pity."

"Oh, I don't know. It looked quite serviceable to me."

Jayas let that one pass. He was not sure how he felt about Tol, and anyway he was not sure he could feel anything much about anything while in this jar. He had nothing to feel with. Life without a body had no pains, but no pleasures either.

"What happened in the warehouse? I was too caught-up dealing with Cremione, or rather failing to deal with her, to take in the whole scene."

Tol laughed. "Our plan did not quite go as intended. Going back a bit, Serriet and I found we needed permits and a warning bell to fly within the city limits. The nobles here build high towers, and keep the defences active all the time. Not full-on counter-siege stuff, but fly too close and you get attacked by winged rats or have choke-dust hurled at you. The permits came through only late in the afternoon, and then Delfe had to brief us, and find the factors for Juleize and Frehuar, who turned out to be the same person. They took some persuading, and my carrot's evening yell upset the local dogs, and then Serriet and I had trouble finding the warehouse from the air, as you can't get too near the waterfront defences either. We were flying around, bells tinkling whenever we came near a warded tower, trying to match our directions with what we could see, patches of fog in the way. In the end, someone left the door open, we spotted light spilling into the street and came down to check. When we came in Yerech was hard-pressed and Seyvyar locked in a stand-off. Serriet put an arrow through one and lanced another. Said it was just like her cavalry days."

Jayas cast around for another topic. Life in a jar was lonely in a way he had never experienced. Before, at least he had a body, with its sensations, prompts, motions and just general there-ness for company. The order in which he had trained had a practical bent, but his lessons had included a little philosophy. The philosophers had been enamoured of the life of the mind, some going so far as to consider existence as pure intellect the highest ideal. Perhaps, Jayas thought, they might reconsider if kept in a jar for a while, say a year or two. He passed this thought to Tol, who chuckled.

"Indeed they might. Those magicians who prose on about the nature of the ether might also benefit."

They bantered on until Tol left, saying she had to sleep. Jayas let his thoughts drift, but sleep did not come to him. If no sleep, he realised, then no dreams. The still silence left no room for anything but thought. He recalled reading that those kept solitary and without a body began to fragment, losing their mental unity until at last there was no whole person, just a set of random associations and proclivities. He supposed this was why ghosts hung around the living, desperate to remind themselves of their own personality. Tol would come back, and he hoped to be back in his own battered case before that happened.

Jayas was not prone to nightmares, the dreams that gripped as hard as reality. His dreams were the usual mish-mash, even the horrid scenes comfortably distanced, himself the spectator at a play scripted by his own brain. He had no fear of the images that presented themselves to him (how could he, when he had no body to feel fear with?), yet the recurrence of the face of that boy, the one he had killed below the tower, dragged at his curiosity. What was special about that boy, among those he had killed? His youth? His fervour? In Jayas' mind he was less an opponent than a sacrifice. He followed that thread.

A sacrifice to whom? That the Hansippif wanted those who had injured it dead was no surprise. Jayas preferred his enemies that way too. He would lie more easily in his jar if Serriet had put a lance through Cremione. A sacrifice, though, was a gift. The powers did not want gifts of death, or gifts of any sort. They wanted what their domains demanded. Baive of the fields wanted good soil, clean water, the right balance between forest and plough and pasture. If the Hansippif wanted death it was a dark power indeed.

His order had tried to make him sacrifice, and he had refused. He had killed rather than lay a part of his soul on a dark altar. That death had been his gift, or so he liked to think. A gift of mercy to the one killed, not of cruelty. At the time he had been driven by an unthinking revulsion, complicated by the need to avoid punishment. As with many of his endeavours, he had succeeded only in part. Jayas brought the memory up from all those years ago.

"NEXT," CALLED THE INSTRUCTOR, and Aymina stepped forward. She took out her dagger, placed the point precisely over the big nerve in the cheek and pressed, then dragged down, across the jaw, over the throat (careful to avoid the major blood vessels), along the collar-bone and down over one breast. Her expression was calm, her hand steady throughout. The subject had been made mute, and was tightly restrained, but still quivered.

"Well done," approved the instructor. "Jayas."

Jayas drew his dagger and approached the woman, considered a moment and then placed the tip delicately between her lips. A slight twist, a tiny cut and the blade was pulled out of his hand, plunging in to the hilt. The woman shivered and went limp.

"Fool boy! What have you done?" The instructor tried to pull the weapon from the body. It resisted, then gave suddenly, coming out to hang limp and bloody, drooping from the hilt. The instructor held it up.

"A leech-knife! Where did you get a leech-knife?"

Jayas looked puzzled. "Forgive me, Dominance. I thought it was my own dagger."

The instructor back-handed him across the face. "Don't play games with me. Where did you get this?" He held the dagger up to Jayas' face. "Tell me or it goes into you."

Jayas bent his eyes on the limp blade, ignoring the flow from his split lip. "The hilt is the same pattern as my dagger, Dominance, but all my gear is marked with my initials. My dagger is so marked on the underside of the hilt."

"Are you saying someone replaced your dagger with this?"

"It is possible, Dominance. I cannot otherwise explain how it came to be in my sheath."

The instructor made to hit him again, then halted his hand. What the boy said was possible, for pranks were common, indeed encouraged. He glared at Jayas and then told the others to stand against the wall, hands high. One by one their weapons were inspected and returned, until he came to Daerkhei. The dagger in his possession had the initials 'JZ' under the hilt.

"Well?" the instructor demanded.

"I do not know how it came there, Dominance," insisted Daerkhei. "Perhaps someone switched our weapons?"

"Someone who had a leach-knife. Did *you* have a leach-knife, Daerkhei?"

"No, Dominance." They had all learned to keep their answers short. The instructor jerked his head and Jayas and Daerkhei rejoined the others at the wall. The instructor stalked along the row of backs. Some one of them had filched an Item and switched weapons between Daerkhei and Jayas. They were all adept in evading simple truth tests, and all practised liars. Of course there were sterner, more intrusive ways, but it was simpler just to assign guilt and deliver punishment.

"You will all do an extra hour on the training course tonight. Daerkhei, you will learn to check your gear. Two days on armoury duty, with a test to follow. Jayas, as you cut the lesson short, you will stand outside the refectory before the evening meal, and each of those who missed out can make their mark on *you,* one each day." He added "Nothing that cannot be healed within the day, else you will run the masters' gauntlet."

This was heard in silence. The instructor let it linger, then gave a further command. "Jayas, Daerkhei – take the remains to the ponds. Keep the portions small. Liszerin, you will see it done properly and report to me after." He left, and Jayas found himself the target of six pairs of eyes, all expressing negative emotions. If there was a slight tinge of forced admiration for his cunning, it was far outweighed by contempt, dislike and, in Daerkhei's case, open hatred. Jayas returned the glares with a tranquil face, and began the messy task of removing the restraints. A bag of treated cloth was on hand to hold the body, but the masters would expect the area to be spotless. Four left, one flicking a kick at Jayas (which he dodged); Daerkhei and Liszerin stood there, neither helping as Jayas scrubbed the straps, wall and floor, then mopped all dry. He picked up one end of the bag and waited. Liszerin silently pointed out a minor speck of dried blood between two tiles, and watched as Jayas took a rag and wiped it away.

The bag was awkward to carry. Jayas went first, along the corridor, down steep and narrow stairs with sharp turns, through the musty basement ways, still narrow and the walls of cobbles roughly mortared, apt to catch on cloth or bruise the careless arm. This place was old, far older than his Order, which had just moved in, like a snake into a burrow. Probably after devouring the previous occupant. They lugged their burden to the lower door, an affair of thick planks bound with iron that gave on to a nook between buttresses. From here the way was through walled gardens, some lethal, others merely dangerous. The ponds were scattered across an enclosure at the far end. Jayas and Daerkhei kept to the centre of the raised path, and eyes to both sides. Some things could leap a long way. As Jayas and Daerkhei heaved the bag on to a stone table and began their messy task the waters nearby roiled in anticipation, tentacles, feeder-fronds and eye-stalks lifting out to sample the air. An armoured slug oozed over a dividing wall and evicted the pool occupant after a short struggle. The ex-tenant, a segmented thing with a barbed spine, crawled up the embankment, only to be flicked back into the water by Liszerin's boot. The slug got what went into that pond, but at least the other thing was not eaten. Not today, at any rate.

The last bone was hurled into a writhing mass of worms, the bag folded and Jayas let Daerkhei and Liszerin precede him back to the house, where no doubt she would report that he had done a poor job. He just had time to wash and change before he took up station outside the refectory. Liszerin would be among those who had a turn at him. She was inventive and still resented that Jayas had refused an invitation to her bed.

IF JAYAS IN THE JAR could grimace, he would. Even now, and even without a body, that memory rasped. Of the five who had missed their opportunity to inflict torture, he thought at least two were friends enough to make no more than a light mark – just enough to satisfy the teachers. No – all five were creatively vicious. Of course Liszerin was the worst. She had wrapped a length of fire-vine around his lower body and watched as skin blistered and peeled. Jayas was forbidden to cry out, but tears leaked from his closed eyes. He got back at them of course: ink-spiders under the table, a sheet soaked in an agent that slowly hardened the skin, a drop of explosive force in a bowl of porridge. A little misdirection led one try at retaliation to weld a master's knees to the underside of his desk, and another to a fall from a third-floor window. In hindsight, the corpse-wasps were an over-reach. It resulted in Jayas being expelled. He had shivered through a cold night, pinned to a courtyard wall, and then been ceremoniously stripped of robes and place before the assembled members before being scourged from the gates. He had been angry at the time, but now thought himself the better for it. Had he stayed, would he be as coldly sadistic as Liszerin, or as carelessly brutal as Daerkhei? He might be a master, tormenting each new group of entrants, or offering dark deeds to tyrants. For all its failures, his life had been better spent than that. For one, he had comrades, not accomplices.

The West Wild, the Hansippif, the tower, Cremione, this jar ... they had all changed his perspective. Wealth was no longer a goal, but a means. To what? *That* he would have to think about.

Jayas turned his attention outwards, to find an aura nearby, a swirl of pastel colours. He followed its movements for a time, guessed it was that of some medical attendant and let his mind wander through a series of idle speculations, then linger on more pleasant pasts. That waterfall on the upper Dinau, the pod of whales near the Fire Islands, afternoons with lovers, a day spent climbing in the hill country behind Sagoy, his first bowl of seafood pot-luck by the harbour in Mer Ammery, Tol swooping up on her carrot, laughing with delight ... Alright, that last one was more a present than a past. Tol was the easiest person to talk to he had ever found; she was calm, intelligent and, unlike most of the people he travelled with, looked to violence as very much a last resort. She was also good-looking, of course. He dwelt on Tol's charms for a time - her bright eyes and alert face, dark hair neatly tied back, sturdy body ...

Tol's return brought him back with a small jolt of embarrassment, as if she could see his thoughts. The hours had passed quickly, but then life in a jar severed one from the ordinary flow of time. Tol's news was that he was likely to go back to his own body the next day, once both kidneys were in place. The poison had been difficult to neutralise, and harder to remove, she told him.

"I didn't know the little creep *could* bite," Jayas said.

“Yerech said it was a demon. You are that familiar with this particular demon?” Tol asked, and Jayas remembered that she was an investigator.

“It was a demon,” he confirmed. “One I first ran into, oh three years ago now. A friend and I were exploring an old working deep in the Sechen Wild. She had been to a different school, and had not been taught never to say a strange name out loud. So she read an engraving, called it and it came. It can create illusions of sight and sound, and draw on your thoughts in some fashion. It led her to her death, disguising a high window as a door,” he ended bleakly. Somehow he felt no reticence about his past while in this state. Or perhaps it was just Tol’s practice of encouraging talk by withholding judgement.

“I nearly went the same way, lunging for her as she fell,” he went on. “But my foot hit the thing, it squealed, and I beat it back into the ether. Like Cremione, it must hold a grudge, for it has popped up twice since, not counting this last. Calling it was my last resource.”

“Well, it worked,” concluded Tol. “It would be interesting to study, as the art needs all illusions to have a material anchor, usually a cognate of the image. It’s a specialised branch of the art, mostly applied in advertising.”

“I’d be happy to see that demon in a cage, along with Cremione.”

“She may be becoming as much your obsession as you are hers,” said Tol drily. That gave Jayas pause.

“Well, she does keep barging in trying to kill me,” he said defensively. “Three times now, or four if you count forcing us ashore on the Hansippif. And getting closer each time.”

“Yes. We will have to do something about her,” Tol agreed. Jayas was heartened by the ‘we’.

MOVING BACK INTO A body *hurt*. So did being ripped from a body, but he had been in so much pain at the time that any extra had passed unnoticed. This time he had the full experience. At first it was just pain, and then it became a whole-body cramp, as if his body resisted his return. He lay there, letting his mind and body adjust to each other again, welcoming even the pain as proof that he could again feel. When at last he could swing his legs out and sit up, then prise his eyes open, Yerech and Tol were there, along with three green-coated healers. As the healers did their tests he sat wiggling his toes, extraordinarily glad that he again had toes to wiggle. When they walked out he was twisting his shoulders, swinging his arms and smiling. He had never appreciated breathing so much.

The healers had watched with amusement as Jayas had strapped himself back into armour. Was his native city so lawless, they asked as he disposed small bottles and a knife about his person. He gave them a quizzical smile and let Yerech go first out the door, to scan the street and sky before Jayas and Tol joined him. Jayas accepted the need and was also mildly irritated. Was he going to need a bodyguard at all times? They turned from the courtyard into the street, where Jayas had his first real view of Frouan. It was a city of steep hills and narrow valleys, criss-crossed by streamlets and bridges. The homes of the nobility perched upon the hills, each a gaunt black pile, windowless, crowned with spikes and angry gargoyles. They varied in height from a few stories to towers reaching into the drifting fog. Tol informed Jayas that the authorities punished the delinquent by removing stories – one for lesser offences, several at once for major crimes. The city maintained a corps of architectural magicians for this purpose.

The street scene was more cheerful. Every few steps a barrow offered some kind of snack, from stuffed pastries fried in oil through mixtures of ice, fruit and sweet noodles to paper cones of spiced peas. If you wanted a drink to go with your food, other barrows provided fruit juices, curds shaken with water, honey and spices, small-beer, teas and liani. Shops spilled their wares on to the pavement, alleys were home to small cafes, and performers attracted crowds in the squares. The central roadway was busy with loads slung under lift-poles, pulled along by overhead cables, while a separate network carried passengers on floating benches. It was all bustle, and a trifle alarming in the cover it offered for surprise attack. Cremione would not even stand out, as dark skin predominated, from the polished ebony common in inland Dravishi (was Yerech still yearning for Jamassein?) through charcoal to something close to his own reddish-brown. The local fashion ran to short cloaks, elaborate headgear (that woman looked as if three pheasants had made a home on her head) and tights, a form of attire good for disguise. He stayed alert until they reached their inn, and only really relaxed when the door closed on the suite. The window bars were too close to admit a vulture.

Tol gave a concise account of the group's doings during his confinement. Delfe and the factor had found it easy to terrify Jaerke into compliance. The Frouan customs officials were nearly as fearsome as those of Mer Ammery and the monkeys were impartial witnesses to Jaerke's crimes. Inquiries had been met with a tale of an attempted robbery foiled with the timely assistance of concerned clients. All cargo was accounted for, the officials were assured. Delfe had arranged clearance and transfer to a vault under the Frouan branch of the Shipwrights' Bank – as secure a place as could be found on this bead of the Necklace. Even dragons were not so bold as to attempt to rob one of the great banks.

Their agreed next step was to convert their loot into a conventional form of wealth, something more portable. The gems could be taken to a reputable jeweller (surely wealthy Frouan had several such), but Jayas could not imagine that there was a large market for so much Pure Silver.

"True," agreed Tol. "Which is why I asked at the Association, as a newcomer, what areas of the city to avoid. Serriet is checking out a few places, as she does a convincing 'tough person looking to connect with crime boss' act." She added "If it is an act."

"I might join her," Jayas said.

"Tomorrow or the next day," Tol said firmly.

18. Cellars

Tol studied Jayas. He looked drawn, uncharacteristically nervous. Having your kidneys removed, rinsed, repaired and replaced would do that, she supposed. Along with several days in a jar and the knowledge that an inveterate enemy might lurk around any corner. She had checked his aura again, of course. The apprehension showed up as a flutter, the time in the jar as tinges of deeper colour. The demon-venom had been purged, but there was a streak of melancholy there now. Extended reflection could do that, she knew. It added another element to an already complex picture. Serriet had said she did not know whether she would greet Jayas with a kiss or a slap, or just share a beer. Tol was in the same quandary, but the beer would be her next move. Or wine. The country around Frouan was famous for good wine, and she could – at last – afford to try it.

Jayas just sat, still enjoying being in his body, going through the mental exercises that relaxed muscles and smoothed out worries until they could be dealt with calmly. That training had never let him down. Cremione was out there, and he did not know what she would do next. He could only be ready. Tol was a restful presence, the light scent she wore a waft of freshness. He would leave other matters until tomorrow. He became abruptly aware that he was very hungry, and told Tol so.

"I'll have lunch sent up. They do a good set menu, white soup followed by fish of the day with greens."

"Sounds good. I would like wine too. Yerech says the Pomaine is very good."

WHEN THE SROSS FAMILY was convicted of champerty, fraud and manslaughter no fewer than five floors of their tower home were removed. The head of the family resented this loss (and the derision of her peers) so keenly that she removed abroad, where she died many years later. Five separate claimants to the property came forward, and the matter was still unresolved after seventy two years of suit and counter-suit, appeal and cross-appeal. Those of new wealth had taken advantage of the confused jurisdiction to build handsome residences on the upper part of the hill, while the part along the lower stream had become a thin ribbon of dubious respectability, convenient to Frouan's financial centre yet apart from it. Here were select gaming houses, clubs for those devoted to particular pleasures, discreet brokerages, shops that sold on personal recommendation only. The Sross tower, now a decaying stub, still brooded over this change in fortune from the summit of the hill.

Serriet studied the Fifth Goat from across the street. It was very different to the taverns, bars and dance-halls she had explored over the last several days, and did not at all look like a den of iniquity.

"Why this place?" she asked Jayas. "Do crime-lords hang out here?"

"Crime pays, but not so much that even a major boss could afford what we are selling," Jayas told her. "Anyway, criminals are not into investment. They just blow the cash on a good time and then go looking for more."

"They have a lot in common with mercenaries then," Serriet remarked.

"What we need are names," Jayas went on. "And this is a good place to start."

They crossed the road and pushed open the polished door. It gave on to a lobby where an elderly clerk looked up from a desk.

"May I help you?"

Jayas slid a sliver piece across the desk, at the same time turning his hand to allow a brief glimpse of an inked mark on his inner wrist.

"We're new to the city, and are looking for a reliable guide. We have a couple of unusual requests."

"That is not a service we provide but, since you are newcomers, our hospitality is open to you. The Green Room is through that door."

The Green Room was quiet. A short bar to one side fronted several shelves of bottles, while booths lined the walls. Serriet at first thought the hush was because it was empty, then noticed that sound-absorbing herbs hung over each booth. The gestures as people within talked made the room into a series of eerily silent puppet-shows. Jayas crossed to the bar and rapped once. A man slid around the corner from the back room, straightening a green apron. He said something then repeated the question in Merllan.

"What can I get you?"

After a short consultation, Jayas ordered two glasses of white wine. As Serriet raised hers he idly traced a shape in drops of condensation on the polished wood of the bar, then sipped from his own glass. "A fine drink indeed." He ran an eye over the bottles. "It's a long time since I saw *rashka*."

The barman wiped the bar clean. "We get a case in from the north from time to time. You here on business?"

"Might do some trading, if we can find the right partner."

The man tilted his head at Serriet. Jayas made a complex gesture with his left hand and received a nod.

"Booth at the back is empty."

"What was all that about?" asked Serriet when they were seated in the booth.

"I just gave him a few clues that I'm connected."

"Connected to what?"

"Just connected. You know how all the martial orders – the Companions, Brothers in Glory, Militant Women and so on – have this mutual recognition thing. You flash your badge and it's good for a free meal at least? The, hmm, grey guys have the same, only not so overt. Sometimes the grey shades to black, and then the self-righteous come calling."

"So you mention *rashka* and you get a free meal?"

Jayas gave a wry grin. "Nothing's free on this side of the line. And that mention only is worth one point in a test where you need fifty to pass. These people are careful, and sometimes lethal."

Serriet cocked her head. "But they trust *you*."

"I've had a varied career. What do you think of the wine?"

They were on the second glass, served with crisp wafers and dried fruit that matched well with the wine, when a man sidled up to their booth. Jayas suppressed a frown. Spies knew better than to sneak around in masks, and competent assassins never wore black. So why did this informant look so very like a weasel? A devious weasel at that, thin, sharp-faced, narrow darting eyes, a twitching lip, hands moving in small circles. Was this a test? Or a joke?

"If I may join you?" in a low breathy voice, Merllan with some kind of accent, not local. Jayas gave a terse nod and shifted over. He had mail under his loose coat, and a bottle or two close to hand, and three knives. Serriet had room and reach, and steel-capped boots.

The weasel's fingers beat a short tattoo on the tabletop. Jayas left ring-finger replied with some irregular nail-taps. The weasel carefully selected a piece of fruit, picking it up in his left hand, and ate it in three precise bites. Serriet wondered how many points each move counted. If fifty was a pass, was Jayas at ten or forty? Was dried-fruit-eating a five point move, or only one? Jayas made a conventional noise of welcome, only with a sort of cough in mid-syllable. Another five points? The weasel made an equally conventional reply. Jayas asked if the weasel would care to join them in a glass of wine. The weasel said that a glass of the Timfne red would be appreciated. Jayas signalled to the bar and then introduced Serriet – 'a friend from the north'. The weasel gave her a sly smile, showing crooked teeth. He really was a caricature, thought Jayas, or else it was a disguise. Who had bad teeth?

"A friend of mine had a few phrases from that way. He used to say '*Tse miraho*' a lot." *Must be close to fifty now*, thought Serriet.

"I don't know that one. Was he from the hill country?"

The weasel shrugged narrow shoulders. "He never said."

The wine arrived, a sip taken, an approving nod. "I heard you are looking for a guide."

Jayas took a matching sip of his wine, then carefully picked a wafer and a piece of fruit to top it. "A guide to those in Frouan who would like to break the chain."

"How big a break? What size of chain?"

"Across the sea, keep a dragon grounded."

The weasel blinked. "Four days. I can recommend the herbed lamb." He slithered out.

Serriet waited until they had left the Fifth Goat before asking. "What was that about?"

"Underworld talk," Jayas told her.

"Chains? Breaks? Size?"

Jayas turned into an alley and took a table near the wall, under an awning. "Two black, well-frothed" he told the waitress in Merllan. To Serriet he went on in Azic "There are opportunities open only to those who have a lot of cash, but that's hard to come by without attention. In Mer Ammery they want to know it's not from piracy. In the Four Kingdoms they tax it, in the Haghar League they seize gold and silver from the Wild unless declared. Then there's guards and special transport and so on if you withdraw from a bank. If you want a secret stash you have to break the chain – create a gap between your payment and the gold in your cellar."

"Ah," said Serriet, enlightened. "So someone can use our haul that way. And the bit about dragons?"

"An indication of the amounts involved, so he does not bother us with anyone less than truly rich."

Their drinks came, and Jayas fussed about with spices and spoons. "That guy did not give us his name," Serriet realised.

"Nor did he ask ours," said Jayas. "He'll try to find out, of course, but that's another part of the etiquette."

Serriet leaned back and regarded him. "How many rounds of this game do we play before we get results? Do we have to go through the whole charade again in four days?"

"Two days. The number changes with the next words." Serriet rolled her eyes. "He must have a few names in mind already."

TO SERRIET, THE NEXT visit was anti-climactic. They entered, ordered drinks and were directed to a booth. No-one dropped by, but when they left Jayas had a slip of paper with a string of numbers. He went to his room and came out shortly to tell them of a meeting that very night. He and one other were to be at a certain street corner one hour after the sunset gong. As before, Serriet would be his companion as 'magicians make these people nervous'.

The warmer part of the year had arrived, but it was still cool in the evenings, and there was the inevitable fog. Jayas led Serriet to a corner by a massive block of black stone and dripping brown brick. The street-level shops were closed, light shone from windows above and wafts of cooking smells drifted down. Jayas paused there only a minute before setting off again, Serriet thought following a person in a long brown coat. They did not hurry, but walked steadily through the thin stream of pedestrians, along to the next corner, across the street, dodging a few last loads squeaking along under tow, two more blocks, another corner, a pause again. When they set off again the brown coat had vanished; now they followed a drab green cape with a high collar below a high-crowned hat. Or so Serriet thought. The cape went straight, but they turned into an alley, off that into another and then halted before a plain door. This opened on to an empty room, Jayas stepped through unhesitating, said something low and clear, followed a dim corridor to a flight of stairs and went down these to a vaulted cellar. Serriet had gone from irritated to resigned acceptance of this mummery.

Two chairs sat between the pillars. Jayas took one, stretching his booted legs out to cross at the ankles, and motioned Serriet to the other. She arranged her axe to hand and perched on the edge of the seat, legs under her. When a sepulchral voice spoke out of the gloom it was so in keeping with all the rest that she did not even start. The language was unknown to her, and Jayas replied in the same tongue. After a little back and forth he spoke in Merllan.

"My companion is one of several partners in this enterprise. She needs to hear what is said."

"Very well. We shall continue in this language," in Merllan. Merllan of the high society of Mer Ammery, each syllable aristocratically crisp.

"We offer," said Jayas from his comfortable pose "a quantity of etherically-pure silver, in bars of twenty-four *tiels* Merllan weight."

"Provenance?" asked the voice.

"We brought it out from a Wild," replied Jayas, perfectly truthfully.

"Tagged?" the voice continued in the same laconic vein.

"Not by any test we have applied. One of our number has expertise in tracing and counter-tracing. They say not."

"Price asked?" *Really*, thought Serriet. *Would it hurt to use a few more words?*

"In Frouan double-towers? Two hundred and twenty per tiel."

There was a silence, probably as they clicked their counting-frames.

"So much?"

"Etherically-pure silver is currently quoted at two-hundred and fifty-four on the Exchange," stated Jayas blandly.

"You are not selling on the Exchange," returned the voice.

"Nor you buying," rejoined Jayas.

"What quantity are you offering?"

"One hundred and sixty bars." Serriet distinctly heard an inward suck of breath. At last the voice came back with "Sample?"

"Certainly." Jayas reached within his coat and laid a gleaming bar on his knee. A tray floated out of the dark, he placed the bar on it and it whisked away. *There go, hmm, five thousand and something something – a lot – of money. What if it does not come back?*

They sat there, Serriet wondering if their hosts would spring for a hot drink, Jayas composed and silent. When the tray came back the bar was on it, and two steaming cups. *Had her thoughts been that loud?* Jayas stowed away the bar and sipped. Serriet followed suit.

"Cover," said the voice. *I'm sick of monosyllables.*

"Thirty-two boxes of rare alchemical oils and essences, declared and cleared," Jayas answered promptly.

"How paid?"

"Transfer to accounts with the Shipwright's Bank."

"Commission?"

"Flat, at your cost."

Serriet thought to detect the faintest of whisperings, a parley of the winds. Then "Two days. By note."

Jayas simply stood and walked away, back to the stair, the corridor and the street. The fog was still there, curling around the brickwork, surrounding each glow-stone with a halo. The traffic had thinned to the occasional wanderer. Jayas set out briskly, keeping to the wall.

"Why not sell on the Exchange?" she asked.

"The buy and sell would be posted. Pure silver trades in small quantities, so this would stick out like a seal on a plate of shrimp."

Serriet could appreciate the consequences of unwanted attention. "Will they buy?"

"I think so. They'll say yes and send proxies for the proxies of their front businesses, and the money will come to us from one account in far Dravishi and another in Reghen."

"Who *are* they?"

Jayas smiled. "I don't know, and that's the point."

IT WAS AS JAYAS HAD predicted. A single word appeared in his mirror as he rubbed a depilatory over his cheeks two mornings later. "Show-offs" he grumbled, and booked a private room. Agents turned up to discuss terms for the sale of the 'oils and essences', contracts were exchanged, boxes left the secure vault and money came into their accounts. They no longer had to guard a treasure, and Jayas nearly whooped with delight as the bank confirmed the last transfer. He was freely, securely, lastingly rich! Two of the stern guards must have caught his emotion, for they sent him warning frowns. The peace of the Shipwrights' Bank was not lightly disturbed.

That night Jayas looked around the table at the group. The food had been excellent, the wines superb and the service attentive but not intrusive. The room looked out over the city, tonight the usual dismal blanket of fog, black towers rising from the moon-lit white like the stumps of trees amid the ashes after a fire. Within all was cheerful, for each one was as rich as he was himself. That they had all made it through was warming; a death would have been a sorrow, a betrayal heart-breaking. Where to now?

Delfe, ever Merllan, was heading back south, confident that his House-Mother would welcome him and any little problems from Hane Bay could be smoothed over with money. Yerech was eager for his homeland beyond the Gate, and Seyvyar keen to visit a new world. If it did not work out he could come back, and how many could say they had been to another world? Serriet was off to Dravishi on her carrot. Frouan gave her the chills, and she fancied playing the wealthy tourist for a time. Jayas could not quite picture her lounging in luxury, no doubt with a handsome companion but – her life. Tol, well, Tol was undecided. She said she had been poor so long that this wealth was unsettling, and she needed time to think. Jayas could appreciate that. He too felt unnerved by the myriad of possibilities open. He likened it to being handed an enormous menu where most of the dishes were unknown to one, indeed many in a foreign language.

He would travel with the others to the Gate, if only to foil Cremione. Once there, well, he would see. He put this decision to Tol, who said she would come along. The uplands were said to be pleasant country, and Frouan gave her too the chills. They had been out shopping together that morning, poking around in an up-market area for magical Items, and had not felt welcome. One shop had refused their custom, another shown them only their poorer wares. He had bought a couple of things at a third establishment and been shown the door with unseemly haste. Even the shady dealer who had sold him a few bottles and another bit of back-up had been surly - and overcharged grossly. They would both be glad to put this city of snobs and fogs behind them.

FROUAN HAD RECENTLY invested in a cableway that ran from the city along the valley of the River Leins as far as Annasleinen. In this way the good folk of the city could be conveyed in ease to their estates, and the lesser enjoy a day in the country, and perhaps a visit to one of the many wineries that dotted the slopes above the river. The three were at the cableway station in the early morning, watched their baggage loaded and took their places in a car. Others boarded in a bustle of leave-taking, a bell clanged, a whistle blew, the cars gave a jerk and they were off. The track was smooth, the crew skilled and they gathered speed between the blocky buildings, rushed under the old city walls, cleared the outlying suburbs and were running along above the river, with Frouan a dark hulk dwindling behind.

The river ran silver below, its waters a backdrop for barges, skiffs and other watercraft, its banks fringed with trees and reeds, meadows and marshy ground rising to the cableway embankment. On the other side fields and patches of woods were interspersed with lawned mansions, and above them vines in full leaf made squares of the deepest green. It was a land of settled peace, content to have humans till and harvest. Seyvyar said that the ether here ran slow and calm, its measures easy to interpret. It was a comfortable land, and not one to stimulate magicians to the higher reaches of the art.

The cars slowed, stopped, passengers alighted at a country station set on the outskirts of a village, set off again. In this way the day went on until at mid afternoon they halted for the last time at Annasleinen. This was a town set above the confluence of the Leins with a smaller river, with stone quays below for barges to tie up, a ferry across the broad Leins, a picturesque ruin on the heights above and several notable hostelries. Tol was waiting at the station, face still fresh from her flight. They made a late lunch on a terrace under the shade of vines, wandered the streets until supper and had an early night, disturbed only by the carrot's evening yell and then again by its dawn greeting.

The next day the ferry winched across the Leins, bobbing as the current contested with the ropes, they swung aboard rented horses and set off on a road that wound up the valley side to a crest from which they could survey a great sweep of country, then on through open lands, villages sheltering in dips and coombes, changing horses at small towns, taking meals with Tol when she swooped down from above, changing guides each day through a succession of chatty youths. As only Yerech could understand them, he bore the brunt of the stream of gossip. They did not hurry, for the Gate grew large or small, open or closed, on a cycle no-one could predict. It would be open or not as the land chose.

Jayas knew Cremione was still on the hunt, but did not let that worry him. He no longer had to shepherd a treasure across the leagues, he had strong companions by his side and, for once, he was within the shelter of the law. He chatted with Seyvyar and Yerech, let the countryside roll by, ate peaceful dinners, walked with Tol at night, both revelling in the clear skies and strewn stars after foggy Frouan and the humid south.

When they topped the last rise to see the Sunrise Gate Jayas was disappointed. The Gate itself was invisible, the small town serving it not much more than another country village. There should be spires, and a monumental arch and a road lined with statues, Jayas felt. Instead there was just the usual clutch of stone houses, a few inns and a caravan yard. When he queried Yerech he was told that traffic through the Gate was limited. The Gate was erratic, there was little to trade and adventurous travellers few. They clopped on, handed their beasts over to the latest guide and went to see about rooms. The Restful Wait was recommended by the guide, and looked as suitable as any.

The features of the woman behind the counter were strange to Jayas. Hair of a startling orange, skin pale as milk, eyes a bright blue, nose thin and high-bridged, clad in a shapeless garment of broad stripes, black and red and gold. He supposed she must derive from that other world, part of the thin leakage that must eventually connect all the varied humanity of the seventeen worlds of the

Necklace. As she laboriously entered their names in a register Yerech asked about the current condition of the Gate. The woman paused her stylus to consider, pursing her lips.

"Came in small two days ago, been waxing since. Be good for going through on foot by the day after tomorrow, I guess."

That evening Jayas sat with Tol in the garden at the back of the Restful Wait. The air was warm, scented from herbs and flowers, the wine a local white, dry, flinty and cool.

"What will you do?" asked Jayas.

Tol sipped her wine, tilted her head back to look at the stars now glimmering into being as the afterglow faded.

"I'm still not sure. I'll go for a long flight tomorrow – I find it clears the head."

After a pause she asked the same question of him.

"I had thought to go through," Jayas said, hesitant. He was not quite brave enough to say that what she decided was important to him. Disappointingly, Tol did not ask for his reasons, but sipped her wine.

"All this money," she said eventually. She turned to look Jayas in the face. "Why did you so readily agree to equal shares when Serriet and I showed up?"

"You saved my life. It's worth quite a lot to me," he answered, then "You had us at a disadvantage. A sierlak hovering, the carriage listing, Cremione circling – if you were against us, or even neutral, we were in dire straits indeed. It was not only a fair offer, it was the only prudent one."

He let her absorb that.

"Do you not want to be wealthy?" he asked.

"I don't want to be poor," she said wryly. "This," she waved a hand at the inside pocket where she kept her bank seal, "feels... *excessive*."

"Then give it away, until you are comfortable again."

"I'm uncertain where my comfort level lies. It has changed since I left my one rented room in Kaber."

Jayas chuckled. "It is a problem many would wish to have."

Tol sighed. "Yes. So tomorrow I will go flying." She drained the glass and stood up. "Thanks for the company. I'm off to bed." She left him to finish his wine alone.

THE DAY AFTER THE NEXT they stood before the Gate. It was a simple affair, two pillars of stone topped by a third massive rock, all roughly squared, standing across a gravel path. It was large enough to allow a cart to pass, and one had rumbled out while they waited, drawn by a strange beast with a woolly coat, two humps, a long neck and a supercilious expression. The three women in the cart were bundled in felt coats, hats with ear-flaps, mittens and knee boots. If they were dressed far too warmly for the weather here, Jayas and the others were sure to be chilled on the other side. He peered through the square. The path continued in shadow, narrowing more than normal perspective allowed.

Jayas shaded a hand and peered all around the horizon. Where was Tol? She had not turned up at breakfast, or at dinner the previous evening. He thought she might be taking the carrot for a last flight, and would meet them here. She would not leave without saying goodbye, would she? He swivelled around again, quartering the sky. Nothing but high clouds and small birds. He looked back along the path to the town, where the cart was jolting along. Nothing there either.

The officer beckoned them forward. "You can go through now." He added "Best not linger – this one is going to wane before the day is out."

Yerech translated, and he and Seyvyar started forward. Jayas abruptly made up his mind. "You two go ahead. Leave a message for me if you can't wait on the other side. I'm going to find Tol."

Seyvyar turned to him. "Are you sure? She must have changed her mind about going through."

"I'm sure. Go on. I'll find you – or not." Yerech was shifting from foot to foot. Seyvyar gave him a calculating look and then, surprisingly, stepped forward to embrace him, followed by the formal double-kiss of final farewell.

"It's been a long road. I will remember you." He followed Yerech and both dwindled as rapidly as if each step they took covered a hundred paces. One step, two, three and four and they were out of sight. Jayas stood to one side to let the only other pair of travellers pass, then started back to the inn at a fast walk.

The milk and sapphire woman was at the desk. She raised a thin eyebrow when Jayas walked in, beckoned and handed him an envelope. Within was a curl of dark hair and a slip of paper. Jayas unfolded it to read the spiky Merllan script.

'*Your friend lives, for now. Be at the third bridge on the road to Harfre two hours after noon. Alone. C.*"

19. Last Throw

Jayas had not made a real effort to learn the local language. He had picked up a few dozen words, and now put these to use. It took some time, but he gained directions to the Harfre road and a rough idea of the distance to the third bridge. He had a little time – now to see if the Association had a presence in the town. If not, was there a senior magician? The Association did have an office, and when he left his purse was lighter.

The Harfre road was a dirt track winding away across the hills. Jayas kept a steady walk and an eye on the country and sky. After half an hour the road dipped into a valley where a huddle of houses surrounded a stone arch over a small river. He drank from a stone basin set above a horse trough and went on, watched with interest by two shepherds and a child dangling a line in the stream. For a fact he did not fit in this pastoral scene, clad in armour, shield on his back, helmet and mace at his side. A word, "Harfre?" the boneless flip of the hand that meant yes hereabouts and he kept on down the road.

The second bridge was of timber laid between stone piers, only wide enough for two people. Wagons and animals used the adjacent ford, where the water ran shallow over stones. The country here was open, at this season largely empty. Insects hovered over the grass and birds darted about, small things scurried from clump to bush, the sun was warm on his head and he kept on. A rise up a long smooth slope, a curve, a turn and a line of darker green below signalled water. Here would be the third bridge. Jayas halted, carefully surveyed the scene.

No-one was visible, but the trees could hide one or ten. The birds were not alarmed, and no vultures rode the winds. He had not seen anyone since the last village. He walked on.

The bridge was another simple affair, timbers laid between stone buttresses over a gurgling creek. There was no-one there, but a chalked message in Merllan said 'track. Hundred paces on left.' Jayas saw no alternative but to do as directed. There was the track, a narrow path between the pines that straggled along the slope. Jayas made a few adjustments, put on his helmet and tightened the straps. Perhaps Cremione would give him a fair fight.

It was stuffy under the trees. Pine needles scrunched under his boots, roots twisted across the path like basking snakes, birds called ahead. Cremione would know he was coming. The path angled across, around a curve and the trees thinned, then gave on to a meadow of rough grass, seed-heads teased by the wind. At the far side stood his nemesis, tall, black, stern, clad in mail of a dull white, eyes invisible under the peak of a helmet. Cremione's sword hung by her side, her shield was to hand. Jayas halted.

"You did come. I'm surprised, but pleased." Her voice carried across the grass without effort, deep and clear.

"I did. You have my friend. What do you want for her?"

"Why, Jayas, I want you, of course."

"Then let her go and we can settle this as you please."

"Yes, as I please."

"As you please, so as you let her go."

"Come closer, Jayas."

"Not until I see Tol, unharmed."

The helmet dipped, a hand went to hilt. Then she gave a hand signal and two figures came from the shrubs behind her. One was Tol, in those absurd leathers she had made for flying. Her neck was encircled by a loop of rope, the other end held by a woman in loose clothing. Jayas noted the copper coils on her forearms, the amber drop on her chest and pegged her as a magician. As far as he could see Tol was unharmed, if deprived of access to the ether. They would not have left her free to speak otherwise.

"Here she is. I will let her go, as she is only the bait. You are the fish I want."

"Then let her go," Jayas replied.

"Not before I have you, trickster."

Jayas simply stood there. This was Cremione's problem to solve, not his. The three formed a silent tableau, a triangle of purposes.

"Shed your weapons and come forward, and I will release her."

"Release her and I will shed my weapons," Jayas counter-offered.

Cremione stamped a foot. The magician muttered something to her and she stamped again.

"Fine. Shed your weapons and armour – every last knife and bottle. In fact, strip to the skin and I will let her go. Then come forward. It will save me chasing you."

Jayas laid his shield under a tree, placed his mace on it, then his belt and dagger. The helmet came off, then the shoulder-strap with its pockets for vials. The armour laces were loosened and the mail dragged over his head. He shook out the rings and hung it over a branch. The boots came off, then the ties holding the thigh-pieces, and they joined the armour on the branch. The padded vest came next, and he stood in shirt and trousers.

"To the skin," repeated Cremione.

"When Tol is free and ten paces away from you."

The magician again said something and Cremione made a curt gesture. The rope was dropped and Tol walked slowly forward. Her mouth was set, her eyes leaking.

"Are you harmed?"

"Not seriously. She killed my carrot. What are you going to do?"

"I am going to do as she asked: strip and walk forward. Enjoy the show."

Jayas unfastened his shirt, folded it and tucked it under the dagger. The undershirt followed. The waistband was loosened, the trousers removed a leg at a time, to join the neat pile of clothes covering the shoulder-strap. Now he was down to a pair of shorts. He gave Tol a grin and slipped those off, added them to the rest and then faced Cremione.

"Like what you see? I'll come closer, and Tol can go." He walked slowly across the grass, mindful of the uneven ground. Tol walked too, so that they met half-way. He clasped her hand when they met, said "Keep going, get out of sight," and walked on, to halt five paces from Cremione, naked and empty hands out.

"Now what? If you want to wrestle, I did not bring any oil."

Cremione's sword slid free from the sheath. "I'm going to kill you."

Jayas ran an eye over the length of blade, the armour, the broad dagger at her hip. "So not a duel then?"

"I'm done duelling with you! You cheat and lie and pact with dark powers."

Jayas sat down, then lay back on the grass, legs together, arms folded. "Not much to say, then. Cut my throat and be done." The magician was clearly taken aback, but not Cremione. She took four long steps, to stand over him with the point at his throat.

"Oh I will," she said.

Jayas exploded. His head jerked sideways, one hand swept her blade aside and held it, the other swung out and down, and a wicked bone blade severed the tendon behind one ankle even as his leg came up to thump into her calf. She cried out as she fell, yet remained a fighter. Cremione went to her knees, sword raised. Jayas' roll and flickering shoulder-spring had brought him to his feet and for a breath they faced each other, he in a knife-fighter's crouch, she kneeling with sword and dagger, face tight with rage. The magician pulled a knife from her belt, her amber drop burst in a flare of orange, she clasped her throat and staggered. Tol clearly had her in hand, so Jayas ignored her to circle Cremione. A darting feint, a stab and the dagger fell from her hand, wrist slashed. He scooped it up, came in again, the dagger slid her sword aside and the bone knife plunged into an eye.

The magician was slumped to the ground, face purpled. Jayas looked down at Cremione, roiled with conflicting emotions. She was dead and he was alive. He was glad of the last, and the first meant he need fear pursuit and vengeance no longer. Yet she had come so far, done so much in her obsession, and been brave to the last. A rasping breath from the magician brought him back to the present. Even as he was there she turned to throw up, but Jayas took no chances. The knife was at her neck, with the warning that a single sound meant death. The retching woman may not have cared.

"If you stop waving your dick in her face she will stop vomiting," Tol said from behind him. "I have your shorts, and she will have some more Inhibitor." Jayas ran a hand through pockets, came up with several vials, thumbed one open and applied a dab to the back of the neck. There, she was now deprived of access to the ether, and her words would be mere sounds. A toss of the knives at her belt into the woods and the magician would harm no-one. It was only with that done he pulled on the shorts Tol held patiently. The magician lay still, pale and sweating.

"You know," Tol said, looking down at Cremione's corpse, "I have not directly killed anyone throughout these months, although there have been deaths along the way. Yet I would have killed this one without hesitating. It was the only way to stop her."

Jayas put an arm around her, and they contemplated the long road together for a moment.

"She was the last tie to my old life, the one where I kept throwing the dice on death or fortune. This time they landed doubles for me and poorly for her, but it could have been the other way. I'm done with that."

Tol considered this, then offered "Life changed when I waked out the door of that dingy room in Kaber, and again when I took ship, and yet again when I kept after you even after the commission ended. We'll see what turns up."

"Yes," said Jayas simply. Then, ever practical, he drew on craft and knelt to lay a hand on the earth.

"The Merllan give their dead to the sea, and that we cannot do. The land here will allow fire enough to burn the body, and the ashes can go into the water later." He added "Cremione was clever. She chose this place because it is close to a domain. No demon would come to my naming. Anyway, let's gather some wood."

"And then I'll fly us back to the Gate," Tol added. "That one," - a jerk of the head towards the magician – "can start walking. But get dressed properly first. You are too distracting that way."

The pale woman was surprised to see Jayas and Tol walk in, Tol in her leathers, Jayas burdened with a bundle of armour and weapons.

"I gave up my room this morning," Jayas said.

Tol pulled at his arm. "I still have my room, and we are going there *right now* to celebrate our survival."

That evening, over a late dinner, Tol got around to asking questions. How had Jayas got hold of the Disinhibitor he had passed her in the field? From the local Association, of course, at a steep price. He had foreseen the need, for how else did one control a magician?

Where had the bone knife come from? He had noticed in the warehouse that Cremione's weapons and armour were not metal, and could transform with her body. So he had asked around in Frouan and bought the knife. It could be hidden within the body, as a weapon of last resort. Tol remarked that, of course it was a last resort – Jayas always had a last trick, and another after that. The final question was the most important: why had he come for her, instead of going through the Gate?

Jayas twirled his wine glass. "You were missing, you could be in trouble. Should I ignore that in favour of more adventures? It would be a betrayal, and I have seen too much betrayal."

Tol absorbed this, then "That's very ... impersonal."

Jayas reached across for her hand. "Well, that it was you, Tol, who compels me to be open. The impersonal only becomes real when it meets the personal. Friendship is a word, a friend is a person. As is a lover."

Tol smiled at him. "I was able to do a lot of thinking before Cremione showed up. I decided that riches don't change who I am, and I'm an investigator. I'm going to go on doing that, only with style. Want to come with me?"

"I do."

Tol finished her wine. "Then let's make that more real."

TOL HAD FINISHED REVIEWING the latest case-notes from her investigators and turned to the letters.

"The treasure you brought from the Hansippif is still making waves. The latest is that another high Brahnak official has been sent into contemplation - that's being put into a cell and told to meditate on your crimes."

"Well, it did force them to cancel a war, so I suppose there were a lot of disappointed people," commented Jayas.

Tol made a hmm noise and went on "Serriet writes that she has been asked to join a party to seek the treasure. She might do it just for the giggles."

"Do you remember the inn in Zyich? There was a poster there about Xanfred - the guy it's named after - offering a reward. That's after twenty years, and this has only been three. Maybe they'll give up in another decade," Jayas sighed. He leaned forward and checked the crib. The baby squirmed and made faint mewing noises. From her desk across the room Tol said "She needs feeding" and went back to reading.

"I know," Jayas replied. The craft had more and better uses than fighting: he opened his shirt, a moment of concentration, a twine of the fingers and he felt his body transform. Breasts grew heavy on his chest. Jayas cradled the child, settled back as the snub nose and rosebud mouth rooted around then latched on. Jayas watched in content as the babe got on with the most important thing in her life. His daughter, in his house. He never before had either.

A partner and a child. Perhaps he could look forward to growing old.

Wealth gives you more choices, he thought. *You still have to choose.*

About the Author

P Thomson lives in Canberra, which most people mistake for the capital of Australia, and passes the time writing and telling stories to children. Authors always mention pets, so they have one dog and at least two possums. The books started with 'what would a world with sensible magic look like?' and went on from there - to lawyers dealing with magicians and trainee spies and sensible middle-aged ladies sorting out the uncanny.

He can be reached at pdt@emailme.com.au

Milton Keynes UK
Ingram Content Group UK Ltd.
UKHW020627021023
429777UK00014B/624